PRAISE FOR SHANNON HALE

# Princess Academy

A NEWBERY HONOR BOOK
A *NEW YORK TIMES* BESTSELLER
AN ALA NOTABLE CHILDREN'S BOOK
A BOOK SENSE CHILDREN'S PICK

★ "An intricate, multilayered story about families, relationships, education, and the place we call home." —*SLJ*, starred review

★ "There are many pleasures to this satisfying tale. . . . An unalloyed joy." —*Kirkus Reviews*, starred review

"A joyful, subversive classic." —Holly Black, Newbery Honor–winning and *New York Times* bestselling author of *Doll Bones* and the Spiderwick Chronicles series

"I learned more from *Princess Academy* than I can ever tell." —Jon Scieszka, First National Ambassador for Young People's Literature

"I know of no other book that provides such a perfect combination of a richly imagined fantasy world with such wise guidance for how to move with grace and dignity through our own world." —Bruce Coville, author of the *My Teacher Is an Alien* and the Unicorn Chronicles series

## Princess Academy
### PALACE OF STONE

A *New York Times* Bestseller

"Proves once again that with quick wit and brave words, one person really can change the world." —*SLJ*

"Powerful and deeply engaging." —*Kirkus Reviews*

"Absolutely incredible. . . . This is the book we have all been waiting for." —Jennifer L. Holm, three-time Newbery Honoree and *New York Times* bestselling author of *Turtle in Paradise*

## Princess Academy
### THE FORGOTTEN SISTERS

★ "Action packed and well paced. . . . This final installment of the Princess Academy trilogy certainly leaves room for more books if Hale were so inclined." —*Booklist*, starred review

# Princess Academy
## PALACE OF STONE

# BOOKS BY SHANNON HALE

## THE BOOKS OF BAYERN
*The Goose Girl*
*Enna Burning*
*River Secrets*
*Forest Born*

*Princess Academy*
*Princess Academy: Palace of Stone*
*Princess Academy: The Forgotten Sisters*

*Book of a Thousand Days*

*Dangerous*

## GRAPHIC NOVELS
with Dean Hale
illustrations by Nathan Hale
*Rapunzel's Revenge*
*Calamity Jack*

## FOR ADULTS
*Austenland*
*Midnight in Austenland*
*The Actor and the Housewife*

# Princess Academy
## PALACE OF STONE

# SHANNON HALE

BLOOMSBURY
NEW YORK   LONDON   NEW DELHI   SYDNEY

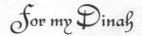

## A princess in her own right

First published in the United States of America in August 2012
by Bloomsbury Children's Books
Paperback edition published in March 2015
www.bloomsbury.com

Bloomsbury is a registered trademark of Bloomsbury Publishing Plc

For information about permission to reproduce selections from this book, write to
Permissions, Bloomsbury Children's Books, 1385 Broadway, New York, New York 10018
Bloomsbury books may be purchased for business or promotional use. For information on
bulk purchases please contact Macmillan Corporate and Premium Sales Department at
specialmarkets@macmillan.com

The Library of Congress has cataloged the hardcover edition as follows:
Hale, Shannon.
Princess Academy : palace of stone / Shannon Hale. — 1st U.S. ed.
p.    cm.
Summary: Miri returns to Asland and calls upon all of her knowledge of rhetoric
and other useful lessons learned at the Princess Academy when she and the
other girls face strong opposition while working for a new, fair charter.
ISBN 978-1-59990-873-1 (hardcover)
[1. Self-confidence—Fiction. 2. Kings, queens, rulers, etc.—Fiction.
3. Sex role—Fiction. 4. Telepathy—Fiction. 5. Mountains—Fiction.
6. Schools—Fiction.] I. Title. II. Title: Palace of stone.
PZ7.H13824Prp 2012      [Fic]—dc23      2012003875

ISBN 978-1-61963-257-8 (paperback)  •  ISBN 978-1-59990-916-5 (e-book)

Book design by Donna Mark
Typeset by Westchester Book Composition
Printed and bound in the U.S.A. by Thomson-Shore Inc., Dexter, Michigan
2   4   6   8   10   9   7   5   3

# Chapter One

*The rock-lined road is the way to work*
*The rock-lined road takes the work away*
*The rock-lined road is the way to take*
*If you take that road away you'll always take that way*
*  back home*
*Take you there and take you home, there's nothing but the*
*  rocky road*

Miri woke to the insistent bleat of a goat. She squeaked open one eye. Pale yellow sky slipped through the cracks in the shutters. It was day—the very day trade wagons might come to carry her off. She'd been expecting them all week with both a skipping heart and a falling stomach. Strange, lately, how many things made her feel two opposite ways twisted together.

Peder was like that.

Miri crept from her pea-shuck mattress to the window. A figure stood in the doorway of Peder's house.

She waved, Peder waved back, and those addled feelings popped inside, her chest light and excited, her head tight and unsure.

She felt two ways about home too, she realized, looking out at the few dozen houses of Mount Eskel, their roofs traced white with dawn light. Her mountain was big. The world was bigger.

A noise called her back. Her sister, Marda, was sitting up, and her pa too, stretching and groaning from the ache of sleep. For them she felt only one way. And for them she never wanted to leave.

Miri talked while she helped Marda stack the mattresses to clear the floor, and talked while she dished up breakfast, and talked while she led the goats from the adjoining room into the sharp light of morning. If she talked, she did not have to think. Thinking only made her stomach fall faster.

"Peder's grandpa says he's seen more bees this fall than he can ever remember, and that means the winter won't be too hard, but if it freezes and thaws all the time you'll have ice everywhere, so I think we should dump more gravel on the path to the stream—"

"We'll be all right, Miri." A goat pushed against Marda's side, and Marda rubbed its ears. "You don't need to worry."

Pa was walking ahead of his girls. His back tensed against Marda's words.

"Pa . . . ," Miri said. She wanted him to say that he would be all right without her.

They reached the quarry, a huge bowl of white stone, rectangles of rock jutting at odd angles. Already dozens of villagers were squaring blocks of linder stone they'd cut from the mountain and were hauling them out of the quarry. The nearest group worked one stone together, singing to keep in rhythm: *"Take you there and take you home, there's nothing but the rocky road."*

Pa halted at the edge. "Expect us for lunch, Miri, so long as . . ."

Miri finished his thought. *So long as the wagons have not come.*

Pa hefted his pickax and strode into the pit. Marda followed, turning to shrug at Miri. Miri shrugged back. They both knew their father's temperament.

Miri tied her goats on a slope where they could graze, then skipped back down to the house. She picked up a letter from the table, as she had each morning since it arrived with the traders in the summer. The letter still seemed as magical as books had when she'd first learned to read.

She had the letter memorized, but she read it again

anyway. It was from Katar, who had left Mount Eskel for the capital several months before.

*Addressing Miri Larendaughter, Lady of the Princess, Mount Eskel*

*Miri,*

    *This is a letter. A letter is like talking to someone who is far away. Do not show the others in case I am doing it wrong.*

    *This fall, extra wagons will go with the traders to bring to Asland any academy graduates who are willing. You are invited to stay one year. I know you, at least, will come. It is a long trip. Bring a blanket to sit on in the wagon or you will get a bruised backside.*

    *At harvest, each province in Danland presents a gift to the king. As this is the first year Mount Eskel is a province, I want our gift to be really fine. I cannot think what we can offer besides linder. I do not think goats would be quite right. Please tell the village council that the linder must be special, perhaps a very large block of it. I do not sleep well with worry. I grow tired of the mocking way the other delegates speak of Mount Eskel.*

    *I am anxious for you to come. There are things happening in Asland. I need advice, but it would be*

*dangerous for me to write about it, I think. I hope it will*
*not be too late by the time you arrive.*

*This letter is from Katar, Mount Eskel's delegate to the*
*royal court in Asland*

Miri put the letter back on the table, held down by a
shard of linder—white stone struck through with veins
of silver. She could not guess what dangerous matters
Katar wanted to discuss with her, but that had not kept
her from trying to imagine all summer long. And summer had seemed very long indeed.

Miri picked up a second letter and could not help
smiling as she read Britta's looping handwriting.

*Miri Larendaughter, Mount Eskel*

*Dearest Miri,*

*I am delighted to write to you! Though I would rather*
*talk to you in person and sit as we used to do in the shade*
*of the princess academy, watching hawks glide. At least I*
*have good news to share. The king has invited the academy*
*girls to come this autumn! Autumn is not near enough for*
*impatient me, but it is closer than next spring.*

*I will brag just a little and claim credit. I made a very*
*pretty argument that the mountain pass might still be*
*stopped with snow in the spring and prevent you from*

*arriving in time for the wedding. And how could the princess be married without the princess's ladies?*

*You girls will room here at the palace. Palace seamstresses will make you dresses in the Aslandian style, so please do not fear on that account.*

*Also, I have wonderful news! There is an open spot for you at the Queen's Castle, the university I told you about. Studies begin after harvest, so you see, another reason I am eager to have you here before spring.*

*More good news. A stone carver my father used to hire has agreed to take Peder into apprenticeship. Gus will house and feed Peder in exchange for a year's labor and one block of linder.*

*There will be so much for us to do here. I can scarcely sleep sometimes for daydreaming! Let the summer fly on hot, swift wings.*

*Your friend,*
*Britta*

Traders came up to Mount Eskel only once each spring, summer, and fall, so Miri had been unable to reply to either girl. She had no doubt Katar was going crazy with worry about their gift for the king. Miri could not wait to surprise her.

Miri ladled morning gruel into a pot and headed out the door. Peder had spent the past three months sweating over the gift. And since his family was short one quarry worker while he labored, the other village families supported Peder with meals. Today was Miri's turn. While her pa and sister worked in the quarry, Miri kept the house and goats.

She ambled over the rock chippings that covered the ground to Peder's house, knocking once and letting herself in.

"Good morning, Peder," she began, stopping when she saw Peder's father, Jons, standing with arms folded. The mood in the cottage had the bite of winter wind.

Peder slumped onto a stool. "My father is reconsidering letting me go to Asland."

"Not reconsidering," Jons said. "Decided. You've already wasted three months carving this thing. Since your sister is leaving us, you'll be staying."

For Peder, quarry work was mindless, endless. He'd been carving bits of linder into animals and people for years, yearning for a chance to do it more. Miri wanted to plead with Jons but checked herself, remembering the rules of Diplomacy she had learned at the princess academy.

"I can understand, sir, why you want Peder to stay. He hasn't worked in the quarry since the summer traders came. Besides, it would be hard on your family to lose both children for a year."

"Just so," he said, squinting suspiciously. "It's impossible."

"I would agree, but in this case, sending Peder to Asland will be much more useful for your family *and* the village in the long run. As it is now, after the traders haul our stone down the mountain, artisans in Asland chip away half of it to make mantelpieces and tiles and such, and they earn a good living doing it."

"Exactly!" Peder said, standing up. "Why shouldn't we do that work here, ourselves? After I'm trained, traders could bring me orders in the fall, then I'd work through the winter and send the carvings down in spring."

"Traders can haul twice as much finished stone as rough stone," said Miri, "which would mean twice as much pay for everyone."

Jons narrowed his eyes further. Miri swallowed but asked the final question.

"I know Peder will be diligent in his apprenticeship and do you proud. Will you let him go?"

She held her breath. She could not hear Peder breathe. Jons turned to look out the window.

"Fine," Jons said with a grunt. He paused to lay his hand on Peder's head before leaving.

"You're amazing!" Peder said, hugging Miri.

He took a step back and smiled as if he truly loved looking at her face. Then he started in on the breakfast.

*Why doesn't he ask?* The thought was so well used it squeaked in Miri's mind like dry hinges. She was of age to be betrothed. Peder seemed to like her and no one else. Yet he did not ask.

Afraid to look at him in case he could read her thoughts in her eyes, she leaned over the mantelpiece he'd been carving. She traced the images of Mount Eskel and the chain of mountains beyond, beautifully captured in linder.

"It's smoother," she said.

"I've been polishing it."

An unmistakable sound reached them from outside. They rushed to the window to see the first in the line of trader wagons, crunching rock debris under metal-rimmed wheels.

Miri was holding Peder's warm, callused hand. She did not know who had reached out first.

They ran to meet the wagons, along with most of the village. Trading began, families selling cut blocks of linder and purchasing foodstuffs and supplies from the wagons. In the past, trading day had been an anxious occasion, each family bartering for just enough food to avoid starvation. But since the previous year, when the villagers were first able to sell their linder at fair value, trading days had become festivals.

Children danced in excitement over ribbons and

cloth, shoes and tools, bags of dried peas still in their shucks, barrels of honey and onions and salt fish. Such items had always seemed magical to Miri, evidence of fabulous, faraway places. How often she'd daydreamed of cities, farmlands, and endless ocean. Now at last she would go. But she did not feel like joining in the dance.

Peder caught up with his mother to help in the trading, and Miri sold her family's stone. Then she went in search of her sister.

"Please come, Marda," she said, panic tightening her throat. Marda was not an academy graduate, but she knew Britta would not mind, and the other girls adored Miri's gentle sister. "I thought I wanted to go, but I'm scared. I need you. Please."

"You're not scared," Marda said quietly. "Or you won't be for long."

"Marda, I'm serious."

"I'm not like you, Miri. Learning about all those places and past kings and wars, it makes me feel like . . . like I'm sleeping on a precipice. I don't like that feeling. I want to stay home."

"But—"

"Pa and I both know you'll be fine. So fine, in fact, he worries you won't come back."

"He does?"

Marda nodded. "So do I."

Miri shook her head. She could not imagine staying away forever by choice, but so much could happen in a year, so many obstacles to coming home. And what dangerous matters did Katar fear? Miri felt her chin start to quiver.

Marda rubbed Miri's back and forced a confident smile. "A few blinks and you'll be back. A year's a small thing."

Marda's words reminded Miri of a line from a poem she'd read in one of the academy books, so she said, "*No small thing, a bee's sting, when it enters the heart.*"

"A bee's sting entered whose heart?" asked Marda.

"It's just a poem. Never mind," Miri said. She should have known Marda would not understand, and that made her feel as lonely as if she were already gone.

Marda put her arm around Miri, tucking her head against her own. Miri noticed her sister had grown taller in the past year. She was older than most Mount Eskel girls who accepted a betrothal, yet no one had spoken for her. Once all the village boys were betrothed, no others would come rushing up from the lowlands to take their place. And Marda was too shy to speak for herself.

As soon as she returned from Asland, Miri decided, she would be matchmaker for her sister. And she'd keep teaching in the village school till every villager could read, including her pa. She felt better making plans like ropes securing her to her mountain.

The trading hurried along, culminating in the trading-day feast. Now it was a farewell feast.

Not all the graduates of the princess academy would be going. Some were kept back at their parents' wishes; others had accepted betrothals and did not want to leave. Miri would travel with five girls: Gerti, Esa, Frid, Liana, and Bena. Each carried a burlap sack filled with her few possessions. Miri clutched her own sack to her chest. The summer had seemed endless, but now that this moment was upon her, it felt sudden and sharp, a hawk in a hunting dive.

"I'll write to you," she told Marda. "Every week. And I'll send the whole stack of letters with the spring traders. And the letters will all say the same thing—I miss you, and I'll be home next fall. Home for good."

Marda just nodded.

Her father approached, his hands behind his back, his eyes on the ground. Miri stepped forward to meet him.

"Don't forget to butcher the rabbits come high winter, when the pelts are thickest," she said. "It breaks Marda's heart to do it, and if I'm gone . . ."

He glanced at her and then away again, frowning into the chain of mountains: brown, purple, blue, and beyond, ghostly gray summits seemingly afloat above the clouds.

"I will come back, Pa," she said.

"I wonder," he said in his low voice. "I wonder."

"I promise."

He picked her up, pressing her to his chest as easily as if she were still a baby. How could an embrace make her feel exquisitely loved and yet heartbroken too?

"I'll always come home, Pa," she said.

But a shiver of uncertainty had entered her.

Miri sat in the back of a wagon as it drove away, her eyes taking in every last image of home: her house built of gray rubble rock, the white gleam of linder shards marking the paths, the jagged cliffs of the quarry, and the magnificent, white-tipped head of Mount Eskel.

She felt night-blind and afraid, as if walking a path that might lead to sheer cliff and empty air. The lowlands were so far away, she could hardly believe they existed. Once she was in the lowlands, would home seem like a dream too?

She glimpsed Pa and Marda one last time before the road bent and, quick as a sigh, the village was gone from sight.

# Chapter Two

⚬⚬⚬⚬⚬⚬

*The city of the river*
*The city of the bay*
*The people of the limestone*
*The people of the clay*

Miri's jaw ached from gaping. First, there were the lowlander trees, their enormous leafy crowns still so vibrantly green it hurt her eyes. Next, farmlands stretched so far they curved with the world, green and golden. Then the wagons rolled onto actual streets, past wooden houses winking with glass windows. The roofs were made of thatch or tile with the occasional one of beaten copper—some new and orange but most a weathered green.

Trying to keep her voice steady, Miri said, "So this is Asland."

Enrik the trader rolled his eyes. "No, this is just a *town*."

That night they camped outside the town. Miri looked up from her supper of bacon and potatoes and met eyes with a thin girl, chewing on a stick. The town girl did not speak, just watched Miri with wide eyes. Had she come to see the backward folk of Mount Eskel? Would she run home and make fun of the way Miri ate? Miri hunched her back and turned away.

By the third day, Miri was accustomed to the rhythm of the journey: woods, farms, town, repeated again and again, the shuddering lope of the wagon constant beneath her. She rarely gaped anymore and almost forgot to be afraid until the day they entered Asland.

The rain began as a mist and thickened into annoying pecks on their faces and hands. Soon it was an onslaught, and the girls huddled together under an oiled cloth in the back of Enrik's lurching wagon. Miri's stomach squelched.

When Bena made sick noises over the side of the wagon, Miri scrambled forward and out from under the cloth, into the rainstorm.

"Death would be better than riding under there," she announced. "Death or rain."

Peder and Enrik shared the driver's bench, huddled under smaller cloths.

"You'll get soaked," said Enrik. With his long nose and thin, stooped shoulders, he reminded Miri of a grumpy vulture.

"Already am." At least the air was warmer in the lowlands.

Peder scooted over, and Miri squeezed beside him. He pulled half of his oiled cloth around her. Their legs touched.

The rain teased her hair, slithered through her clothes, and lay against her skin. But in the fresh air her stomach settled, so she hugged her arms and was glad at least to be looking out at the gray-blue world. She'd fantasized many times about her first glimpse of the capital. Her imagination had not planned on rain.

"I'm so nervous," she whispered to Peder, her teeth chattering.

"You sound it," Peder said.

"No, my jaw's pounding because it misses the sound of quarry hammers."

"Or else you're cold and should get back under the larger cloth."

"And deprive you of my company? I'm not so cruel."

Until that year, no mountain villager had journeyed to the lowlands. But so much had changed since the priests divined that Mount Eskel was the home of the future princess. The court-appointed tutor had established a princess academy there to teach the rough mountain girls to read and to introduce them to other subjects each should know in case the prince chose her as his bride. But from the academy books, Miri and the other girls had learned much more, including how the village could sell linder for better prices.

Because of the higher profits, every daylight moment no longer needed to be spent working in the quarry, and Miri had started a village school for anyone who cared to learn. Mount Eskel had been elevated from a territory to a province of Danland, the graduates of the princess academy were named ladies of the princess, and suddenly the world beyond the mountain view was no longer a frightening mystery but a place Miri could visit or even inhabit.

The rain was softening into a fine drizzle. The low clouds lifted, sunlight melted the mist, and Miri saw that they were already in the middle of a city larger than any from her imagination.

Street after street, gardens and fountains, buildings like giants. The bench beneath Miri seemed to drop away, and she felt as if she were falling through the whole, huge world.

Peder pressed his shoulder against hers and opened his eyes wide. She widened her eyes at him and nodded back.

They crossed a bridge over a river. Houses six stories high crammed the banks, so tight they presented one great wall. Each house was painted a different color—blue, yellow, red, brown, green, rust, turquoise.

SHANNON HALE

"Why is that farmland gray?" Miri asked. Downriver, the buildings stopped abruptly, bordering a huge empty plain.

Enrik laughed. "That's the ocean."

"The *ocean?*" The lowlander traders always went on as if the ocean were the most wondrous thing in the world and the Eskelites were fools for living so far from its glory. But it was just a flat, lifeless sky.

*Poor Asland, with no mountains,* she thought. *They have to paint their houses to have something pretty to look at. They have to marvel over a boring ocean.*

The bridge ended, and the wagon veered away from the river toward the center of town and a white stone palace in a sea of green park.

"Linder," Miri whispered. "It must have taken a hundred years to quarry all that."

The other girls were sitting up on their knees and watching the approach.

"It's so big," said Frid.

"So are you," said Miri. It was true—Frid was dwarfed only by her mother and six big brothers. "And if it came to a fight, I'd pick you over the palace."

Frid laughed. "What's it going to do, fall on me?"

"It's like a huge piece of Mount Eskel," said Esa, Peder's sister.

18

"Then we should feel right at home," said Miri, trying to give herself courage.

The wagons entered the palace grounds around the side through a gate that opened into a large courtyard.

"The entire village and quarry could fit inside here," said Peder.

"Indeed," said Enrik. "Perhaps next the king will make this courtyard a province."

"Very funny," Miri said, reaching out to knock Enrik's hat over his eyes.

An orange-haired girl left a crowd of people and ran at their wagons. Katar stood taller than Miri remembered, regal even. Miri recalled the "dangerous" matter of Katar's letter and looked for a sign that they were not too late.

"Did you bring a gift for the king?" Katar said, skipping over greetings. Peder hopped into the wagon that contained the mantelpiece and removed the cloth.

Katar nodded. "It's something at least."

"It's *beautiful,*" Miri said, nudging Katar with her tone of voice.

Katar blinked, looking at Miri, then Peder. "Oh. Right. It's beautiful."

"How has it been for you here, Katar?" Peder asked.

"They all hate us, of course. What would you expect?"

Then she whispered in Miri's ear. "I need to talk to you alone, as soon as we can."

Miri nodded. The sun had steamed much of the rain from her clothes, but she shivered with new cold.

"I would have liked you here yesterday but at least it's not tomorrow," Katar said. "You'll have to get settled later. It's time for the gift giving. Mount Eskel goes first, since we're the newest province."

The king had come out of the palace and was standing on a dais built in the courtyard. Around him stood what Miri assumed were his guards and family. She recognized Prince Steffan alongside yellow-haired, red-cheeked Britta. Miri jumped up and down, waving, and Britta happily waved back. Katar glared at Miri to behave. She directed the wagon driver to follow her across the courtyard.

"Your Royal Majesty," said Katar, bowing to the dais. "The people of Mount Eskel, in honor of your noble reign, offer our harvest gift."

The king glanced into the wagon without leaning forward. "My first gift from my favorite mountain. The crown gives thanks." He lifted his hand in dismissal, and the wagon drove on.

Peder's hopeful expression stuck to his face, as if he were afraid any change would show his hurt. Three months he had slaved over that stone. It was the greatest treasure Mount Eskel could offer the king, and yet it was worth no more to him than a moment's glance.

Miri put her hand on Peder's shoulder. His muscles were stiff.

No doubt the rest of the provinces would offer impressive gifts and grand displays of wealth. Miri readied herself to feel humiliated once again for being from poor, lowly Mount Eskel.

A white-haired man spoke to the king.

"He's the delegate from Elsby," Katar whispered as she rejoined Miri. "Full of mines."

"In years past," the delegate was saying, "we have honored you with but a handful of gems. In thanks for your kind attention this year—and for the many tributes you've requested from us—Elsby wishes to honor Your Royal Majesty with the *greater* portion of our excavations."

He pulled the tarp off a wagon and revealed a heap of loose gravel. There was a quiet gasp from the dais.

"What's happening?" Miri whispered.

Katar's mouth hung open. "That's probably the dirt that they dig the gems out of. I don't understand. . . ."

Next, the delegate from Hindrick approached the dais with a dozen others, each carrying a sack in his arms.

"Your Majesty, you have been much on our minds, given the tributes you so often request. In the past we've sent you bushels of culled grain while always keeping to ourselves a substance our workers sweat and bleed to produce. Even now, great king, twelve wagons heaped with golden dross arrive at your granary." With a flourish, the delegate and his men upended their bags, and dusty bits drifted onto the king's boots.

"Dross?" asked Miri.

"After the grain is removed from the wheat stalk, dross is what's left over," Katar whispered. "Good for nothing but stuffing itchy mattresses."

The king was on his feet. He whispered furiously with an impressive-looking man dressed in green with black sashes across his chest. Katar said he was Gummonth, the king's chief official.

"Have any of you come with an honest gift?" Gummonth asked.

The remaining thirteen delegates were waiting their turn. Miri saw one holding a jug of water; another was in a wagon stacked with cattle bones. Some seemed uneasy while others stared back with defiant smiles.

A delegate with a jar of worms answered the king.

"Of course normally we would present our beloved monarch with our very best silks," he said. "But the tributes this year—"

"His Majesty has suffered enough of this farce," said Gummonth.

The king started down the dais steps, royal guards gathering around him.

Katar was shaking her head. "I was so determined we wouldn't stick out as the ignorant poor folk. And yet we did anyway. The other delegates planned this, and they excluded me."

Miri did not completely understand what was going on, but she could see the confused alarm on Britta's face as she and Steffan followed the king.

A man in fine red clothing approached the royal party.

"One last gift, Your Majesty," said the man. His trousers hit above his ankles and his jacket above his wrists, as if he'd borrowed the clothes from a smaller man.

"Is that one of the delegates?" Miri asked.

Katar shook her head.

"Which province do you represent?" asked Gummonth.

The man said, "The shoeless!" and pulled something out of his jacket.

Miri had never seen a pistol before and did not know until later that the loud *crack* and sizzling light came from the spark of gunpowder shooting a lead ball down its barrel and toward the king's chest. But the king's guards knew, and as soon as the man pulled it out, the guards were in motion. One jumped at the king, pulling him

23

down. Others leaped between him and the man in red, while several more shot their long-barreled muskets. A volley of *pops* scratched the air with smoke and lashed Miri's ears.

When the smoke cleared, several people lay on the ground. All but two stood up again—the guard who had thrown himself into the bullet's path, and the shooter, downed by the guards' muskets.

Miri seemed to see it all from far away, and she felt rather than heard herself scream.

# Chapter Three

❧

*A queen there was in a palace of bread*
*Sing blue, sing white, stay up all night*
*She nibbled the walls and gobbled her bed*
*Sing white, sing blue, sing ballyhoo*

*The folk begged crumbs from their robust queen*
*Sing blue, sing white, she ate all night*
*She shared not a thing until it turned green*
*So white, so blue, the mold it grew*

M iri was not the only one who screamed.

Guards massed around the royal party, pushing them into the palace. The crowd that had gathered for the gift giving was running for the gate. The courtyard felt like a cage.

"Inside!" said Katar.

The Eskelites followed Katar across flagstones toward a palace entrance, skirting wide the two bodies on the ground.

A group of guards blocked the doorway, their

expressions a study in menace. Katar explained that she was a delegate and the girls were all ladies of the princess, but the guards held tight to their spears.

Britta came from inside. She looked darker, her hair no longer touched by sunlight. Her cheeks, often mottled, flushed a deeper red.

"Yes, let them pass, please," Britta said, and at last the guards budged.

Tension filled the palace like smoke from a stopped-up chimney. When Miri had pictured her reunion with her best friend, she'd never imagined gunshots and bodies. Britta signaled Miri, Peder, and the rest of the girls to follow her down a corridor and into a large room. She shut the door and locked it.

Miri could no longer hear the clamor and calls from outside. Peder was beside her, their arms touching. Britta shut her eyes. Gerti, the youngest of the girls, was visibly trembling. Miri guessed that none of them was ready yet to talk about what had just happened.

She cleared her throat. "So, is this where we'll be staying?"

Gerti took a breath and looked around, seeming relieved to have a distraction.

The room reminded Miri of how they had slept at the princess academy, all the girls in one open chamber. But that chamber had been bare. This one had carpets on the floor, mattresses on wood frames, and curtains hung from the ceiling so each girl could dress and sleep in privacy. The fabrics were colorful, patterned in florals, stripes, and swirls. Miri supposed it was meant to be beautiful, but she found it jarring.

"Yes, this will be home for the next year," said Britta. "Please try not to worry. I'm sure we're safe in here. The guards will take care of everything. Is this all of you? We won't need as many beds then. My room is just across the hall."

"We will live in the actual palace?" said Liana. Her dark eyes were wide, taking in the scene with pleasure.

"I thought the palace was made of linder," Gerti said, brushing the cream limestone wall with her fingertips. Her father was head of the village council and built like a bear, but his daughter was more of a bird—thin, fair, and likely to sing.

"Only the king's wing," said Britta. "We're in the south wing. There are strangely strict customs—that only the royal family may live inside linder walls, servants and guards can spend no more than eight hours inside before having to rotate to another section of the palace, that sort of thing." She shrugged. "Crazy lowlanders."

Miri laughed, and Britta smiled at her.

"Katar," said Britta, "I thought you would want to stay with friends from home while they're here, so I had your things moved from your room in the delegates' wing."

Britta smiled, sure she had done right, and did not seem to notice Katar's hesitation.

Katar had never had friends, though Miri believed any cruelty on her part in the past simply stemmed from unhappiness. Perhaps now that she had left Mount Eskel and the father who had never loved her, she might be ready for friendship.

"You can have my things brought in too," said Peder, throwing himself on the nearest bed. He groaned as he sank into the soft mattress and rolled onto his side.

"Um . . . I don't think boys are—" Britta began.

"Don't mind me!" Peder pulled a blanket over his head.

Miri did not know how he could even pretend to nap. She could barely keep from pacing.

"Don't worry, Britta," said Esa. "We'll kick him out before night. Off to your fancy apprenticeship, big brother."

She nudged Peder's shape under the blanket. Peder made an exaggerated snoring noise.

There was a knock at the door, and Miri startled. A voice called out, and Britta opened it to an official.

"I guess with all that's happened there are bound to

be meetings." Britta sighed and met eyes with Miri. "I'm sorry this has been such a strange welcome. I *am* happy you're all here!"

As soon as Britta left, Katar grabbed Miri's wrist and pulled her to the chamber's seating area. Miri hesitated at the soft, long benches Katar called "sofas." Surely something so fine was not meant to be sat on like a common stool. But Katar yanked Miri down beside her.

"Oh!" Miri said, cozying in. "I have a feeling this sofa and I will become good friends." Katar glared, and Miri pretended she did not notice. "That man shouted something about 'the shoeless' before—"

"Before he tried to shoot the king." Katar explained about bullets and gunpowder, as well as the classes in Danland. "Nobles are the landowners. Commoners pay tribute to the nobles, who own the land they live on. Some commoner merchants and artisans are well off. But the poorest of the commoners—the farmers, laborers, and servants—are called the 'shoeless.'"

Miri supposed that she and everyone from Mount Eskel were considered shoeless as well. "What does it mean that he tried to kill the king for the shoeless?" asked Miri.

"I guess it means that it's begun," Katar said. "It's what I wanted to talk to you about."

Katar glanced across the room, but the other girls were busy claiming their beds and investigating wardrobes full of clothing.

"*Revolution,*" Katar whispered.

Miri had never heard the word before, but it gave her a cold kind of thrill.

"Some commoners came to me after I arrived here in the spring," said Katar. "Even though I'm a delegate, they thought the daughter of a quarry-worker might be sympathetic to the shoeless. Things have been rough for the shoeless the past few years. The king keeps demanding higher tributes from the nobles. In turn, the nobles take higher tributes from the commoners on their lands. The shoeless must give so much of their crops and income to the nobles, they fear starvation. When people are afraid, Miri, they do crazy things."

"Like that man in the courtyard."

Katar leaned closer. "These rebels want me to pledge my loyalty to the commoner cause and be a spy among the delegates."

"Did you agree to spy for them?" Miri asked.

"No! I said I'd think about it and have avoided them since. If the king's officials even suspect I spoke with such people, I could lose my place as a delegate. Or something worse—like my head."

"Don't talk to them," said Miri, suddenly afraid. "Avoid them."

"I do. But they send me messages; they wait for me outside the Delegate House with questioning looks. I don't think they're bad people. Just desperate. And probably half starved." Her voice quieted even more. "You and I both know what it feels like to go to bed hungry."

Miri nodded. Hunger ran through her childhood like a string through a bead necklace. But surely Katar was exaggerating about the poor of the lowlands. How could anyone go hungry in a land of such abundance?

"What we did last year—what *you* did, Miri—that was revolution. Turning things around. You said just because things had always been one way didn't mean they couldn't change. You persuaded the village council to refuse the traders' terms and fight for fair value. That was pretty brave."

Miri blinked, too surprised by a compliment from Katar to say anything but "thanks."

"The gift giving is a tradition as old as Danland, but today the nobles used it to mock royalty. The nobles still pay the king's tributes—they don't dare oppose him and his royal guard. But the anger must be spreading if even *nobles* are refusing to honor the king. And one

commoner with a pistol tried to overthrow him entirely."
She shuddered and rubbed her arms as if pretending she
were simply cold. "Maybe he acted alone, or maybe
there are thousands like him, uniting. I wish I knew.
Things are pretty good for Mount Eskel right now. If
the commoner cause is doomed, joining them against the
king is *not* a good idea."

"And if it's not doomed?" Miri asked.

"If they overthrow the king and create a new government? Then Mount Eskel had better be on their side—
and quick. We're too small to stand alone. We *must* be on
the winning side, or we'll get squashed. I'd rather not see
our fathers hanged as traitors of either side."

Miri shook her head. "Whenever our academy tutor
or the traders talked of the lowlands, they made it sound
so perfect."

"Nothing's perfect," said Katar. She picked up an
orange pillow and tucked it under her arms. "I figured at
the Queen's Castle you're in the best position to meet
people outside the palace and figure out the situation."

"So it's too dangerous for you to be a spy, but that's
exactly what you want me to do?"

"I'm a *delegate*," Katar said. "The king's officials would
notice if I went slinking around commoners."

"Fine, I'll learn what I can."

"Carefully. Don't tell anyone what you're doing—even

Britta, all right?" Katar looked down, playing with the tassels on the pillow. "This may shock you, but I'm not eager to attend your execution."

A new thought shivered in Miri. "Wait . . . Who *owns* Mount Eskel?"

"What?"

"You said only nobles own land, and there haven't been nobles on Mount Eskel for hundreds of years."

Katar looked at the ceiling, as if the white molding held the answer. "I guess the king owns it all."

"If commoners pay tribute to their landowners, why haven't we had to pay the king?"

There was a burst of laughter so sudden Miri jumped to her feet in alarm. Bena and Liana had pushed Peder out of the bed and onto the floor. He in turn leaped on Liana's bed, clinging to it and laughing as the girls tugged at his ankles.

"So, are you two betrothed?" Katar asked.

"No," Miri said shortly.

"Ohh." Katar smirked, one eyebrow raised, and she looked altogether more like her old self. "It appears I stumbled upon a topic of conversation even more dangerous than revolution."

# Chapter Four

❦

*Open sky, cat's-eye*
*Honey drop, treetop*
*Flag stripe, plum ripe*
*Pipe smoke, ancient oak*
*Pine knot, moon shot*
*Rose bed, raven's head*

The carriage had windows of glass, but they were shut, curtains drawn. Miri felt as boxed in as she had huddled under the cloth in the back of Enrik's wagon. But these seats were covered in red velvet, and she rode beside her best friend.

"I really don't think I'm in danger," Britta said. "That poor man yesterday was crazy. Besides, he's . . ." She paused. "Still, Steffan wouldn't let me come out with you unless I promised to keep the curtains closed. I hope you aren't feeling ill."

Miri put her hands to her stomach and made an exaggerated grimace. "The egg bread I had for breakfast was so delightful . . . *ulp* . . . I think I'll take another look at it. . . ."

"Just mind you do not sully my dress, your ladyship," Britta said, sitting up primly and using a mock high voice. "It is the very *latest* from Morland."

"You mean to say," Miri said in an equally pinched tone, "in Asland it is not fashionable to decorate your gown with your breakfast?"

"You must think us so backward, my dear."

"Shocking indeed!" Miri smiled, but she could not quite forget. "That guard . . . He knew he might be killed, yet he put himself in the path of the bullet."

"To save the king." Britta briefly shut her eyes. "That's the oath the royal guards swear when they enter service."

Miri nodded, but she actually did feel queasy, and not just from the jostling of the carriage. She wanted to ask Britta about the stirrings of revolution, but Katar's warning silenced her.

"Don't worry. I'm sure the king and his officials are taking care of any problems," said Britta. "What matters is you are here! I'm sorry to rush you off, but we'll have all year together, and I knew you wouldn't want to miss the first day at the Queen's Castle."

Miri parted the curtain a slit, squinting past her own reflection in the glass to see what waited beyond.

The carriage was starting onto a bridge. The river split in two around a rocky island where a red-brick building rose, the top peaking into towers roofed in the now-familiar green copper.

"The Queen's Castle," Miri said softly.

The name alone delighted her. Surely all the knowledge of the world was contained inside. If only she could learn it, she could teach the others at home, and at last Mount Eskel would have the same advantages as the lowlands.

Miri started to open the door before the carriage had completely stopped.

"Wait!" Britta said. "It's bad manners to fall to your death on your first day! Besides, you're supposed to wear these over your dress. They're your scholar robes."

"What's a scholar?"

"Well, *you* are. A person who wants to know things, whose job is to learn."

Miri pulled her arms into the wide sleeves and did up the hooks in the front. The robes were pale blue, the Mount Eskel sky in the morning. A crown and an open door were embroidered over her heart.

Britta gave her a cheek kiss and wished her well. "The carriage will return for you at the end of the day. Go learn for all of us."

Miri knew Britta meant the sentiment in kindness,

but the words felt heavy. *Go learn for all of us.* For the other academy girls, for her family, for all of Mount Eskel. As well, she needed to meet other commoners and find out for Katar if it'd be safer to join in their cause or to stick with the king. Miri could not let anyone down.

*I won't*, Miri promised herself.

The robes were thick and long, made to cover clothing and keep it clean, not to be pretty. And yet as Miri walked through the massive wooden doors into the stone entry, she felt as beautiful as she had in a gown at the princess academy ball. She, little Miri of Mount Eskel, was an Aslandian scholar.

And apparently she was one of thousands.

The castle teemed with people in robes just like hers in a dozen different colors. She stared. And stared. So many! And so many gray heads. She smoothed her own brown hair. She'd noticed Aslandian girls often wore their hair down, so Miri had not braided hers that morning. It felt strange hanging free.

A group in orange scholar robes jostled her in passing, so she moved out of the way. A scholar in brown bumped her, and she scurried into a corner. Her toes curled in her boots; the thuds of her heart were achy. She let her arm hang at her side and pretended her sister was holding her hand.

An older boy in blue robes stood where Marda was

not. He glanced over and Miri winced, waiting for him to remark that she looked too young to be a scholar. And then she'd have to explain that she was not as young as she seemed, just short, thank you very much. But perhaps she *was* too young after all. Perhaps there had been a mistake and she'd be kicked out and—

"The robe colors represent different courses of study," said the boy.

"Oh. I didn't know."

"You have that first-day look in your eyes. It hasn't been long since I rubbed that same look out of my own. I arrived last year, full of hot powder and ready to learn! And then I stood in that very spot, waiting for someone to tell me what to do."

"And did someone?"

He shook his head. "Everyone was too busy being scholarly. If you don't mind skipping the part where you wander this castle aimlessly, you can follow me."

She looked him over as they walked. His hair was so pale it seemed more white than yellow, and he had a good face with a prominent mouth. She was not sure why she noticed his mouth.

"Um . . . Does light blue mean novice?" she asked.

"Precisely. Every first-year scholar wears open sky, as they call it. Cat's-eye," he said, nodding toward a clot of green-robed scholars, "indicates a focus on teaching."

He taught her the chant that named all twelve fields of scholarship. "Once you reach master status, you wear raven's head—the black robes."

"Ha," Miri said, and then wished she had not.

"What's funny?" he asked.

"Nothing. I was just thinking, clearly the masters are the smartest. This pale blue will show every smudge, but if the masters don't wash their black robes, no one will notice."

"Until you are downwind from one," he said, fanning his nose.

Miri smiled. Perhaps scholars were not too serious to laugh.

"How long does it take to become a master?"

"Twenty years or so."

"Twenty . . ." She felt her heart plummet. How could she possibly learn enough in only one year? "Wait . . . If you were here last year, why are you still wearing blue?"

"I didn't finish the year out, so I am starting over," he said, and something in his voice told her he did not want to talk about it.

They made their way up more stairs than Miri had imagined possible, at last arriving in a chamber of gray stone tiles, wood-paneled walls, and narrow windows overlooking the river. Three dozen scholars in open-sky robes milled about, and Miri was relieved to see a couple nearly as young as she. The sole black wearer in the room, a man of white beard and hair, raised his hand. Everyone quieted.

"I am Master Filippus. You are either beginning your scholarship at the Queen's Castle or you are trespassing. If your name is not on my list"—he lifted his paper and made a throaty whine—"I will be forced to send you to the Green for summary execution."

Miri thought he was teasing. He *had* to be teasing. No one laughed.

"You will tell me your names, and I will check you off the list."

Master Filippus waved his hand at the nearest scholar.

"Hanna Wengerdaughter of Elsby," she said.

Master Filippus peered at his paper. "Mmm, your name is present and so it appears you have avoided the ax. For now. Next."

After the first dozen names and provinces, Miri lost track. The older boy she'd met was called Timon of Asland. His name she would remember.

She was gazing at a painting above the fireplace when Timon nudged her. It was her turn.

"Oh. I am Miri Larendaughter of Mount Eskel."

The master's eyebrows twitched; he was interested in something at last. "Our first student from Mount

Eskel. Mmm . . . And where did you do your preparatory studies?"

Miri blinked. "My preparatory studies?"

"Which schools did you attend previously?"

"Oh, the only school there was. The princess academy."

Now *everyone* seemed interested. Miri smiled nervously, afraid they might have mistaken her for Britta.

"I was just one of the girls there," she explained. "Not the princess. I mean, none of us were princesses, obviously. But I wasn't who Prince Steffan chose for his bride. He chose Britta, so now she'll be the princess. Not that I mind. I mean . . . um . . ."

*Shut it, Miri*, she told herself.

"A graduate of the princess academy," said Master Filippus. "Tell me, did you study more than just Reading?"

"Oh yes, we studied everything."

"Everything?" He blinked slowly, his lips pursed in scorn. "I'm not acquainted with that subject. Is *Everything* a science or an art?"

"Um, I mean, we also studied Commerce, Diplomacy, Geography, Kings and Queens, Poise, and Conversation —"

Someone snorted, and Miri blushed. Perhaps real scholars did not bother with Poise and Conversation.

"That is a good beginning," said Master Filippus.

Beginning? What other subjects could possibly exist?

"Of course, in order to graduate to tutor status, one must also have a basis in Mathematics, Science, Engineering, Law, Music and Art, Astronomy, History, Logic, Rhetoric, Theology, and Ethics."

"What is Ethics?" she asked. In truth she had never heard of several of the subjects he'd named, but she'd already forgotten the others.

"Ethics . . ." He turned his gaze to the painting above the mantel. "I notice your attention is drawn to this work of art."

Miri nodded. Before coming to Asland, she'd seen only one painting and had prized it almost as much as her six books. Now it seemed inconsequential. This painting was not only larger but more vivid. It showed a girl pouring milk from a jug and looking out the window at the night, and yet Miri *felt* as the girl must be feeling. That her home was small and safe. That the world out there was huge and scary, but it called to her. Would the girl stay home and keep pouring milk? Or would she leave?

"It is one of the few surviving works of the master painter Halstein. Notice the way the candlelight outlines the girl's cheek, mirroring the shape of the milk pitcher and the curve of the moon. Perfection."

"Yes," Miri agreed.

"Now, imagine the Queen's Castle catches fire. Besides yourself, there is only one other person in the building—a confessed murderer of a child, chained in the dungeon. If you save the murderer, he will not harm you but will live the remainder of his life in another prison, and the painting will burn. If you save the painting, the man will burn. Which would you choose—the murderer or the painting?"

*The painting of course*, was Miri's first thought. But suspicious that she was missing something, she just said, "The painting is irreplaceable. . . ."

"And so is the man," said the girl Hanna.

And with that began a debate so rapid Miri could scarcely note who said what.

"The painting inspires, but the man kills."

"Unlike the painting, the man is alive and so has endless potential for good—"

"Or evil."

"The painting gives us beauty."

"Beauty isn't a useful commodity. Simply calculate what's worth more: the painting or the work the man can do."

"Oh, it's always about gold and silver with you. What about right and wrong?"

"Who has the right to weigh the value of any person?"

"Is any object of greater value than human life?"

"He nullified his life by choosing to end another's."

"And that, Miss Miri," said Master Filippus, raising his hand to quiet the voices, "is Ethics. The science of right and wrong."

"It's an impossible question," Hanna said.

"As impossible as life itself," said Timon.

It did not seem that impossible to Miri. Once a thieving bandit had tried to kill her. He was dead now, and Miri was not sorry. Besides, the painting *was* beautiful.

They spent the rest of the morning on Mathematics, and though Miri worked hard with her slate and chalk, she kept glancing at the painting. The ethics question seemed to hang in the air before her, a dust mote that she could not quite catch in her hand.

At the end of the day, Timon fell in beside her on the stairs going outside.

"You aren't lodging at the Queen's Castle?" he said. "I live in town too. We could walk together."

"Well . . . there's a carriage waiting for me." She tilted her head, letting her hair slide over her face. Only the wealthy had carriages, and Miri felt like a fraud riding in one.

"Are you staying far from here?"

"At the . . . the palace."

He blinked. "You are a courtier?"

"Um . . . I'm a lady of the princess?" she said as if she were not sure.

"I see." He hesitated and then walked ahead of her toward the bridge.

Miri watched him go, feeling a failure as well as a fraud. How could she hope to learn anything for Katar? She could not exactly say to Timon, "Lovely weather, I like your shoes, and by the way, can you tell me about the revolution?" She might as well holler at the city: "Everybody who wants to get rid of the king, raise your hand!"

Suddenly two children came at Miri. They were very thin, about five and seven years of age, and their feet were bare. With bony hands they seized her robes and made a raspy, keening noise.

"A quint, please, be kind," said the little boy.

Miri knew from her reading that a quint was a unit of money. "I don't understand. You want a coin?"

"A quint for me, a quint for my sister, or one for us both, be kind, a quint for us both, be kind."

Miri had no coins, neither heavy gold nor light copper, and she told them so, but they kept gripping. She gently tried to remove the boy's hand, and he resisted, his voice getting louder.

"A quint, a quint, be kind," they repeated over and over, eyes wide but without hope.

Miri told them firmly to let her go, she tried to push them away, but the children pressed harder, backing her against a gate, their hands gripping like hawk talons. She could smell their hair and clothing, so rancid it stung her nose. Their voices sawed at her, relentless. "A quint, a quint, be kind . . ."

Then Timon was there. "Here," he said, giving each child a small silver coin. "Now go on."

The children clutched the coins with both hands and ran, disappearing into the traffic on the bridge.

Miri felt like crying. "I told them I didn't have any, but they wouldn't believe me."

"They're used to people saying no. If you haven't eaten in a day or two, hunger makes you desperate. And there are far too many poor and desperate in these streets."

"Poor? But this is Asland."

"There are poor in Asland, Miri. Didn't you know? There are poor everywhere."

Katar had said the shoeless often went hungry, but until seeing the children Miri had not quite believed it.

Then Miri recalled the thin girl from the town on their journey. The way the girl had watched Miri eat. How she had gnawed that stick. Her bony legs, her bare feet. Miri's throat felt tight. She wished she could go back to that moment, say hello to the girl, share the meal.

"No, I didn't know. I'm sorry," she said, both to Timon and to the girl in her memory. "On Mount Eskel, almost all our food came from the lowlands—I mean, from Asland and the rest of Danland. I guess I thought there were endless mounds of food here."

"Plenty of people in the *lowlands* do just fine," Timon said. "But too often the children of farmers starve while the noble landowners grow fat. When the changes come—"

Timon stopped. He looked around, as if to see if anyone else had heard him.

"I shouldn't have said . . . I didn't mean—excuse me." He started to go.

*Changes?* Did she dare ask? She started after him, but fear pushed against her, and it seemed to take an hour just to catch him on the bow of the bridge.

"Timon, wait. Yesterday at the palace something happened."

He turned back. "You mean the attempt on the king's life?"

Miri stepped closer and whispered, "If there are *changes* coming, I'd like to know more. I'd like to help."

Timon's eyes brightened. "Truly? But—"

SHANNON HALE

"I'm staying at the palace, but I'm not one of them. I hope you will trust me."

She'd promised Katar. And now the memory of that thin girl goaded her on.

"I can't speak freely," he said, "but . . . I'll talk to you as soon as I can. There is much happening."

His icy blue eyes flashed, and he smiled at her. Miri found herself smiling back. A tickle in her stomach slid up to her heart. Timon knew things, Miri was certain, and for the first time she wondered if perhaps the unknown changes to come might be wonderful.

# Chapter Five

A quint, my lord, a quint for some grain
A quint for the rent, a roof from the rain
A sip of hot soup to fill empty space
An old wool scarf to warm my face

So what did you do today?" Miri asked, entering the girls' chamber. She posed in the doorway, in case they wanted a good look at her scholar robes. No one glanced up.

"We *sewed*," said Bena. She was wearing her brown hair unbraided as well. It hung long to her waist and made her look even taller. "Ladies of the princess help in the wedding preparations, which apparently means sewing."

"And spinning," said Esa.

"How much thread does a wedding need?" Gerti asked, incredulous.

"I miss the quarry," said Frid with a sigh. She was holding her hands out while Esa wrapped them with yarn. "I miss hitting things."

Liana lay on her side, accentuating the curve of her hip. "The *servants* bring us food. We don't even wash our plates. Being a princess's lady actually *means* something. We have *rank*."

"I'm surprised Britta couldn't get more girls into your special academy," said Bena. "She *is* the betrothed princess."

Miri removed her robes and looked around for Katar, eager to tell her about the conversation with Timon. Katar was gone, but Inga, their gray-haired chaperone, gave her a smile full of wrinkles. Inga sat on the sofa, neither sewing nor spinning. Just watching. Her king-appointed task was to keep an eye on the girls, and it seemed that was all she meant to do.

"I'm sure Esa would like to attend the Queen's Castle," said Bena. "And I wouldn't mind, if you would know. Instead of sewing in this room all day—"

"And spinning," said Esa.

"And eating food the servants bring us as ladies of *rank*," said Liana.

"I thought something smelled rank," Miri mumbled.

"What?"

"Nothing, Liana." Miri sat on the floor and tossed a pillow in the air. "I learned some stuff today I didn't know before. If I tell you about it, then it's almost as if you attend the Queen's Castle too."

"I want to hear," Esa said, turning so she could see Miri and still use Frid's hands as a spool. Esa's left arm, injured in a quarry accident years before, hung limp at her side.

Miri recounted Master Filippus's introduction of the different subjects. But when she got to Ethics and a painting versus a prisoner, the girls began to argue so passionately two palace guards stormed in.

"We're fine, really," Miri told the bewildered guards. "Which is more than I can say for that murderous prisoner if Frid gets her hands on him."

"He killed a *child*." Frid was on her feet, gesturing with yarn-wrapped hands. "And you're talking about freeing him!"

Esa touched her arm. "It's just a made-up story."

Frid's face was wide open—all eyes, mouth, and flexed nostrils. "Why? If I were going to make up a story, it wouldn't be about someone killing children. It'd be about cutting blocks of linder and being so strong I could lift them over my head. And it would be *funny*. All stories should be funny."

One of the guards scratched his beard. "So you girls are all right?"

"You may go," Liana said with a wave of her hand.

Supper came, and Miri asked Inga if she could go eat with Britta. Inga nodded as if she did not care one way or the other.

51

In Britta's chamber, there were several wardrobes painted as brightly as the river houses, and an enormous bed stuffed with feathers and dripping with blankets, but no Britta. Miri sat on the floor and had begun to eat her fish and potato cakes when the door opened.

"Miri!" Britta caught Miri around her shoulders and knocked her back onto the carpet in a running embrace. "I almost forgot you were here and when I saw you, I had that happy jolt all over again. Isn't that wonderful? How was your first day?"

"Amazing! And a little daunting." She told Britta about the grand castle, old Master Filippus, Timon of Asland. "He has hair so pale it's almost white. He's only a little older than we are, but he talks like a master scholar sometimes, I guess because he's read so many books. Oh, do you think you could get Esa into the Queen's Castle? And maybe Bena too? I hate to ask for Bena—she can be such a pain sometimes—but she seems interested."

"I'm sorry, I can't. I wish I could."

"That's all right." Miri thought of what Bena had said. Shouldn't a princess be able to do such a thing? Miri smiled weakly at Britta and wished she could make the smile stronger. "Um . . . How's Steffan?"

"He's well. I think he is, anyway. I only get to see him at meals, with his mother and father sitting there watching us, and the occasional chaperoned walk in the gardens, and . . . and . . ."

Britta pressed her hand against her mouth and took a sharp hiccup of a breath.

"Britta!" Miri put an arm around her. "Don't be sad. What did I do?"

"I'm sorry, nothing, I'm fine." Britta pushed the heels of her hands against her eyes. "It's just all so much. The duties and the worries and the way the king and queen look at me, and my father is at court too, looking at me, everyone looking at me. Except Steffan. I'd never been in Asland with Steffan before. Perhaps he is always so distant around his parents. Or perhaps . . . he does not feel for me what I feel for him."

"I don't believe it. He adores you. That was very clear when he came to Mount Eskel."

"I thought so too. Maybe he changed his mind. And I don't know what to make of the attempt on the king's life and all the whispers and frowns and . . . never mind. I just want to be glad you're here."

"Well, I'm glad I'm here, even if I'm not sure where here is. Asland is overwhelming."

"I don't worry about you a bit. You know, you would be a better princess. The king and queen would have approved."

"Yes, indeed," Miri said, pursing her lips dramatically. "Their most Royal Highnesses long for a girl who knows a billy goat from a nanny and the business end of a soup ladle."

"I mean it."

Miri shook her head. "Britta, you're being silly. Steffan chose you and that's that."

*Besides, I have Peder,* she thought. *Don't I?*

Miri went to bed that night surrounded by the slow breathing of the other girls, her curtain pulled so she could read by candlelight without being seen. It was the first day in a long time that Miri had not seen Peder. And it was the first day she had known Timon.

Autumn Week Six

Dear Marda,

I have been in Asland nearly a week. There are still at least five months until traders will carry my letters to you along with the barrels of salt pork and bags of onions. But I want to talk to you now. I wish I could quarry-speak all the way from Asland.

Each day a palace carriage drives me to the Queen's Castle, where I take my studies. I am glad of the carriage. I dare not edge a single toe onto a busy Aslandian street. Are you surprised that I am such a trembling baby?

There are so many things to learn at the Queen's Castle my head hurts. And even more things I am supposed to learn, and those scare me some. I feel like a tiny bug, and the world is a hungry bird looking down at me.

I have not seen Peder in five days as he is only free at week's end. Britta says Gus's stone-carving workshop is close enough to walk to, but then I would have to enter the streets of Asland. The ones that terrify me to trembling. Are you laughing at me yet? I hope so.

I do not see Britta much. She is very busy preparing to be a princess. I do not see the other girls much as I am in my studies all day. How can anyone be lonely in a city seething with people? If you were here, you would poke me and tell me I am doing a fine impersonation of a grumpy old billy goat.

I miss you. I miss Pa. I wonder if I was wrong to come.

*Perhaps when it is time to send this letter, I will feel much, much better. That is hard to imagine. It is easier to imagine that you are here. It is easier to imagine rain is honey and stones are bread.*

*If you have not guessed yet, this is from your trembling baby of a sister,*

Miri

# Chapter Six

*'Tis I, my sweet, your rough-and-ready man*
*Well hid by night to beg your fine white hand*
*Though king of bandits, draped in chains of gold*
*I'm poor in love and suffer grief untold*

In Asland, most people did not wake at dawn. Even the poor were rich in candles and fuel. They could afford to light a house after sundown and stay up late in the evening, window after window golden and flickering. Miri was in awe of the homemade sunshine of candles and kerosene lamps and hearths fat with wood and flame. Such a luxury to be awake while the sun slept, and then to ignore dawn and sleep while the world lightened.

*I'm an Aslandian now,* Miri thought. *I'm richer than morning.*

The girls woke slowly, stretching in their beds like cats in a patch of sunlight. It was week's end, and Miri did not have to rush into a carriage.

Their chaperone, Inga, shuffled in. "Wake up, girls. His Majesty the king invites you to the royal breakfast."

Katar sat up. "The king? When?"

"Now," Inga said.

There were several gasps, and then the room was all squealing girls scrambling for dresses and stockings and shoes, rubbing water from pitchers on their faces and underarms, and elbowing for space at the mirror.

Inga hastened them down several corridors to the threshold of the king's wing, where guards asked the password. Inga gave it and motioned the girls forward, but no one moved. The walls, floor, and even the ceiling were made of polished linder, rich as cream. Miri could *feel* the stone surrounding her, a kind of silent hum, a subtle vibration that lifted the hairs on her arms.

Gummonth, the chief official, approached, telling them to hurry along. But the girls just stared, mesmerized. Never had any of them been completely surrounded by linder, and Miri was tempted to see if quarry-speech worked differently here.

The people of Mount Eskel used quarry-speech to communicate in the quarry, where clay earplugs and deafening mallet blows made it impossible to hear instructions or shouts of warning. Miri had discovered that quarry-speech moved through linder and communicated with memories, not words—the speaker's memory nudging the same or similar memory in others.

"It's as if we're *inside* Mount Eskel," Esa was saying.

"I miss home," said Gerti. "I even miss sleeping beside the goats."

Miri quarry-spoke of the academy tutor running terrified through the village, chased by a particularly saucy nanny goat, an event Miri knew the other girls had witnessed. It was more like singing in her mind than thinking, the way she silently poured the memory into the linder. Usually only a quiver in her vision accompanied quarry-speech, but this time the memory burst into Miri's mind so full of color and motion that for a moment she seemed to live it again.

The girls inhaled sharply, apparently experiencing the heightened quarry-speech as well, and then they laughed. Gummonth looked around in vain for the cause of the hilarity. That made the girls laugh harder. Only people of Mount Eskel were able to use quarry-speech, though by the end of her year on the mountain, Britta had seemed to recognize faint sensations.

Gummonth looked over them with a dead-eyed expression. "Bumpkins and peasants. I am made to bow to the children of goats."

The girls frowned, straightening dresses and smoothing hair. Miri had thought Gummonth a handsome, striking man, but now she noticed his sour mouth, his pinched voice. As the girls followed after him, Miri sniffed her braid just to make sure she did not smell goaty.

They entered the royal breakfast room, where King Bjorn and Queen Sabet perched on high-backed chairs before a dining table.

"Your Royal Majesties," said Gummonth, "the ladies of the princess."

"Hm?" The king was spooning cream and raisins onto a dish of rye bread. "Yes, all right."

The queen barely glanced up from her tea. She had dark hair and skin as pale as parchment.

The academy girls sat at a table opposite Britta, Steffan, and other members of the court. Britta waved at Miri and then quickly resumed a ladylike posture.

There seemed to be enough food for a village. Miri devoured a pecan-encrusted fish, and oat porridge with several globs of honey. The king and queen did not look at the girls. They did not look at each other. No one spoke.

Then Miri noticed the mantelpiece over the hearth.

"Oh! Mount Eskel's gift!" she said. "Peder, the boy who did the carving, will be so happy to hear you had it installed. Thank you, Your Majesty."

Katar kicked Miri under the table. Should she not have spoken? But it would have seemed rude not to acknowledge the kindness.

*Though perhaps not as rude as kicking someone*, Miri thought, rubbing her ankle and glaring at Katar.

The king frowned, his beard bristling around his lips,

and he waved a spoon at Gummonth. The official stooped and whispered to Miri, "You are not to address His Royal Majesty. Ever."

Miri felt the heat of shame burn her face. She watched the king dribble fish broth in his beard and wondered for the first time if Danland actually needed a king.

After breakfast, the academy girls accompanied the king and queen to the chapel for services and then to the palace theater. On a stage, a troupe of actors in extravagantly colored costumes enacted a play about forbidden lovers: a noble girl and a bandit king. Miri knew her mouth hung open, and she did not care. It was the most enchanting thing she had ever seen.

*I hate bandits*, she reminded herself.

But she could not help cheering the bandit in the story, with his expressive eyes and lavish words. She squeezed her arms, anxious for the lovers to triumph over evil.

When at last the noble and her reformed bandit wed, Miri had to stifle a happy sob. She spied the royal couple in the first row. The queen stared at some point above the stage. The king snored.

Britta came to find Miri at the end of the play.

"I'm sorry this has been so formal and dull—"

"Dull? That play was . . . was . . ." She exhaled grandly, lacking better words.

A tall boy with dark hair and a square chin came up beside Britta, his arms behind his back, his face impassive.

"Speaking of formal and dull . . ." Miri shook her head. "Now, Steffan, don't tell me you're working on your imitation of a stone column again."

"It's good to see you, Miri," he said, his mouth finding a smile. "I hope you've been keeping out of mischief. For once."

"None to be had in Asland," she said, playing at a haughty tone. "This place is just so boring."

He knocked her with his shoulder, and she knocked him back.

"Let's get into mischief together, shall we?" Britta said, hooking arms with Miri and Esa. "I've been dying for the week's end so we could finally—"

"Lady Britta?" An official in a green dress approached. "If your ladies are available, then we should begin fitting you for your trousseau."

"That is mischief I'm not fit to tackle," said Steffan, nodding farewell as he departed.

"Trousseau?" Miri whispered.

The official started to walk and clearly expected the girls to follow. "Lady Britta will need a ball gown, a chapel gown, and a marriage gown, as well as receiving gowns . . ."

In Britta's chamber, the seamstress unrolled fabrics and went over the styles of sleeves and trains and skirts and bodices. The Mount Eskel girls stared. How could there be fourteen different kinds of skirts?

"Traditionally, the ladies of the princess do the lace-work on the marriage gown," said the official.

"Um, we'll be helpful if Britta needs a stocking darned," said Miri.

"Or a block of stone quarried for her wedding," added Esa. "But lacework . . ."

The seamstress clicked her tongue.

"Then we won't take up any more of your time," said the official. She ushered the girls out. Miri caught Britta's forlorn expression just before the door shut.

"What is lacework?" said Frid.

They'd started back to the girls' chamber when Katar pulled Miri aside.

"Learn anything?"

"Not yet," said Miri, "but I met someone who might help me."

"Hurry. If enough commoners are serious about making change, who do you think they'll come for after the king? The delegates, that's who. And then the rest of the nobles. If the commoners will succeed, Mount Eskel needs to side with them right away, or we'll be taken for royalists and tossed onto the fire with the rest."

"And I'm somehow supposed to find out on my own?" said Miri.

"I told you, I'm a *delegate*," Katar said, annoyance in her voice answering Miri's grumpy tone. "And do you really trust the other girls to keep—"

Katar straightened. Gummonth was strolling down the corridor, shoulders back and chin up, sure of his importance. No, Miri decided, he was definitely *not* handsome.

"So many Eskelites," he said. "It does make one ponder. I don't think the king has ever received a tribute from your people."

Miri froze, still as a mouse under a hawk's shadow. She heard Katar hiss under her breath.

"I must check the books. Surely Mount Eskel has a hefty debt to pay. Delegate Katar," he said, nodding as he walked past.

"Lord Gummonth," Katar said, as if his name tasted like moldy cheese. As soon as he was gone, she cursed.

"How much tribute could the king take?" Miri whispered.

Katar slumped against the wall. "As much as he wants. A common tribute is a gold coin per person."

Miri thought of the two gold coins her family kept wrapped in her mother's old shawl. At least once each day, she and Marda would unwrap the red shawl and marvel at the coins, beautiful as tiny suns. They'd never had money before this year. Coins meant hope, coins meant safety.

The threat of the tribute made the palace feel like a cage, and her longing to be with Peder sharpened into a keen ache. Miri told Inga she was going for a walk and ran outside.

Her fear of what Gummonth might do displaced her fear of the city. Britta had described the way to Gus's workshop. Hoping she remembered, and with a deep breath before the plunge, Miri entered the streets of Asland.

When she was not killed instantly, her mind returned to churning over tributes. What if two gold coins were not enough? Would the officials demand a goat as well, or even all five? No more milk and cheese. No more meat during a hard winter. Even with goat milk, some families nearly starved before spring.

"Watch it!" yelled a man, reining in his mount just a handsbreadth from trampling Miri.

Miri bolted to the nearest building and hugged its wall. Her legs wobbled as if afraid the ground beneath her would give way.

She took a shaky breath and continued on, determined to keep focused. There were a few more near misses with carriages, but she was mostly unscathed when she found the entrance to Gus's workshop, a narrow alley between a grocer's shop and a potter's. Down the passage she discovered a small courtyard hedged by other buildings. Cluttered with stone blocks, heaps of rock chippings, an open shed, and a small square house, the workshop was like a slice of home hidden in the middle of the city. Despite the fear that tributes and thoroughfares had rattled in her, she could almost relax.

Gus was a stout man, his forearms thick with muscle and his belly thick with fat. Miri tried very hard not to stare. She had never seen that much fat on a person.

"Umph," he said when she introduced herself, and he nodded in the direction of Peder on the other side of the shed.

Peder was leaning over a table, examining an intricately carved block of gray stone. Miri stood behind him.

"Whoa, did you do that?" she asked.

Peder spun around.

"Miri! Cough or something before sneaking up. You're like a she-wolf in winter." He straightened his filthy apron. "It's Gus's work. He's very good."

"He's not the only one. The king installed your mantelpiece in the royal breakfast chamber!"

"Oh no," Peder groaned.

That was not the reaction Miri had been expecting.

"I'm so embarrassed, Miri. I had no sense of proportion, no understanding of scene movement, no depth."

"Oh," said Miri, not sure what that all meant. But he seemed so disheartened, she did not want to burden him with worries about lost savings and goats. Besides, the king could not really be so cruel as to rob and starve an entire province, could he?

Peder rubbed the stone with a cloth. "I need to work harder."

He evidently meant to work harder right then, because he got to it, sweeping up rock chips and hauling a stone slab onto the worktable. Miri could not help but notice how Peder's muscles flexed as he lifted the stone. She felt her own arm, sure her muscles lacked the same definition. The hair on his arms was paler than his sun-soaked skin. The hair on his head was so curly, when he slid a piece of chalk above his ear, it stayed.

Twice she tried to renew the conversation, but he answered her questions briefly or drifted off mid-sentence, distracted by his work. After a time she wandered into the shed. She found a sock stuck with a needle, a hole half darned. She lay back on a pile of straw, finished the job, and started on another sock, idly singing a quarry song. Peder picked it up, and they sang together while she sewed, he carved, and the dim Aslandian stars began to throb in the sky.

*Autumn Week Ten*

*Dear Marda,*

I never imagined how many people there must be in the world. Every day hundreds of people with no names cross my path. Well, I suppose they have names, I just do not know them. Then again, perhaps nameless lowlanders spend all day walking in circles just to make the city look busy and confuse poor little mountain girls.

I hope you laugh at that. I miss making you laugh.

I have made friends with a lowlander, and he has a name: Timon. He has read hundreds of books and sailed to three other countries. Each morning for the past few weeks, he has waited for me under a tree near the palace, and we walk together to the Queen's Castle. Yes, I finally learned to navigate Asland's streets! I suppose the walk is fairly long, but it seems short because our conversation is always longer.

When I asked our chaperone, Inga, if I could walk to the Queen's Castle instead of ride in a carriage, she shrugged. She does not seem to care much where we go or what we do. I thought I would enjoy such freedom, but it makes me feel lonely.

Timon has invited me to a Salon night. "Salon" is a fancy word for "room," though I do not know why lowlanders need fancy words for things. We should call our cottage "Laren's Palace" and the goats "mighty horned ones."

Timon told me that on Salon nights nobles invite scholars and artists into their fancy rooms to talk. I think I know what we might talk about, and so I am nervous. Some things, I am learning, are dangerous even to say.

Should I go, Marda?

I want to invite Peder, but he is always so busy. I will anyway. All I can do is keep going to see him until he asks me to stop pestering him for good. Right?

This is from your very fancy sister, who does have a name,

Miri

# Chapter Seven

⬳⬳⊙⬱⬱

*No small thing, a bee's sting*
*When it enters the heart*
*Not so benign, the growing vine*
*When it tears stone apart*

M iri sauntered into the thoroughfare. She'd made her way through the labyrinthine streets many times over the past few weeks, and that gave her a little bit of swagger. She stopped for an oncoming carriage just in time. A loose cabbage caught beneath its wheel and shredded.

*At least it wasn't my head,* she thought.

In Gus's stone yard, Peder was marking a slab with a piece of chalk. She cleared her throat.

"She-wolf creeping in," she whispered.

"Hello, Miri," he said without looking up.

"Hello." She waited. She was wearing a yellow silk dress, a lace shawl, and a fur-lined cloak, her hair painstakingly curled beneath a feathered cap. Lately she was often surprised at how good wearing clean and pretty clothes made her feel.

"I didn't expect you tonight," he said, squinting at his drawing and then rubbing out half with his thumb.

"I came with an invitation."

She waited again. She was wearing a silk dress. Her hair was curled.

"Right now? I—" He looked up. "Oh. You look . . . fancy."

She smiled.

He smiled.

She smiled even broader.

"How do girls do that . . ." He twirled a finger beside his head. "The curly thing with the hair."

"We heat an iron rod in the hearth and then wrap a lock of hair around it. It takes forever, but some of us aren't as lucky as you." She ran her fingertips through his curly hair. She could feel the heat of his scalp and pulled back, tucking her hands against her sides.

"Timon, another scholar from the Queen's Castle, invited me to meet some people at a noble lady's house. Will you come?"

"Maybe. I . . ." Peder looked at the dirt on his hands, wiped them on his apron, and then yawned against the back of his hand. "I'm so tired, Miri."

She felt her shoulders slump.

"It turns out that being an apprentice means carrying water and stone and wood, and sweeping and cooking and doing everything *except* carving. After Gus finishes his work for the day, he lets me practice on his spare stone, so I stay up carving till after midnight and I feel like I barely sleep at all before I'm up for more fetching and carrying. . . ." He yawned again. "Sorry."

"All right. I'll see you at week's end?"

He nodded and stooped back over his stone. As she walked away he called out, "You do look pretty, Miri."

And with that, her step had more spring than swagger.

Miri found the red-painted house Timon had said was Lady Sisela's, though it seemed impossibly large. She tapped on the door, ready to flee, but a man in servant's black opened it and seemed to expect her. His hair was a dusty gray, and he leaned on a cane.

"They are in the Salon. Right this way."

The entry floor was tiled in linder—brilliant white with pale veins of green. Miri dragged her toe along it in a kind of greeting.

She tensed her stomach before the Salon door and tried to prepare her face, lest she gape. The preparation was in vain.

The walls were papered in exotic patterns, the floor inlaid with polished tiles of blue, reddish orange, and cream. Deep-green plants grew in pots (inside the house!), and there were so many sofas and chairs Miri did not dare count. How could a regular, non-king person live in all that richness?

Someone was playing a cart-size musical instrument Miri learned later was a piano. The song was just ending as she entered. The couple dozen listeners applauded, so Miri did the same, hoping that was right. She could not see Timon.

Miri wished for Marda or Peder beside her and leaned against the papered wall as if to blend in. But a woman seated near the piano was looking at Miri, her dark eyes lightly outlined in black paint. Her back was perfectly straight and a large white feather shone startlingly bright against her black hair.

"Good evening," said the woman.

Was Miri supposed to introduce herself? "Um . . . I'm Miri Larendaughter." She paused, trying to keep her voice from squeaking. "Of Mount Eskel."

Everyone was quiet, the thick kind of quiet that seemed to buzz. And then those nearest Miri arose and bowed or curtsied.

It was clearly a mockery, Miri knew. No one curtsied to a Mount Eskel girl. Their princess academy tutor had been clear—Aslandians would consider Eskelites lower than servants. Miri almost preferred the prattling insults she got from Gummonth and others at the palace. Anger and shame surged inside her, and she wanted to shout that she was just as good as any of them, but all she could do was run.

She ran past Timon, who had entered behind her. She ran past the startled servant. She was almost out the front gate when Timon caught up.

"Are you unwell?" he asked.

"I'm fine, don't worry." She forced herself to slow to a walk as she stalked out the gate. She was already despising herself for leaving so easily. What a pathetic spy, she thought. How quickly she had failed Katar, and Mount Eskel too.

"You seem upset."

*You seem pushy*, she thought, but only said, "I get tired of being put in my place again and again. You were kind to invite me, but I understand. I'm an ignorant mountain girl who's trying to be a princess's lady."

He kept beside her as she hurried down the walk-way. "But you don't understand, Miri. . . . The way they stared, and those who bowed, you thought—"

"They're making fun of me."

"No, Miri, they're not. Truly. We know what you face in this confused and lopsided kingdom. But in the house of Lady Sisela, you will always receive the respect you deserve. Miri of Mount Eskel. Lady of the academy. You are honored here."

Miri stopped. Timon's smile was slight and tinged with a frown, afraid she would not believe. She wished she could, but she shook her head.

"Allow me to show you?" he said.

He held out his hand, and she took it before realizing that she had never held any boy's hand besides Peder's. On Mount Eskel, girls often held hands while walking together, but when a boy and girl held hands, it was a sign of attachment.

*Perhaps in the lowlands it's just casual courtesy,* Miri thought, letting Timon lead her back inside. His hand was warm, his grip firm.

The others smiled as she entered, as if nothing had happened. The pianist was playing again, the music erasing any tension. The dark-haired woman gestured for Miri to sit and introduced herself as Lady Sisela, the mistress of the Salon.

"I'm sorry I was rude," Miri said. "I didn't think I belonged here. For one thing, I'm . . ." She looked around. Only Timon and Hanna from the Queen's Castle seemed near her age. "I'm *small.*"

"'No small thing, a bee's sting,'" Sisela quoted.

Miri marveled that Sisela would cite a poem as if she

assumed Miri were well-read enough to know it. And in fact, she did! She'd spoken that very line to Marda, though her sister had not understood.

Miri added, "Not so polite, an Eskelite, when she runs from your Salon."

Several in the room laughed. She blushed again, though this time the burn felt welcome.

"The linder in your entry is beautiful," Miri said quickly, talking over her embarrassment. "It's very old, the oldest kind quarried on Mount Eskel."

Lady Sisela nodded. "This house was built before the kings kept all linder for themselves, even while paying those who quarried the stone the barest fraction of its worth. That is, until recently—when you yourself, I believe, learned its true value from books at the princess academy and bartered for better prices."

"You know about that?" Miri asked.

"The happenings of Mount Eskel may not reach many ears, but we in this room have been *very* interested. You started a . . . well, a revolution, and your village changed for the better."

"We could use a little revolution here," Hanna said.

Someone shushed her, and Hanna bowed her head, mortified. Miri realized they must be afraid to speak freely in front of her, a stranger and a palace resident.

"We were elated last year when the priests designated Mount Eskel as the home of the next princess," said Lady Sisela. "Surely we would have the first commoner princess in the history of Danland! But instead the prince chose the only noble girl at the academy. How did a noble come to be on Mount Eskel?"

Hesitant to talk about Britta, Miri said, "She lived there . . . before the academy."

"I see. Miri, I, too, am a graduate of a princess academy."

"Really?"

Lady Sisela nodded. "I danced with King Bjorn when he was a prince, and waited to hear if he would choose me. He did not. At the time I was *heartbroken*."

The lady put a hand to her heart and swooned tragically. Miri smiled.

"He was charmed by Lady Sabet—beautiful but quiet and a little dull witted, I'm afraid."

"Clearly you're not quiet or dull witted enough for him," said Miri.

Lady Sisela laughed. "Bless you, you wise thing! But years go by, as they tend to do, and now that I see what Bjorn has become, I'm entirely grateful for my narrow escape. Bjorn is . . . Well, surely you've met him by now. What is your opinion of our king?"

The room was quiet, everyone watching Miri. Her

mouth felt dry. If she was to learn more for Katar, she had to convince them she was on their side.

"He eats large breakfasts and falls asleep during plays," Miri said.

There was a hushed sound of relief as many in the room exhaled. Timon stood beside Miri, a hand on her shoulder, as if claiming her as one of their own. The touch was gratifying. She continued.

"I expected the king to be like the head of our village council—the biggest, the strongest, the first and last at work each day. But King Bjorn—does he do *anything?*"

"Besides grow fat off the labor of the shoeless?" said Timon.

"It is a shame. What marvels a ruler could accomplish." Lady Sisela's smile hinted at secrets and possibilities. "If Bjorn had married someone like me or you, Miri, instead of his pretty, dull-witted doll, Danland's changes might come from within the palace itself. We could enter a golden age! Ah well. In the end, I married a fine man, even if he was a *noble.*" She smiled to show she was teasing, but then her smile faltered. "He opposed the king's tributes and was executed."

"Oh!" Miri covered her mouth with her hands.

"It was some time ago. The heartache no longer grips me, but I cannot forget. I need not explain justice to a fellow academy graduate. You and I, we are sisters of a kind, aren't we?"

"I hope so, Lady Sisela."

"Call me Sisi. No title, not from your lips."

Miri had no memory of her mother, but at that moment she began to imagine, even to hope, that she had been a lot like Lady Sisela.

Clemen, the lanky, thin-nosed pianist, transitioned into a more rousing song. A couple of the women sang about the downtrodden workers of Danland, repeating the chorus: *"We will march this kingdom down, we will break the golden crown."*

"'The Shoeless March,'" said Clemen, trilling out the last notes. "A composition from Rilamark."

Lady Sisela said, "Miri, are you familiar with the news from Rilamark?"

"It's the kingdom east of Danland," Miri said as if spouting information for a test.

"Not a *kingdom* any longer," Hanna said happily.

This time no one shushed Hanna, and Miri suspected she had been taken into their trust.

"The people of Danland know what the king allows them to know," said Timon. "The only legal news journal is the one his officials write. But the master scholars in the Queen's Castle exchange letters with the university in Rilamark."

SHANNON HALE

"Just months ago, Rilamark was a kingdom like our own," said Lady Sisela. "A monarch in a crown ruled in riches while millions of commoners went hungry. Now Rilamark is a nation governed by its own people, no king or queen to rob them of their goods. At the harvest giving, even Danland's nobles showed they tire of our king."

"That's good, right?" Miri said. Surely nobles had more power than commoners and a better chance of making change. "If the nobles and commoners work together, we could make sure Mount Eskel—and any province—didn't have to pay heavy tributes—"

"The nobles don't care about us," said a woman in servant's black.

"It's true, Miri," said Timon. "Nobles have done next to nothing to improve the lives of the commoners on their lands. All they care about is their own wealth and power."

"But . . ." Miri looked at Lady Sisela, who was clearly a noble herself.

"Even I will attest to that," said Lady Sisela, raising her hand.

Some in the room chuckled.

"We here have taken a solemn pact to educate the shoeless," said Lady Sisela. "It is in their power to transform this kingdom, if only they believe it. Hope

80

spreads like wildfire. We *shall* follow Rilamark's brave example. We shall create a nation ruled by the people, where everyone has the chance to thrive."

As Lady Sisela was speaking, Clemen began the march again. Some shouted "For Danland!" and "The Shoeless!" Some danced, merry just at the idea of the changes to come.

Miri swayed, full of the rhythm and tempted by the gaiety. Again emotions wrestled inside her—joy with anxiety, eagerness with shyness.

*Britta.* What would happen to her if the people really did topple the king? Britta did not seem that attached to Steffan's father or too concerned about being a princess. Perhaps Britta and Steffan would be happier giving up the duties of royalty and living in Lonway. Still, the thought made Miri uneasy, and she glanced at the door.

But Lady Sisela put her soft hand on Miri's cheek, leading her gaze back. Her voice was low and only for Miri's ears.

"I knew, the moment I saw you, that you are a girl of much power, Miri of Mount Eskel," she said. "Having you on our side is an honor."

"Thank you. I mean, the honor's mine. I'm just happy to be here." Miri felt a timid giggle tickle her chest and forced herself to keep it down.

They talked and ate and sang for hours, it seemed. Yet it was still night when Miri stepped outside, as if time had paused. Rain had fallen. Glass lanterns hung from lampposts, kerosene-powered flames flicking gold into the air, sprinkling amber starbursts into puddles.

Timon asked to walk her home.

*Not home*, she reminded herself. *To the palace.*

A man and woman with feathered caps nodded at Miri and Timon as they went by. A man in black stepped aside to let them pass.

"I thought only scholars wore uniforms," Miri said, "but everyone in Asland seems to. Some wear black—"

"Servants," said Timon.

"Why do master scholars wear the black of servants?"

"Scholars are meant to be servants to all."

"I see. Some men wear flat caps and brown jackets."

"Commoners," said Timon. "The women wear the same flat caps but with—"

"Knit shawls? Other women have lace shawls and feathered caps."

"Nobles."

Miri shook her head. "Poor nobles, dressing in bright colors. If they were as smart as master scholars, they'd choose nice stain-hiding black."

"Nobles aren't concerned about washing their own delicate fabrics."

"Of course, the servants do it for them. Noblemen wear feathered caps . . . and swords too, right?"

"Yes, because they have the right to use them."

"Wait . . . What am I wearing?" she asked.

Timon stepped back to inspect her yellow silk dress and lace shawl, prepared for her by a palace seamstress. Miri could feel his gaze on her as if it were a wind that blew.

"You, Lady Miri, are dressed as the noble that you are."

*I'm a noble now?* The realization made her strangely uneasy. She noticed Timon was wearing a flat cap, no feather, no sword. He placed her hand on his arm and continued to walk.

"All graduates of the princess academy were named ladies of the princess, a title of nobility. Your father and sister, however, remain commoners. If your sister wore your clothes in Asland, a noble could employ his sword."

"What? You can't mean that!"

"You see why so many in this kingdom yearn for change," he said.

"And what do you yearn for, Timon?"

"I want a country where all have the chance to succeed, regardless of who their parents are," he said, his voice warming. "I want freedom to speak my mind without fear of execution. I want to live in a nation of possibilities, not a kingdom where the noble-born get richer and the poor get poorer."

Her heart beat harder as he spoke, and she scolded herself. She was supposed to be a spy, not jump into a dangerous movement with people she barely knew. Her pulse was pounding in her temples, and she rubbed at her brow.

"Do you ever feel like you're learning too much too fast?" Miri asked. "My skull feels like a goat-bladder balloon blown up too tight." She peered at him from under her hand. "You don't know what a goat-bladder balloon is, do you?"

"I don't!" he said pleasantly. "Here is something you can teach me. I'm sure you're an excellent teacher."

She was about to tell him that she was the teacher in the village school, and that whenever the boys got to daydreaming, she would say something silly to get their attention, such as "The first king of Danland was Dan the Hearted, and the second was his son, Jons Herring-Breath" or "Lowlanders will pay us high prices for Mount Eskel's treasured goat hair, which they sprinkle on potatoes" or "And that's why we wear underpants on our heads."

But before she could speak, he bowed over her hand and kissed her between her second and third knuckles.

She forgot her words.

"I very much hope you will be a regular at our Salon nights, Lady Miri," he whispered.

He kissed her hand again and left. No one had ever kissed her hand before.

*Probably just another lowlander custom,* she thought.

Her heart pulsed in her vision now, and it took her a few moments to look around and realize she was at the gate to the palace.

She wandered through the dark corridors, her head still popping-tight, her hand now tingling. She wanted to talk to someone about Lady Sisela, "The Shoeless March," and Timon. Perhaps Britta was still awake? She held up her fist to knock at her door and then stopped.

The king was Steffan's father. Would Britta feel required to tell him? Better, perhaps, to follow Katar's advice and keep it to herself until she knew more. Besides, Lady Sisela's husband had been executed just for saying he disapproved of the king's tributes.

Some ideas were safer left unspoken.

*Autumn Week Twelve*

Dear Marda,

Each morning I wake, eat, dress, and run out to meet Timon. We walk to the Queen's Castle, where I study all day. I get back to the palace just in time for supper and "Miri's Salon." That is what the girls call our evening chats, when I teach them some of what I learned that day. And then I study till I fall asleep on my books.

I am sorry to report that I am the dullest scholar in all of Asland. I have had so little schooling compared to the other students, I have to work twice as hard to keep up. When Britta is free, she helps me study. Her worried face relaxes when I enter her room.

I should attend another Salon night. Katar pesters me to learn more. But when would I go? Besides, their talk scared me some. I wish I were as brave as you think I am. Maybe everything will work out without my help. I hope so.

I worry that much of my letters makes no sense to you, Marda. I do not want to think anything separates us but the distance itself. I do not want to become someone you would not understand.

Your dull and bewildered sister,

Miri

# Chapter Eight

Melted salt, drenched air
Rocking ground, fish lair

Master Filippus marched down the walkway, the scholars in blue robes surrounding his black robes like the iris of an eye. He lectured on the classification of vegetation, but Miri suspected the focus on Natural Science was just a ruse to get outside. Even master scholars could appreciate a sunny winter day.

Soon the ocean rose into view. Miri could see now that its waters did not pour like a river or stand like a pond, but were constantly moving in great heaving bursts. And it was huge!

Miri pressed her lips together, determined to be grumpy. Liking the ocean seemed a betrayal of Mount Eskel. Both could not be magnificent.

As they neared the dock, Master Filippus's lecture turned to Commerce.

"Fish account for a third of Danland's sustenance. The sunny shores of Fuska province give us salt, salt

preserves the fish, salt fish is carted to all parts of Danland, and no one goes hungry."

Miri shook her head. Some salt fish did make it all the
way to Mount Eskel. Even so, Miri and Marda had spent
many nights curled up in bed, their knees and arms
pressed to their middles, as if pushing against the hunger
would make it go away.

On the docks, mountains of crates awaited shipping.
Merchants bought arriving goods to resell in their shops.
Nets full of fat fish lay on ship decks. Seagulls circled,
their cries rising above all other noises, a high, carefree
harmony to the melody of work.

"Well, Miri?" Timon said. "Still think the ocean is dull
and overrated?"

"When compared to my mountain, of course," she
said, embarrassed that she had confessed that opinion
on one of their walks. "But the ocean is becoming more
interesting."

"Would you like to get a closer look? Perhaps from a
ship's deck?"

"Well, yes, but . . . we couldn't, could we?"

Timon just smiled. He went to a nearby ship and
returned a few minutes later.

"Master Filippus," he said, "if you wish, that captain
there is willing to take us all for a short sail."

The master agreed and the scholars climbed aboard.

Miri passed Timon as he shook the captain's hand, and she heard the captain call him Master Skarpson.

A smaller boat helped tug the ship free of the harbor. Sailors scrambled around the deck. The sails lifted, and the ship charged into the open water faster than Miri would have thought possible. She stood at the foremost spot, holding on to the railing and breathing in the cold sea spray. What would Pa think to be on a ship, skipping across water as big as the sky? How would Marda look, her hair full of wind? Miri's imagination failed her. She could not seem to remember their faces.

"What net catches your thoughts, Miri?" Timon asked, standing beside her. He kept his balance without holding on.

"Home," she said.

He nodded. "And when you were home, did you think about Asland?"

"You're right! If I were a cart, I'd dream about pulling a horse."

"I've missed you at Lady Sisela's. I hope we didn't scare you away."

"Not at all. Sorry, I'm just . . . busy."

"You didn't . . ." Timon tugged on his thumb. "You didn't tell your princess friend about us? Sisela and the rest, they are good people, and I'd hate to see any of them hauled to the Green."

"No! Of course not. Your secrets are safe with me. I admire you. *All* of you," she added, afraid she'd sounded too personal.

"Thank you." He looked at her long. His nose and cheeks had turned red in the brisk air. "I told Sisi we could trust you. We speak of you often."

"You do?" The thought made Miri's stomach feel funny, but in a mostly pleasant way.

"She is surprised the prince did not choose you. I . . . I am as well." Timon cleared his throat. "I never understood how this noble girl came to be on Mount Eskel. Wasn't she from Lonway province?"

Miri's gaze was lost in the waves. The ship's rocking was lulling, and she spoke without thinking. "She came up a few months before the academy. We thought she was an orphan with relatives on Mount Eskel."

"You mean she tricked you?" said Timon. "She lied?"

"Oh! I shouldn't have said that. You have to understand, Britta and Steffan were friends as children. As they grew older, Britta realized she loved him and believed he loved her too. It's not fair that two people who love each other can't wed! Even so, Britta never would have come to Mount Eskel if her father hadn't forced her."

"And how long had you been friends before Britta admitted she wasn't an orphan?" Timon held on to a rope, his knuckles white. "How long before she revealed she went to your mountain so that she could rob from you the right to be the princess?"

"No, it wasn't like that. She was sure Steffan would be appalled to see her there, and she hid from him at first."

Timon shook his head at the sky. "I'm tired of nobles seizing whatever they want. Why should birth determine worth? You are better than she is, Lady Miri of Mount Eskel, with a title you *earned* and the hands"—he lifted her hand and touched her palm, nodding as if satisfied—"the hands of an honest laborer."

His fingers traced the calluses on her palm. It had never occurred to her that a callus was a thing to be proud of. Her heart bumped like a fly against a windowpane.

The wind blew her hair back and billowed her blue robes. Salt spray touched her lips; sunlight lay on her cheeks. The heaving rhythm of the deck began to feel familiar to her legs, and she considered Timon, as once she had only considered Peder.

*Don't take the ocean lightly,* she thought.

Timon was still touching her palm.

"Just calluses," she said, hoping he could not feel her rapid heartbeat in her hand. "I take care of our five goats, you see, and they pull on their ropes. . . ."

He smiled. "I'd like to see the king manage five goats at once."

The image made Miri laugh. "Or even milk one nanny."

"It's a skill, as noble as any."

"I wouldn't say *noble* exactly, but since you said it first, I won't argue."

"Aha! There you go being noble again!"

She smiled demurely. "You should see me in a feathered cap."

"Indeed, you come from a noble place, Miri—noble in the truest sense. I wish I could see your mountain."

"It's the most beautiful place on earth," she said simply.

He nodded. He was rubbing warmth into her cold fingers. Should she pull her hand away? Should she stop blushing? *Yes*, she decided, she should definitely stop blushing.

"Have you chosen a topic for your Rhetoric paper? Why not write about the academy and the princess? Perhaps recording the events will allow you to see them in a new way."

"Maybe I will, Timon Skarpson."

He let go of her hand. "What?"

"I heard the captain call you that. Skarp is your mother's name? Who are your parents?"

"Merchants," Timon said shortly.

"Merchants of what?" she asked. His reluctance made her even more curious.

"We buy goods and ship them between provinces and countries." He hesitated. "This is one of my parents' ships."

Miri looked around. All that wood and rope and sailcloth must cost a fortune. "One of? How many ships do they own?"

Timon pressed his lips together. "Twenty-two."

Miri allowed her mouth to hang open and then pressed her chin up with her hand to close it. Timon smiled as if against his will.

"I was afraid of what you'd think of me if you knew I was—"

"Ridiculously wealthy?" she said. "Swimming in gold coins?"

He shrugged. "We pay tribute to the noble who owns the land we live on, the same as all commoners. Still, the wealth of the sea has been good to my family. My father is determined to make so much money the king will be forced to offer him a noble title. He thinks I'm a fool to fight for change."

"He's wrong," Miri said, feeling certain of the words.

Timon's smile seemed grateful. "Last year I tried to sell one of his ships and use the money to help families whose tenement was destroyed in a fire. He sent me back to the Queen's Castle because he didn't know what else to do with me. If I don't turn into a reformed, obedient boy, he'll ship me off to the far-flung territories to see how much I like the poor once I become one." He laughed. "But I don't care, Miri. Some things are more important than one person. Lady Sisela showed me that. I don't want to live a comfortable, small life. I want to change the world."

They were returning, sails down. A group of people had amassed on the dock, and even from the ship's deck, Miri could hear angry voices.

As soon as the gangplank hit the deck, Timon said, "Come on." He grabbed Miri's hand and pulled her along.

Merchants mobbed together, grumbling. An official in green clothes was affixing pieces of paper to large earthenware jugs. One paper blew free and stuck to Miri's boot. She picked it up. It read: *Claimed in tribute for the king.*

"Now he's taking cooking oil," Timon said, shaking his head.

"The attempt on his life spooked the old boy, that's what I think," said a nearby merchant, nearly as short as Miri and with a fuzzy brown beard. "He keeps enlarging the royal guard—and claiming more tribute to afford them."

"He can take whatever he wants?" said Miri.

"He's the king," the merchant said.

"Why, he's nothing more than a bandit," she said.

"They're bandits and robbers, the lot of them," the merchant agreed.

"The king already claims a portion of all grain and meat brought into Asland," said Timon. "If he takes oil too, the oil merchants will raise the price of what's left over. The rich can afford to pay more for oil, much as they'll resent it. It's the shoeless who can barely afford bread as it is. I doubt the king even cares that his greed causes starvation."

"If anyone stole something on Mount Eskel—even the head of our village council—my pa and his friends would tell him to give it back or else."

"The king has his own army," said Timon.

"Well, it's time someone told him to stop being a bandit."

Timon's eyes lightened. "You're right, Miri. It's time."

He ripped the paper off the nearest jar and crumpled it into a ball.

Miri held her breath. She had not meant he should get himself arrested. What of Sisela's husband? Instinctively, she tried to quarry-speak. *Stop.* A common warning, but there was no linder underfoot to carry her message, and anyway his lowlander ears would not hear it.

Timon ripped off another paper. "No," he said.

Two soldiers stood with the official, their silver

breastplates and tall stiff hats marking them as members of the royal guard. One had noticed Timon. Frowning, he approached. Miri covered her mouth with her hands.

Timon grabbed at all the tribute notices he could reach, saying "No! No!"

Both soldiers were nearly upon Timon. One was drawing his sword.

Then the short, bearded merchant said, "No."

Another joined. Another. The soldier hesitated.

"No!" Timon said again, and with that, the general despondency flashed into anger. The merchants moved closer to Timon and began to chant "No, no," as they ripped the notices. The soldiers took a step back.

To Miri, never had any word seemed so powerful. And dangerous too. What would happen if she joined in? Would the official recognize her from the palace?

"No," Miri breathed, not moving her lips.

The chant was nearly a song, a "Shoeless March" kind of thrumming music that got inside her head, slid down into her muscles, and made her want to *do* something.

"No," Miri whispered, thinking of two gold coins in a shawl and five goats that lifted their heads at the sound of her voice. "No," she said, imagining how the tributes would impoverish her entire village. "No!" she said, because never had she felt so powerful. She was not one person, she was a crowd. She belonged to the mass of bodies and voices, strong in number, united in purpose. Two soldiers were insignificant compared to thirty merchants, and the scholars and sailors now lending their voices too. Who could stop such a force? And what outcome would not be worth joining in?

"No!" Miri shouted. "No!"

The official and his soldiers were backing away. The crowd closed in, tossing papers and shouting. The official ran as if afraid for his life, the soldiers on his heels.

The mob's shouts turned joyous, and still they called out, pumping their fists and chanting that powerful word. Miri did not want the moment to end. She felt tall and strong, as if she and this mob could move together like a giant, striking down any obstacles, remaking the whole world.

As soon as the official disappeared around a corner, the chanting broke into cheers, and merchants and sailors and scholars alike thumped one another on backs and shook hands. Timon pulled Miri into his arms, spinning around. The world seemed so large, and yet Miri felt so much a part of it.

Trade resumed, with merchants buying the oil and loading it onto their carts to sell across the kingdom. Master Filippus could not rally the scholars into any semblance of a group and released them for the day.

Miri found herself walking on her toes as if the wind were tugging her up, up into the sky. Timon laughed with delight.

"It's begun!" he said. "When one voice shouts, dozens will join. Thousands! Real change comes soon, Miri. So soon."

He kissed her on each cheek, then took her hands and kissed them too, as if so full of fervor and happiness he could speak in nothing but kisses.

*Lowlanders kiss hands an awful lot,* Miri thought, feeling as if she, too, could kiss the whole world.

Timon continued on to Lady Sisela's to give her the good news, and Miri went to Peder's.

Her head was aswim with words like "no" and "change" and "soon." The words felt heavy and good, like a hammer in the hand. She could not wait to tell Katar that they need not worry. The commoners had started the revolution, and surely a commoner government would not demand tribute from the shoeless of Mount Eskel. Miri would no longer have to spy. She would join them and help change Danland!

Miri walked to Gus's and found Peder sharpening tools. He startled when he saw her, dropping a chisel. It bounced against the spinning whetstone and flew off in another direction.

"You forgot to cough!" he said.

"Sorry." She coughed.

"Your sneakiness is dangerous. Next time that chisel will lodge itself in my head."

"Now, Peder, there's plenty of stone around here for carving. No need to practice on your own face."

He stroked his chin. "You're right, my jaw is already chiseled to perfection."

She agreed, but she felt too silly to say so aloud.

"Some things happened at the dock today," she said, her stance bouncy. "The king was going to claim jugs of cooking oil—just take them, like a common bandit—but people shouted and refused to give them up."

"Really? I didn't think anyone could say no to a king. At least he's not taking stuff from Mount Eskel."

"But he might. He robs all the other provinces."

"Robs?" Peder wiped his brow with his sleeve and got back to sharpening.

She still had not told him about Gummonth and the tributes, but it was hard to talk about such important things to his back.

"I've been coming up with a new plan for when we go home," Peder said as he worked. "If I get good enough, I could train others, and the lot of us could carve all through winter. Everyone could have a choice of occupation besides just the quarry. And with increased profit, Mount Eskel could prosper, you know? Not just get by.

Someday we could be the very center of fine stone craft in the kingdom. Lowlanders would come to *us* to learn sculpting!"

He turned to smile at her.

"Yes, that's a good idea," she said.

"Why aren't you more excited? This is exactly the kind of plan that usually makes you hop about."

"Sorry, I'm just distracted. There's so much going on in Danland, more problems than I ever dreamed of when we were home."

"I guess that's true. But we can't worry about everyone. Even you can't change the whole world."

He said it lightly, as if to goad her into a smile, but she could only shrug. She was definitely not going to tell him about the threat of tributes now.

She left him to his work and started back to the palace, scanning the streets for any gathered mobs, listening through the bustle of traffic for chants of "No, no!" Nothing seemed changed. Nothing besides Miri herself.

She tensed at the palace entrance, but the guards accepted her password without hesitation. Perhaps news of the riot at the docks had not spread that far. Perhaps no one knew she'd been involved at all. She felt relieved and yet a little disappointed too.

When Miri entered the girls' chamber, they gathered for Miri's Salon.

"Liana, we're starting," Esa said.

Liana stayed on her bed, her feet resting on the head-board. "I. Don't. Care," she said through gritted teeth.

Bena rolled her eyes. "She's been in a mood *all day*. We had tea with some ancient courtier, and she made the mistake of saying Liana was *almost* as pretty as her granddaughters."

"Must be hard for her, being in Asland with so many other girls," Gerti whispered. "On Mount Eskel, she was always the prettiest."

"I can *hear* you, you dolts," said Liana.

"Go on, Miri," said Esa.

"Today I . . . Today we . . ." Miri stopped. What if one of the girls mentioned Miri's involvement to someone else? The academy girls were no longer isolated in their room, sewing and spinning. The wedding official had seemed displeased with their work and stopped bring-ing them tasks. And lately Inga spent much of her time sneaking around outside after a tall, gray-haired gar-dener, so the girls could do as they pleased.

Liana and Bena often visited courtiers in their palace apartments, eating dainty food and gossiping.

Frid had made friends with the workers in the palace forge. They called her "mountain sister" and let her pound red-hot steel on the anvil.

A palace musician had overheard Gerti singing to

herself in the garden and invited her to sit in on symphony rehearsals. They were delighted with her ability to improvise songs—a common activity in the quarry—and asked her to sing to their music. A young man gave her a six-stringed lute, and Miri joked it had become her third arm.

Gerti clutched the lute now, gently plucking the strings as if unaware of her action.

"Some people believe noble titles cause harmful divisions—" Miri started cautiously.

Now Liana sat up. "I *love* being a noble. Anyone who doesn't is *stupid*."

*You're stupid*, Miri wanted to say, but stopped herself. A rule of Rhetoric: Attack the argument, not the person.

But Liana's comment filled Miri with more unease. What was safe to say?

"Um . . . This week Master Filippus introduced us to Rhetoric—the art of communicating. He said if you learn the rules, it's easier to explain your thoughts and persuade others. The basics include listening, expressing your own opinion as succinctly as possible, offering stories instead of lectures, and allowing silence for consideration."

Sometimes talking about communicating was easier than actually doing it.

*Winter Week One*

Dear Marda,

You must be thigh-high in snow. My mind knows it is winter, yet my eyes cannot believe it. Although I count some lowlanders as friends, I have to admit they are a flimsy lot. A breeze rises from the ocean, and all shiver as if ice rain were falling. Nobles go about in thick fur coats. And the shoeless . . . well, they put on shoes, if they have them.

Today was amazing. Something bad was going to happen, but then someone took a stand and dozens joined him. I want to be one of those people. The standing ones.

I have been afraid lately, too afraid to talk to anyone about it. Afraid that all the changes on Mount Eskel were useless. That things will soon go back to the way they were, the linder sales buying barely enough food for survival, nothing extra for warm clothing or better tools, every moment working, no time for the village school or making music or anything. Like that, or worse. I have been afraid. But today I was not.

It feels good, Marda, not to be alone, to be surrounded by people who want and think the same as I do.

I should be asleep but my thoughts blaze, and I do not want to douse them yet. I am so full of hope and ideas I might float right off my bed.

*Ships are bigger than houses and yet they sail with the speed of* the wind and the power of a hundred horses. I rode a ship with Timon today. He noticed my callused hands and thought they were beautiful.

    This is from your very silly but always hopeful sister,

Miri

# Chapter Nine

*King Dan sat on his stallion fierce*
*Swords did slice and spears did pierce*
*But in a tree upon the field*
*Perched a small, keen-eyed blackbird*
*And the blackbird did not sing*
*No, the blackbird did not sing*

Miri's sleep was fragile that night. The rhythmic snores of the other girls mimicked a slower chant of "No, no . . ."

In the morning, Miri dressed and left without breakfast. She passed the corner where she usually met Timon, her feet too impatient to wait. She weaved between carts and carriages, wagons and horses, feeling as sleek as a ship on water. Change was coming, and she was part of it.

Surely all the scholars at the Queen's Castle would be readying for the next action. *Revolution.* What an exhilarating word. She wanted to ring it like a bell; she wanted to pound it like a piano. She wanted revolution to be a song she could sing so loudly all the world would hear!

But at the Queen's Castle, the scholars in blue were gathered in their room as usual. No changes in sight.

"An interesting experiment yesterday," Master Filippus said when Timon entered late, his shoulders stooped. "The will of the people versus the king. History shows us several examples of the common people attempting to overthrow the crown. Each failed."

"But it worked at the docks," Miri said. "People said no, and the official ran off."

"The royal guard visited merchants later yesterday afternoon and seized jars of oil," Timon said, slumping into a chair. "No one protested."

"It's exciting in the moment, mmm?" Master Filippus said, his eyes half closed. "But you, my hasty young scholars, forget History. You must study the past to know what will work in the future."

Miri rubbed her face. She'd felt so strong yesterday as part of that mob, but it had been a false strength after all. One day later, nothing had changed. There was still a king who could take whatever he wanted—jugs of oil, wagons of grain, two gold coins wrapped in a shawl. She glared at the girl in the painting. What was she about, gawking at the moon while pouring precious milk? If she did not pay attention, she would spill it. *Stupid girl.*

Master Filippus took the class down to the Queen's Castle library, lecturing as they walked.

"Yet one must study carefully to uncover truth. For example, Dan the Hearted, beneficent first king of Danland? You know the stories of his wisdom and compassion."

Miri nodded with the others. She had grown up singing "Dan and the Blackbird," in which the king stopped a battle to save a blackbird's fallen nest.

"Such stories are likely myths. The actual records we have from Dan's time reveal nothing more than his skill in warfare. In fact"—Master Filippus hummed a little laugh—"one historian claims he was called Dan the Hearted because he wore his enemies' hearts around his neck."

Miri was about to say "ugh," but they'd entered the library, and she could do nothing but stare in wonder.

Once she'd thought all the knowledge in the world was contained in the princess academy's thirteen books. Now she faced thousands. She wondered if she should curtsy as if she were entering a chapel.

Filippus directed them to select a volume of history, read it, and write a paper questioning some part of the historian's account.

"Choose a history of a province other than your

own," he said. "That will not be a problem for you, Miri, as Mount Eskel has never inspired a historian."

He led them to the History section, and Miri searched the shelves, eager to prove him wrong. Perhaps just a general volume of Danland history would have a section on Mount Eskel? But she found nothing.

All the others except Timon had selected their volumes and gone off to read.

"You're upset," said Timon. "Perhaps there's no record in this library, but surely Mount Eskel keeps its own history."

"Until the princess academy, we had no books. No one could read or write."

"History can be found outside books," he said, his smile hopeful. "In graveyards, for example, you can find names and dates."

"We don't bury our dead. We wrap people in their own blankets and lower them into the Great Crevasse. There are no grave markers. There's no means to mark the passage of time at all, except empty quarries abandoned by previous generations. Our only history is holes."

Timon had no response but to lay his hand on her shoulder before turning away.

She paged through various books but felt too discouraged to choose one. According to this library, there was no Mount Eskel.

*Tragedy*, she thought, a word she had learned only the week before.

She had seen a play with Britta, another story of two lovers kept apart, this time a brave soldier and a girl who was betrothed to another. Expecting this play to be like the first and end with marriage and laughter, Miri was stunned when the soldier was slain and the girl died of a broken heart.

"Oh," Britta had said as the curtain closed, "I didn't know it was going to be a tragedy."

*It's just a story*, Miri had reminded herself that night, curled up in bed and crying over the lovers.

She felt similarly struck now, her belly cramped, her head heavy. *Tragedy*. Because no one on Mount Eskel had learned to read or write, their history was lost forever.

She realized Master Filippus was at her shoulder.

"Having trouble selecting a volume?" he asked.

"There are so many," she mumbled.

"Well I know it. I've read them all."

"Really? How long did it take?"

"Mmm, half of my life. One must, to reach master status."

Miri swallowed. She had less than a year left in Asland. The weight of all she did not know felt like a boulder on her back.

"It is a shame you plan to go home after the summer.

With just one more year you could become a tutor. Cat's-eye green would become you, Miri of Mount Eskel."

"Just one more year?" she asked.

He nodded. "Or stay two years, don the honey-drop robes, and become the first historian of Mount Eskel. You have a keen mind. One day you could wear raven's head."

She was glad when he walked away. His compliment did not cheer her. Rather, she felt even more pressed down by that boulder, the heaviness of impossible expectation.

Still determined to find something about her home, she turned to the massive Librarian's Book on its pedestal. The librarians over the years had cataloged the contents of every book in the library. She located a mention of Mount Eskel in a royal treasurer's account book, over a century old, and she hunted down the volume.

I find not a record of linder's strange history, so I relate here what others have spoken. Two hundred years past, workers were recruited to quarry a linder cache on Mount Eskel. The stone minister reported to the king that "working with linder has altered the people," though the details remained mysterious.

King Jorgan abolished the stone-minister post, leaving the Eskelites to fend for themselves. Only the hardiest of traders risked the trip up the cursed mountain, lured by the promise of reselling the stone to the king himself, who began building a linder palace.

When I was a lad, a common game named one child the Eskelite. If the Eskelite touched another child, he or she became infected and turned into a monster. It seems to me children no longer play this game. People do forget to fear Mount Eskel and the poisons of raw linder.

Poisons? Surely not. For much of her life, Miri had breathed in linder dust and drunk stream water white with it. Besides, if past scholars believed linder was dangerous, then why did the kings build their palace from it? Clearly the royals were not afraid of the stone.

Miri replaced the book on the shelf. There was no reason to believe the account. Still, her stomach felt full of stones, and when she tried to read a history of Lonway province, she could barely focus on the words.

*Winter Week Three*

*Dear Marda,*

Today was a rest day. Esa and I spent the morning with Peder.
At lunch the girls gathered for Miri's Salon, and I reviewed what
I'd learned about Logic. Logic teaches that truth can be reasoned
out using proof and careful thought. We can rid ourselves of
emotions and rely on solid arguments instead.

Esa said, "My ma says truth is when your gut and your
mind agree." I nodded but really I was ashamed. Surely a
thousand years of scholars know more than Esa's ma. Still,
I am ashamed that I was ashamed. Marda, I hope you are
not ashamed of me for being ashamed. If so, shame on you.
Or on me? Which is logical?

After chapel, Britta and I sat beside her fire and talked for
hours. It eased my homesickness for you some. When Britta says
Steffan's name, her eyes change. I want to say they glow, but they
do not light up like embers flickering with quiet fire.

I am trying to choose words carefully, you see. Master
Filippus lectured on the importance of word choice in our Rhetoric
lesson. Words can fall hard like a boulder loosed from a cliff. Words
can drift unnoticed like a weed seed on a breeze. Words can sing.

So no, Britta's eyes do not "glow" exactly. They widen, I
guess, as if she is so full of the thought of Steffan, her head cannot
contain it and tries to make more room. He is everything to her.
And I think she is everything to him.

*Peder works very hard. I do not think I am everything to him.*

*I am eager to return to Lady Sisela's, but I am nervous too. For one thing, everyone there is so clever. Do they think me dull? Perhaps I should assure them that our goats enjoyed listening to me for hours on end. I am certain their bleats meant "Do go on, Miri, darling. You are immensely entertaining."*

*Your immensely entertaining sister,*

*Miri*

# Chapter Ten

*All hail brave King Bjorn*
*All hail our noble king*
*He is always victorious*
*Congenial and glorious*
*Ever meritorious*
*All hail our daring king!*

Miri and Peder sat on the straw in Gus's open shed. Last visit, Esa had come too. Miri had been impatient for next week's end and time alone with Peder, but now that she was here, the only news they shared was silence. He seemed too tired to talk. Her own head ached, stuffed full of History and tributes and kings. Twice that week she had spied Gummonth at the palace and slinked off in the opposite direction, afraid that if he saw anyone from Mount Eskel he would remember his threat to seek their tribute.

Miri opened her mouth to spill all her worries on Peder. But instead she yawned.

A tickle on her tongue made her choke. Peder had

stuck a straw into her open mouth. Miri harrumphed and scooted farther away, yawning again despite herself. Peder threaded one straw into another, and another, creating a piece as long as his arm. He wiggled it threateningly before her face.

She gasped with fake shock and made her own extended piece of straw. It was longer than Peder's and she managed to stick it in his ear. He hit hers away with his and they began to battle, beating each other's straw swords into pieces and remaking them, both their faces earnest, until Miri could not help it any longer and laughed out loud.

The sound broke the game. Peder looked at her. He reached out, and she thought he meant to grab her straw or perhaps yank her hair as he used to when they were little. But he put his hand behind her head and, leaning forward, pulled her face to his. He kissed her. One long, slow kiss. At first she felt nothing but shock, but he held his mouth against hers long enough for the heat from her lips to melt down her neck into her middle and out into her fingers and toes.

He let go. She opened her eyes, wide now. She became aware of the city noise, dim and hollow in their little courtyard like an echoed mountain shout, and she felt shy, as if all of Asland were watching. But they were alone.

"My ma used to say 'Miri's laugh is a tune you love to whistle,'" he said quietly. "Only your laugh always made me want to do something besides whistling."

Miri stared. She was sure he would run off now, as he had after the first time he'd kissed her—a cheek kiss at the spring holiday, sudden and soft.

Peder stared back, perhaps waiting for her to flee too. Such a kiss was too remarkable to go unnoticed, too much to talk over, too lovely to let fade away.

They both stared. Neither ran.

At once, both began rebuilding their extended straws and they renewed the fight. Peder laughed this time. And Miri understood the impulse to kiss the lips that laughed.


Miri stayed with Peder for the rest of the day, mostly not talking at all. Next to Peder, in that quiet courtyard of stone, she felt so close to home she could almost smell snow behind the breeze.

At dinner hour Gus sent Peder back to work and Miri away. She let her feet wander with her thoughts, and the farther she was from Peder the less sure she felt about anything. Part of her longed to get lost in the crooked streets of that endless city. The longing frightened her.

She thought of the villagers in the coming spring, excited to hear the trader wagons approach, anticipating goods and letters but instead meeting officials who demanded all their savings. She imagined Marda's face when they took the gold coins, and Pa's when he realized he could not fight this kind of bandit. Miri's heart ached.

How could she face her family again if the king's tributes reduced them to poverty worse than before? Even Katar credited Miri for changing Mount Eskel, but the tributes would undo anything she'd done, and she had no idea how to prevent it.

Perhaps if Peder realized how useless she was, he would not like her at all.

She pulled her shawl around her, more aware of winter as the sun plunged into the horizon. She had to do something. She had to figure out if change really was coming to Danland, and how to help it along before Gummonth had a chance to send officials up the mountain.

Timon would be at Sisela's that night. Miri's hair was not curled, her dress was not her best, but she suspected no one at the Salon would think less of her for it.

The same gray-haired servant opened the door to Miri and walked her to the Salon, his cane rapping the linder floor stones. Miri smiled at him and felt warmly toward Lady Sisela, who kept the elderly man on despite his limp. Miri knew enough of the lowlands now to suspect other nobles would have let him go.

When Miri entered the Salon, a woman was reciting a poem about rabbits and squirrels defending their offspring by overthrowing a bear, which was supposed to be metaphorical and quite dramatic. But every time the woman intoned the line "The rabbits roused and the squirrels squeaked," Miri had to hold her breath to lock down a laugh. The thought of laughing reminded her of Peder. She touched her lips.

When the poem concluded, Sisela arose.

"Tonight, dear friends, instead of just speaking fondly of the poor, let us again go to them."

They did not have to walk far to find the shoeless of Asland. One block away, wooden tenements grew like weeds between brick-and-stone buildings. They made their way through apartment after apartment, leaving baskets of food along with leaflets questioning tributes and the king.

The families looked worn and sleepy, usually crammed in one room, their bedding on the floor, where rats ran. No clean mountain air, no comforting snuffles from goats, no beauty from a chain of mountains springing away into forever.

"Thank you," said a man, taking Miri's offered basket.

"We had no lunch break at work. I could eat the basket and all!"

"But today is rest day," said Miri.

"Bless you," he said. "There's no rest day for factory workers."

Even on Mount Eskel, where each block of linder sold was one stone away from starvation, the quarry workers had taken a rest day. She could not imagine endless labor, no break to attend chapel or even wash a shirt.

Miri stepped out of the sour air onto the landing, where Sisela and Clemen were huddled with three men in laborers' garb.

". . . a supply of grain from Hindrick arrives with only a handful of royal guards," one of the men was saying. "Might be a good time to—"

He noticed Miri.

"Who is this?" he asked, staring pointedly at her feathered cap and fur-lined cloak.

"Don't let her nobleness fool you," said Clemen. He put an arm around Miri's shoulder and blew her feather out of his face. "She's one of us."

Miri felt the warmth of those words as if they were a blazing hearth fire.

Another apartment was stuffed with girls—Miri counted twelve, and all younger than she. Miri asked if they attended school, and their faces lit up at the idea. However, all but the youngest worked in a glass factory, their blistered fingertips proof.

"I'd thought all lowland—I mean, *Aslander* children went to school," Miri said when they'd returned to Sisela's house.

"There are some schools, but few shoeless attend," said Sisela. "Nobles demand higher tributes every year. Children must work alongside parents just to earn enough to eat."

"Most of the adults can read, so we leave the leaflets," said the woman Cristin, still wearing her servant garb.

"We must be able to do more to help," Miri said.

"I agree." Timon paced before the window, hands in his pockets. "All we do is write leaflets. Talk without action. When will the people finally rise up?"

"Patience." Sisela put a hand on his back and he stopped pacing, his shoulders still tense. "We are gathering straw and stacking it high. All the fire needs is a spark."

"We should seek outside help," Timon said in a low voice.

He looked at Sisela, and she nodded and then shrugged, and Miri had the idea that an entire conversation had just passed in silence.

*What do you mean by outside help*, Miri was about to ask, but Clemen began to punch out a tune on the piano.

"When the spark comes," said Clemen, "the fire will burn bright enough for the whole kingdom to see. We already have many on our side. Including our very own lady of the princess!"

Miri recognized his music as "All Hail the King," an anthem to the monarch. Cristin coiled a scarf and placed it on Miri's head like a crown, and a couple of the young scholars put Miri on their shoulders and spun her around.

Miri blushed and laughed, but took off the play crown as soon as her feet touched the floor.

"I don't mean to betray Britta by being here," she said. "She's not like the king and queen. I'm sure when she's princess she'll look after the shoeless. I mean, *if* the changes don't come like we hope."

Sisela draped the scarf over Miri's shoulders, as though dressing a doll. "Think with your mind and not your heart. Is it right that the poor go hungry while the wealthy feast?"

"No, but—"

"Is it right that our very lives are subject to a man who did nothing more than be born to a queen?"

"No."

"I need you to believe, Miri, that things *can* change. If you don't believe, you who changed your own home, how can we convince a country?"

"Lady Sisela—" Miri started.

"Sisi," she corrected gently. She patted the lounge beside her, and Miri sat.

"You're a noble," Miri said. Judging from the others' clothes, Sisela was the only noble in the room besides Miri. "Why do you work so hard for the commoners' sake?"

Sisela tilted her head and smiled. "I don't need to tell you this, Miri, not you of all people, but there is right and there is wrong. Even a *noble* should be able to tell the difference."

"We could try to unite nobility and commoners to bring change together," said Miri. "Others must think as you—and I—do. I mean, nobles can't all be bad, right?"

"Show her the ledger," said Timon.

Clemen looked at Sisela, and she nodded. He reached under the piano, removed a slat of wood, and brought out a thick leather-bound book. Timon placed it on Miri's lap.

The title was *Ledger of His Majesty's Grievance Official*. In her course on Law, Miri had learned that if commoners accused a noble of a crime, they had the right to petition the king. Past kings heard grievances in their linder palace, but King Bjorn did not take the time. Instead he sent a Grievance Official to the provinces.

Miri opened to a random page.

CLAIM: Farmer accuses Lord Jemel's guards of stealing his horses.

> FINDING: Perhaps the farmer ate his own horses.
>
> RULING: In favor of Lord Jemel.

CLAIM: Miller accuses Lady Katarina of excessive tributes, resulting in the starving death of his son.

> FINDING: Millers are often unreliable.
>
> RULING: In favor of Lady Katarina.

CLAIM: Farmer accuses Lord Halffword of ill-using his daughter.

> FINDING: The daughter is thirteen and too young to be trusted.
>
> RULING: In favor of Lord Halffword.

Miri paged through the ledger, searching for any instance when the Grievance Official believed the commoner.

"Every claim's ruling is in favor of the noble," Timon said, guessing her thoughts. "For twenty years, every single claim. Nobles bribe the officials. Commoners never have a chance."

Miri might have thrown the book across the room then if Clemen had not taken it first, putting it back in its hiding place.

"They can't get away with it!" Miri said.

"They already do," Sisela said. "You see why I scorn my own kind. Nobles are as selfish and untrustworthy as royalty. They know the king overreaches his power—they scorned him with rubbish at the gift giving—and yet they do nothing for the commoners. The changes we dream of will only come if commoners seize their own future."

Miri nodded, but she shivered as if just realizing how cold the world was. Sisela put a warm arm around her, and Miri was tempted to rest her head on the woman's shoulder. She missed Marda and Pa. She missed home.

A group in the corner were laughing as they sang. Clemen was again playing "All Hail the King," but the group had toyed with the lyrics.

*He is ever inglorious*
*His laugh is laborious*
*His smell is notorious*
*Impale the herring king!*

Pounding knocks at the front door surprised the song from their tongues. Miri had not imagined that Sisela could look afraid.

"It might not be—" Clemen began.

"But it might," said Sisela. "Go!"

There was a scramble. Timon took Miri's hand, leading her to the rear door of the Salon. She glanced back. Clemen began a casual tune at the piano, and Sisela plucked the feather from her hair and reclined on her lounge. All the rest were running. The Salon door was opening. Timon yanked her out.

They raced through a maze of rooms, all dark, cold, and empty. Miri kept expecting to trip over a chair or table or anything at all, but their passage was clear. They exited the house in the back, sidled down a crack of an alley into the street, and then stopped. Timon placed Miri's hand on his arm and began to stroll. She darted one glance back. An official and several soldiers stood outside Sisela's house. One met Miri's eyes and frowned. Miri forced herself to look up at Timon and even managed a carefree smile.

"What a droll little play," he said, loud enough for his voice to carry. "Did you enjoy it?"

"Indeed!" she said. "Wasn't the jester amusing?"

Miri and Timon laughed until they were around the corner. She let go of his arm.

"What happened?"

Timon frowned. "It's illegal to meet in groups to discuss politics."

"It is? But those officials couldn't know what we talked about. It might have just been a party."

"They don't have to prove it. If they find us assembled together and even suspect we were talking about laws and the king, they could take us to the prisons, where people often die of disease and neglect before they reach trial."

Miri shook her head. "Things were simpler on my mountain."

"Asland is the better for your presence, Miri. We need you."

"I wish I was smart enough to help in any way at all," she said. "I want the world you imagine, Timon. I want it so badly."

"I knew it!" His step bounced. "I knew we were of the same mind. And heart. Miri, I should confess something. I don't want to lie to you, not the way the robber princess did. I already completed my open-sky year. I enrolled in Master Filippus's class just so . . . so I could meet you."

They were passing through the light of a lamppost, and Miri was glad to reenter the dark and hide the expression on her face.

"Is that true?" she whispered.

"Yes," he said. "I heard that a graduate from Mount Eskel's princess academy was enrolling, so I asked my father to send me back. I was curious to meet you. But . . . curiosity has long since been replaced by stronger emotions."

"Oh! Um . . . I should tell you . . . maybe I misunderstand . . . but I just wanted to say . . . you might want to know about Peder. He's a boy. From Mount Eskel. And he's my . . ."

*My what?*

"Your betrothed?" Timon said.

Now Miri's face felt as red as a firebrand and no shadow could hide it.

"No."

"Aren't you of age?"

"Yes," Miri said miserably.

"Then he hasn't asked . . . and yet you still feel committed to him? Well, whatever he feels for you can't be as strong as what I feel. He met you on Mount Eskel, where you were just one of a few girls. I chose you out of the entire kingdom."

Miri became uncomfortably aware of the pounding in her chest. "Even though it isn't spoken, Peder and I do have a commitment. I mean, I think we do."

"I am not giving up so easily," said Timon. "This boy has not seen fit to speak. But I will speak for you, Miri. You blush because I'm too bold! I'll be bolder still. Together we will change Asland. And then Danland. For our wedding, my father will give us a ship. We'll sail to Rilamark and Eris, explore coasts with white sand and crystal waters and trees dripping with fruit. We'll befriend scholars in faraway universities, and everywhere we go we will change things."

She could see all he promised, as if actors on a stage portrayed the adventures of Miri and Timon. She squeezed her eyes shut and shook her head. "I can't do all that, Timon. I'm from Mount Eskel."

"We choose who we are. The name, rank, and affluence of your parents, the feather in your cap—none of that matters. You are your own person. I am *not* my cold, ambitious father. And you, Miri, are not bound by your birth. You can be who you will."

*Is that true?* she thought. *I am not simply Laren's daughter or Marda's sister or the girl my mother held for a week before she died. I am not formed from the mountain alone. I am the girl who left the mountain. I am the face in the mirror, the thoughts in my head. I am not made of them. I am me.*

"You can be who you will," he repeated. His voice softened. "And if you will have me, I will be the one beside you."

He did not ask for an answer to his proposal, and she did not feel ready to give one. But he leaned down and kissed her lips. She forgot to startle away, she forgot to blush, she forgot to do anything but hold her breath and feel cold and hot like lightning shoot through her. The kiss lasted just one beat of her heart, though it felt as long as a night.

She could not dismiss that kiss as an innocent low-lander custom. She knew exactly what it meant.

He put her hand back on his arm, and in silence they walked their usual path to the palace.

She was accustomed to the city now: the hiss of the kerosene lanterns on the posts, the grumble of cart wheels on cobblestone, the chill in the breeze when it lifted off the river, the salt tang when it stretched from the sea. The buildings and thoroughfares did not panic her. The endless books of the Queen's Castle library thrilled her, as did one word: revolution.

But this was not home. Was it?

She repeated to herself her plans for the future: speak for Marda so she might wed, help Pa learn to read, teach in the village school, and one day marry Peder.

Why did those ties to home feel thinner now? Maybe Marda did not want to wed. Almost certainly Pa did not care about reading. Esa and some of the other girls enjoyed teaching in the school too. And Miri was no longer certain of Peder. In the vast history of Danland—in the frighteningly enormous history of all the world—would it really matter if Miri of Mount Eskel ever returned home?

*Winter Week Five*

*Dear Marda,*

*Do you know the feeling you get when you are awakened in the middle of a dream? The dream story is still real and full of color, but the waking world is rushing back into your mind. And for a moment both worlds are true, and you cannot quite tell them apart.*

*I feel that way. There is Mount Eskel. And there is Asland. The two bleed into each other, and I am not sure which is my home and which is the dream.*

*Everything was simpler when the world was smaller. Everything was simpler when I knew no more than twenty boys, and Peder was the only one I noticed. But never mind. I am not sure I am ready to know what I think about that, so I dare not write it out.*

*I like how Timon cannot help pacing and gesturing when he is talking about something important. And how the things important to him are important to me too. I always know exactly what Timon is feeling and thinking. He never leaves me guessing. I am so tired of guessing.*

*I miss you. I miss Pa. I miss my mountain. But I am not sure if missing a place and loving a place are enough to call me back.*

*I know I will not send you this letter come spring. I just need to write down these thoughts, Marda. I need to tell someone that I am not sure about anything anymore.*

*But I do know I am still your sister,*

*Miri*

# Chapter Eleven

*A need, a need, a need have I*
*A wish, a wish, a wish, I sigh*

It was a quiet rest-day morning in the girls' chamber. Winter rain deluged the city, and the patter on the window glass made a drowsy song. Miri lay on the sofa, reading a book for her studies. Tucked inside an essay on Law she came across a dangerous but beautifully logical idea: *A king is a servant to his people. He rules by their consent. If the king fails his people, it is their right to rebel.*

Miri could almost hear Clemen's spirited music accompanying the words. She had spent every evening that week at Lady Sisela's. Later, if the weather cleared, she would either join Timon at Sisela's or go visit Peder. The thought of Timon made her blood feel hot and fast, while the thought of Peder made her smile.

Then suddenly she was thinking about Esa without knowing why.

"Where's Esa?" Gerti asked.

"I was just going to ask the same thing," said Miri.

"So was I," said Frid.

Miri was about to remark on the coincidence when her mind leaped to a memory of Esa at the princess academy, reading aloud beneath the bookshelf. Esa's ma, Doter, always said *Listen to your second thought, or the third might be too late.*

"Frid, come with me to look for her?" asked Miri.

"Maybe we're thinking about her because she's quarry-speaking," Frid said as they checked in Britta's empty chamber.

"We're not on linder," said Miri. "Then again, we're near a whole lot of it."

The closer they got to the king's wing, the more panicked Miri felt, until finally she broke into a run. They passed over the linder threshold and into a quarry-shout so intense Frid lifted her arms as if to shield herself. Images pounded in Miri's head: the time the shelf at the princess academy had broken, dropping the precious books onto the floor; the night Miri had used quarry-speech to shout all the way from the academy to home, a plea for help. The memories came one on top of another, askew and throbbing.

Miri tried to walk forward into the linder wing and the shout, but guards blocked the way, spears tipped forward.

*Where?* Miri quarry-shouted back, using a memory of playing hide-and-find-me.

No response but the same images slamming into her head: Esa at the academy, a fallen shelf, Miri calling for help.

"Please let us through," Miri said to the frontmost guard. "We're trying to find our friend. She's in trouble."

"Not without the password," he said. "Tell me where she is and I can dispatch a man to her."

"In one of the linder rooms. A shelf may have fallen on her."

The guard narrowed his eyes. "Why would you think that if you don't know where she is?"

Miri made an impatient gesture, and the guard shrugged and nodded to another, who began peering into rooms. One by one. Frid paced, as patient as a rolling boulder.

How could the guards hear nothing of it? Indeed, how did the stones themselves not rend and tear? But even as Miri thought it, she noticed small vibrations through the soles of her feet.

"Is Britta within?" Miri asked the guard. "Or—"

Steffan walked by. He started to smile and then seemed to sense her anxiety.

"Miri, is everything—"

"Oh Steffan, help!" she said. "I think Esa is trapped somewhere. Tell the guards—"

"Let them in," he said.

Miri took Frid's hand, and they ran.

At first she thought she could follow the vibrations in the stone to Esa, but they seemed to radiate in every direction. Corridor after corridor, through large chambers and narrow rooms, it all seemed the same in their rush: linder floors, linder walls, finery that tired their eyes. Miri wanted to see Esa, not another sofa.

"Did her quarry-speech make you think about a bookshelf?" said Miri.

"Yes, the time it fell at the academy," said Frid.

There could be a bookshelf anywhere. Surely the king could afford as many books as he wanted.

Miri rubbed her face. Her bones no longer shook from the ferocity of the shout, and that was so much worse. Esa's voice was dimming.

Steffan jogged around the corner, following after them.

"A place with books," Miri said. "Somewhere in the king's wing?"

Without wasting time to ask why, he ran forward, motioning them to follow.

*What a marvelous boy!* she thought. *No wonder Britta loves him.*

The quarry-speech was so faint now, Miri felt only a thin, dry wail. She quarry-spoke a memory of Frid, Esa, and Miri together at the academy, hoping Esa would understand they were coming.

"Esa!" Frid shouted. "Esa!"

"The palace library," Steffan said over his shoulder, and he pushed two great doors inward. Miri cursed herself for not thinking of a palace library. The Queen's Castle library had seemed large enough to support the entire kingdom.

Down a row of shelves, a massive bookcase lay toppled, and the ends of Esa's yellow-brown hair splayed out from beneath it. Frid seized the case and inched it up. Esa took an audible gasp. Steffan helped lift while Miri pulled Esa free. Frid and Steffan, groaning at the weight, let the case thud to the ground behind them.

Esa breathed and coughed. Miri smoothed the hair off Esa's forehead. It was the same color as Peder's, and she imagined their mother, Doter, touching their hair like that when they were sick or hurt. Doter always knew what to do.

Mount Eskel had never felt so far away.

"Don't die," Frid said, her bottom lip trembling.

"All right," Esa croaked.

Steffan was hurrying out and called back that he'd find a physician.

Moments later the door opened to Queen Sabet.

Her gaze took in Esa and the upset case, books strewn about.

"I'm sorry, Your Majesty," Esa said. Her voice trembled. "I reached for a book and the whole thing came down."

"Well," the queen said in her slow, high voice, "books can be dangerous."

She motioned to someone in the corridor. Several black-clothed servants appeared. They righted the case and began to reshelve the books.

"I'm sorry," Esa repeated. "I won't come here again if you don't want me to."

The queen frowned with a press of her chin. "Someone may as well use this room. It *is* pretty." Her hands fluttered, unsure, and she left.

Miri and Frid had helped Esa move to a library sofa when the physician arrived.

"The longer I lay there, the harder it was to breathe," Esa said as the physician examined her. "I thought I was dying."

"Yes, when the breath stops, death usually does follow," said the physician. "But you got out in time. I spy nothing worse than two broken ribs, and if you don't bother them, those bones will knit themselves back together."

He gave her a dose of something for the pain. Esa

thanked him, but as soon as he left, her face scrunched up and tears fell.

"Does it hurt too much?" Miri said. "What can I do?"

Esa shook her head. "Nothing. I just . . . I'm angry. I'm so angry!"

Miri and Frid took a step back and looked at each other. Esa was not one to yell, and especially not minutes after her life's breath had been nearly squashed out of her.

Then Frid said in one rush, "I'm sorry I ate your roll this morning, I was hungry and I didn't think you wanted it and you can have mine tomorrow!"

Esa laughed softly, as if the effort hurt.

"I'm not angry at *you*, Frid." She was still clutching a book with her right hand, her limp arm lying on her lap. "The other day, the queen saw me reading one of Miri's books in the conservatory and said I could use her library. I thought, how pleasant it will be to browse stories, but do you know what I found?"

She held up the book. Miri read the spine: *Maladies*.

"There are herbs for pain and others for heart palpitations and some to bring on sleep," said Esa. "There are things you can do to help get a baby out right and keep the mother safe, and make sure a cut doesn't go bad—and if it does, it tells how to cut off a limb and save the person from dying."

"That's some book," Miri said.

"I remember a little brother," Esa continued. "He had fat cheeks. My ma lost four babies, Miri lost her ma, but in the lowlands they're off at horse races and plays and banquets while their libraries hold secrets about how to help keep a person alive. Why didn't they bother to tell us?"

"There's so much distraction here," Miri said. "I guess they don't think about us much at all."

"I guess." Esa took back the book and spoke softly, the anger fading. "But *I* won't get distracted."

Miri had been studying in the grandest school in the kingdom, but she did not think she'd learned anything so important. Esa would go back to Mount Eskel and save lives. Meanwhile Miri still did not know if she would save the painting or the prisoner.

"You can have my roll tomorrow anyway," Frid said, paging through a book called *Anatomy*.

"Thanks," said Esa.

Frid snickered. She held up the book, open to an illustration.

"The artist forgot to draw some leggings on this fellow."

Esa barked a laugh and then schooled straight her expression. "If I'm going to learn doctoring, I'd better get used to it."

Miri left Esa and Frid studying Anatomy and wandered the stacks. It was so quiet compared to the Queen's Castle library and its constant rhythm of footsteps, whispers, and flipping pages. This room had an air of abandon. Rain-gray light seeped through the high windows and dusted the books below.

On the back wall a small bookcase stood alone, proclaiming its significance. Miri examined several of the books, realizing with dawning awe that they were the actual diaries of kings. She picked up one covered in gray, cracked leather, but it slipped. She lurched and caught it just before it hit the floor. Some things could never be replaced if lost: a king's diary, the history of a mountain village, a painting of a girl looking at the moon.

*And my mother, and Esa's fat-cheeked baby brother,* Miri thought.


The queen offered library access to all the girls, and Miri meant to return soon, but it proved difficult to find time between the Queen's Castle and Sisela's Salon. She missed her nightly chats with the academy girls, but she just had to meet up with her Salon friends. Protests had begun to crackle around Asland. Angry over the rising cost of food, commoners gathered at the roads into the city, where officials exacted tribute on incoming wagons of winter vegetables. They complained, they hollered, and sometimes they fought.

"It *is* beginning," Timon said, seizing Miri's hands. "At last."

Miri squeezed his hands back. Each protest was a tiny spark, and they believed the revolution would explode any day now. Miri longed to be in the middle of it and planned to accompany Sisela and Timon to the next protest, but that morning she'd woken up congested and sore.

"I never get sick," Miri said when Britta brought her juice and toast. Her voice sounded loud in her stuffed-up head and made her ears squeak.

"No one gets through an Aslandian winter unscathed," Britta said.

Britta dodged officials and appointments for a week, sneaking to Miri's bedside to help her keep up on her studies and bring gossip. Demonstrations continued, and Miri realized there must be dozens of Salons full of rebellious commoners. But the royal guard always quelled the protests, and no mobs neared the palace.

One morning Inga delivered a package that had come for Miri. The box held twenty-five books, many times more than currently existed on all of Mount Eskel. Miri inhaled the sweet and dusty smell of ink on paper, rich as the air in a bakery.

"They must be worth a wagonload of linder!" said Esa. There was a note.

*For Lady Miri,*
*Who deserves a library of her own. May these serve*
*as a humble beginning.*

*Timon*

Miri passed the books around but held the note to her chest.

*What if* . . . Miri shied away from the thought, but it had already started to form. She saw herself in the black robes of a master, showing young scholars the Queen's Castle library and nodding demurely that *why yes*, she had read every volume. She imagined standing on the bow of a ship, skimming over foreign seas, carrying the message of freedom won in Danland.

Timon had said first Asland; the rest of Danland would follow, and then all the world. His promises felt as real as paper in her hands, just awaiting the ink strokes of action.

But Miri was not the only one who took sick that winter, and revolution proved no match for a head cold. Salons emptied, as did the Queen's Castle. Now Miri found time to haunt the palace library.

Master Filippus had said they needed to study

History to understand what had worked in the past. Miri found the Librarian's Book of the palace library and started to read all she could on tributes, hoping for clues on how to defend Mount Eskel. There were laws that limited how much tribute nobles could take from commoners, but as Miri had seen from the Grievance Official's ledger, if they took more anyway, no one could stop them. And no laws limited the king.

Discouraged, she moved on to any mentions of Mount Eskel or linder. She read a curious entry in the diary of the previous king, the father of King Bjorn and grandfather of Steffan.

Sweyn's cruelty toward Bjorn has grown worse. He torments the boy and says his brother has no business inside linder walls. I regret telling Sweyn about linder wisdom so soon, but after my illness in the spring, I feared my own mortality and wished to pass on the secret before Sweyn became king. Now it seems I was premature.

I will send Bjorn to the Summer Castle to keep him safe from his brother. Besides, Bjorn need not be raised inside linder walls as he will not be king.

But Bjorn did become king, and now he did indeed live inside linder walls. Surely the passage she had read in the Queen's Castle suggesting linder was toxic had been wrong. But what was the royals' secret connection with linder?

*Linder wisdom*, Miri repeated to herself. Could the royals have quarry-speech?

Impossible. Although Steffan did not share Esa's exact memory of a fallen bookshelf, surely he had experienced something similar enough to understand. If the royal family could quarry-speak at all, Esa's quarry-shout would have nudged a similar memory in Steffan or the queen. But they had heard nothing.

Miri read the diary and pieced together the story of the two brothers. Sweyn, the prince heir, harassed Bjorn from a young age, threatening and striking him. On one occasion he locked him up and would tell no one where. It took nearly a day to locate the boy in a storage pantry. Bjorn did not call out or even cry—just shivered till his teeth clattered. It was soon after that Bjorn and his mother moved to the Summer Castle in Lonway.

The king's diary ended abruptly, so Miri found a historian's account to learn the rest. The king grew ill, and Sweyn ruled as prince regent. Sweyn attended the ball of a princess academy in Hindrick province and chose his bride. Just months after his parents had died and he had been made king, Sweyn was racing carriages and was killed in a crash. He had not yet married.

And so Bjorn—the shivering boy locked in the pantry, raised in the country, kept away from the palace and politics—became king.

Whatever linder secret the king had passed on to Sweyn the prince heir, Bjorn likely had never learned. What was this knowledge royalty took to the grave?

The rest of the dreary winter afforded Miri many more afternoons of reading. Esa was rarely in the library anymore. A palace physician had taken her on as an aide.

All the ladies of the princess kept busy. When they were not helping Britta memorize names of nobles and rules of court conduct, Frid was at the forge, Gerti at her music, and Bena and Liana on social visits.

And Miri kept reading.

Whenever Britta was free, she joined Miri with a book of her own, resting her head on Miri's legs. Sometimes the queen sat nearby, flipping through books with illustrations, humming to herself when she discovered something she liked.

*Royalty is the enemy of common people*, Sisela had said, and Miri suspected it was true. But the sentiment was hard to hold when the queen directed a servant to take Miri a tray of mint tea and snacks.

"I felt you were thirsty," the queen said, not making eye contact before leaving the library.

*She* felt *I was thirsty?* Miri wondered. Her thirst could not have been obvious. She had not been panting like a dog.

The phrase reminded Miri of something she'd read. She looked back over a previous king's diary: *The ambassador from Rilamark was all pomp and swagger, but I felt his insecurity tinged with fear.*

It was an odd note, but Miri dismissed it, thinking perhaps the royals had their own peculiar way of speaking.

When Miri could not read another word without going cross-eyed, she left the library, with more questions than answers, and walked into the city with Gerti and Frid. They had coins, an allowance given to the ladies of the princess, and they planned to buy Aslandian treats for their families.

"Traders will head up soon. Just about two weeks till spring!" Gerti smiled, lifting her face to the sun.

"They think it's spring already," Frid said, pointing to blue crocuses peeking between cobblestones.

"I bet our miri flowers are coming up," said Gerti.

Miri had been named for the flower, a tiny pink native of Mount Eskel that bloomed between rocks. But as she stared at one of the blue crocuses, an uncomfortable sensation burned in her chest. She could not name it. Perhaps if she wrote to Marda she could figure it out.

Lately she did not quite know what she thought until she wrote it down.

Letter writing was a lot like quarry-speaking—a soundless call from far away. Would Marda have similar enough memories to understand what Miri was trying to say? How could she communicate the whole world to a quiet sister on top of a mountain? She would try. She needed a pen and paper and a way to see her thoughts.

*Winter Week Eleven*

*Dear Marda,*

*Did you know there are histories written about every province in Danland except Mount Eskel? We might as well not exist. I have been reading so much that I know more about the lowlands' history than I do of our own.*

*I saw a crocus today, blooming between cobblestones. It made me sad and I did not know why. But now I think it is because I feel more like that blue crocus than a miri flower. My feet are planting in city earth. I cannot imagine leaving here forever.*

*Every night I close my eyes before sleep and try to see home. All the bits of my life here take up space in my head till it cannot fit the memories of before. I know the streets of the city now, the faces of my fellow scholars, the feel of my bed. I know Asland. And there is so much I want to do still, a lifetime of doing.*

*I am not the only one changed by Asland. I wish you could see Gerti as she plays the lute and sings with the palace musicians, or Esa after she helped birth a baby, or Frid working in the forge. After a luncheon with Lady So-and-So and Lord Something-or-Other, Liana and Bena are "happy as a goat drinking her own cream," as Doter would say. And then there is Peder with his carvings.*

*Pa was right. Though short as always, I have grown so much bigger, I do not know if I will fit anymore in our little house in our little village. I do not know if any of us will.*

I am afraid this letter might make you sad. It makes me sad too, because I cannot imagine going home for good. My heart aches as I write those words, and yet at the same time my shoulders feel lighter just from admitting the truth.

Still your sister,

Miri

# Chapter Twelve

*Hear the leaves applauding*
*Hear the wind hurrahing*
*Hear the surf guffawing*
*The ways of old are dead*
*The queen has lost her head*


T he day was a stale kind of cold—no breeze, no brightness. The sky was as gray as Miri's mood. It had been some time since she'd spoken to Katar, and she wanted to talk things through before hurrying to the Queen's Castle for the day. When Miri finally found her, Gummonth had found her first. They stood together in the brown winter garden, Gummonth smiling as he spoke, Katar's posture wilting.

Miri watched from behind a leafless tree and exhaled when the official finally left.

"He must have been an unpleasant, sickly infant," said Miri as Katar approached. "What mother would hold a beautiful baby and say 'I know! I'll name him *Gummonth!*'"

Katar's glower made Miri swallow.

"What . . . what did he want?" she asked.

"To gloat," said Katar. "He convinced the king Mount Eskel has long been in neglect. Officials will travel with the traders in the spring to take a tribute of two gold coins for each villager, to make up for lost years."

Miri sat down hard on a low rock wall. The ground seemed to tilt. The gray sky was the stone ground, and Miri was crushed between it all.

"My family doesn't have that much, Katar. I doubt anyone has."

"Then the officials will take the goats and some linder too. You can be sure that trading day won't be a festival anymore."

Miri covered her face with her hands, further darkening the day. She prayed the entire world would just disappear. She peeked. Unfortunately, the world was still there.

Katar sat down beside her. "Gummonth was going on about some leaflet he read about Mount Eskel that made him determined to see us pay our dues."

"We can't let this happen."

"Perhaps we can barter for a reprieve."

"Barter with what?"

"Information," Katar said, sitting up straighter. "You've cleverly cozied up to the rebels. Expose them in exchange for freedom from tributes."

"No! Katar, we can't turn our backs on the shoeless. There's right and there's wrong. People are hungry and suffering all over Danland."

"And you expect to help them all?"

"More and more commoners gather at each protest. Once enough of them join together, nothing will stand in their way. They only need more time, and if the commoners create a new government in Danland, there won't be outlandish tributes anymore."

Katar folded her arms. "You've had *months* and you offer me 'wait and see and maybe the commoners will succeed and be nice to us'? That's pretty disappointing, Your Royal Shortness."

Miri flinched. "I may be short, but at least I'm not nasty."

"That depends on who you ask."

"Remind me never to ask you anything!"

Miri stalked away, feeling like a frayed bit of twine. She wanted nothing more than to unburden her thoughts on a friend. She knocked on Britta's door, still undecided about what was safe to tell the girl who would marry the prince.

"Have you seen it?" Britta asked the moment Miri was inside.

"Seen what?" asked Miri.

"'The Mountain Girl's Lament.' Oh Miri, it's . . . it's

awful. There are always leaflets circulating the city, but Gummonth says people are really riled up about this one. It complains about royalty, as many such leaflets do. But this one—it attacks *me* specifically. And it was written, most definitely written, by someone who was at the princess academy."

"What? Who?"

"There's no name, but the leaflet includes details I don't remember telling anyone besides . . . well, besides you." Britta examined her hands. "I thought you might know something, you could explain. . . ."

Britta looked at Miri fearfully.

"Britta, I don't know anything about this. I'm so sorry."

Britta exhaled. "Yes, of course. If you'd *known* that . . . that one of the girls was writing this, you would have told me. I just . . ." Britta's brown eyes brightened behind tears. "I just don't know what's going to happen. Everyone's so upset. At my father for sending me to Mount Eskel under a lie, but at me too. What if they decide Steffan and I can't marry after all? And maybe we shouldn't."

"Don't be ridiculous."

"The princess *was* supposed to be from Mount Eskel." Britta held up a hand before Miri could sputter a protest. "I know you understand why I did what I did and you forgive me, but it was still wrong, wasn't it? If not for me, Steffan would have chosen you, I just know it. He's always thought highly of you. And if . . ." Britta's chin started quivering, but her voice got stronger. "If it would be for the best, I will leave, and you could marry Steffan."

Miri laughed despite herself. "Britta! I am not going to marry Steffan. None of the Mount Eskel girls would. Steffan chose you. Anyone else marrying him would just be . . . *weird.*"

Britta laughed too and seemed surprised by it. "I think Liana would be willing."

"You're probably right, though I hardly see that as a blessing. Don't worry. Steffan loves you, you love him. I'm sure that won't change, even if Danland does."

"But the leaflet was so angry, and when people get angry, violence often follows. The Rilamarkians killed their queen last year. Did you know that? They chopped off her head in front of her palace. People watched as if it were a show at the theater. When the ax fell, they . . . they *cheered.*"

Miri put her arms around her and stayed till Britta no longer cried.

By the time Miri returned to the girls' room, her heart was boiling.

"All right, who did it?" she said, slamming the door behind her.

"I suppose you're talking about this," Bena said, waving a printed piece of paper.

Liana strolled around the room, her hands held behind her back. "We were just saying that it must have been you."

"Me? I would never speak against Britta."

"It does kind of sound like you, Miri," Frid said.

"Why don't you just admit you did it?" said Liana. "All this show is getting silly."

"You used to spend the evenings with us, teach us things," Esa said. "You've changed recently."

"You *are* the most likely one," said Bena, "off in that school all day."

Miri took a step back. "So you're attacking me because I attend the Queen's Castle?"

Bena fanned herself with the paper, her lips pursed. Miri tore it from her hand and stormed out.

She was so busy stomping and fuming that she'd exited the palace gate, heading to Peder's, before she read the leaflet. The first sentence sounded eerily familiar. The second was decidedly so. By the third, she had to sit on a crate outside a grocer's, the paper shaking in both her hands.

I never really believed the lowlanders would allow a crown to sit on a mountain girl's head. We were used to being tricked by traders, to being cursed and mocked and forgotten. When the chief delegate came to Mount Eskel to announce the king's priests had divined our village as the home of the future princess, we assumed it a cruel joke on us.

And yet, after some time at the princess academy, I did begin to hope, and then even believe, that things were changing for Mount Eskel. If the priests of the creator god thought we were special enough to produce a princess, then perhaps we were.

They were Miri's words, taken from a Rhetoric paper she'd written at the Queen's Castle. When Master Filippus handed it back, Timon had asked to see it.

I first met Britta the summer before the academy. She said she was an orphan and had come to live with distant relatives on the mountain. We became friends. It was not until the day Prince Steffan chose his bride a year and a half later that I learned the truth: Britta's parents lived, and her father had sent her to our mountain so that she could be chosen.

Miri put a hand over her mouth. *What have I done?*
The paper gave details of Britta's youthful friendship with Steffan—secrets Britta had confided in Miri. She

winced now at the sentences that had once made her proud. She'd meant to write a true portrait of events, but she had been self-congratulatory too. *Aren't I such a good friend to forgive her lie?* she seemed to be saying. *Aren't I so generous?*

There was an added paragraph at the end that Miri had not written:

And so we see how nobles lie and cheat to keep down the most hardy, diligent, and innocent Danlanders. Sacred custom was mocked and the shoeless robbed of opportunity. Instead of the first commoner princess in our history, we get yet another pampered noble girl. The priests of the creator god remain silent, as they so often do. But I speak out. And I say, enough. Danland has outgrown royalty like a child outgrows baby clothes. Cast them off. The time of the people has dawned. End the oppression. Stand up and be heard.

"Thoughtful, isn't it?"

Miri looked up. The grocer was stacking apples into a golden pyramid. He nodded at the paper in her hands.

"Those Mount Eskel girls were done a cruel turn. Poor innocents, barely scraping by, and when one of them gets the chance to be royalty, a noble girl steals it away. Turned my stomach. I usually tear down any leaf-lets I find on my store, but this one I decided to keep. If enough of us display the leaflet, the royal guard can't arrest us all."

A copy was affixed to his shop window. Several more were stuck to the wooden stand holding the apples.

Miri crossed the street, away from Peder's, and headed instead for the Queen's Castle. She pulled down many leaflets as she went but soon gave up. There were hundreds. She might as well try to empty the river with a bucket.

Miri was late; Master Filippus's class was in the library. She found Timon and placed a leaflet over the book he was reading.

He smiled up at her. "Isn't it wonderful? We've gone back to the printer three times. He says it's the most popular leaflet he's ever seen!"

"Timon, these were my personal thoughts. How dare you steal them from me?"

"Steal?" He smoothed the paper with his palm. "But I asked if you'd be willing to share it—"

"I thought you meant with *you*, not the entire city!"

He winced, as if surprised by a stab of pain. "I was certain you'd be thrilled at the response. We've been in this together. Aren't we in this together?"

"We're not in *this* together," she said, shaking the

leaflet. "It makes Britta look like a thieving, dishonorable snob."

"Isn't she?"

"No!"

"We are what we do," he said quietly.

"But the leaflet will make people hate her." She sat in the chair beside him, planting her head facedown on the desk. "This is really, really bad."

"I *am* sorry, Miri. I have a tendency to get excited and act without thinking. But your words were so perfect! I added my own at the end, but I believe them true and important enough to risk execution. Is the part you wrote true?"

"Well, yes, but it's not that simple, Timon."

"Why not? How can telling the truth be bad? This kingdom is blind. It's our job as scholars to keep speaking out and describing the world as it is until the people can truly see it."

"But Britta—"

"People are afraid to challenge a king in his palace surrounded by his army. He seems too large to overcome. But a robber princess? That's an easy rallying point."

"She's my friend!" Miri said.

Timon flipped open a book to a genealogical chart of the kings and queens of Danland.

"History is names on a page. Years from now, your *friend* could be just another meaningless name school-children memorize. Or hers could be the name that ignites the change. You are smart, Miri. You know you can't support both your friend the princess *and* the commoners' fight for fairness."

No, she had not known that. The idea hit her like a stone.

Timon was on his feet, his cheeks flushed. "Let the people question a princess. That will give them the courage to keep asking until those questions shake the kingdom. The people will rise, the crown will fall, noble titles will be abolished, and at last everyone will be equal."

When Timon spoke that way, her mouth wanted to shout and her feet wanted to march. People rising, kings questioned, a country changed! Her heart beat, but her stomach rolled, sick with guilt. How had things gotten so complicated?

Miri took genuine comfort in studying Mathematics that day. She could sort numbers into two simple ideas: true and not true. Unlike numbers, words were rarely just one thing. They moved and changed, camouflaging and leaping out unexpectedly. Words were slippery and alive; words wrestled out of her grip and became something new. Words were dangerous.

*One and one will forever be two*, Miri thought.

She looked at the girl in the painting. Had her expression always been so forlorn? The girl seemed trapped, aching to go explore the world but unable to put that stupid jug down.

*I'm sorry*, Miri thought at the girl in the painting, because she needed to apologize to somebody. *I'm so sorry.*

# Chapter Thirteen

Goodness knows she is too fierce for you
Goodness knows she has eyes for a lord
Goodness knows she yet will prove untrue
Her cheek's blush is as false as her word

Miri did not wait for Timon at the end of the day, hurrying back to the palace alone. Words tumbled about in her head, but she could not form them into pleasing sentences. Nothing she could think of to say to Britta would make it better. She knocked at Britta's chamber and cracked open the door.

"Miri, come in!" Britta said with a grateful smile. She was not alone. Britta introduced her guests, Aslandian noble ladies seated primly on the sofas. "And this is my dearest friend, Lady Miri of Mount Eskel."

Miri curtsied, wishing she could have her dearest friend alone. The truth of the leaflet was a live coal in her gut.

The conversation dallied on the weather, preparations for the royal wedding just days away, and the best

toppings for custard. Miri was about to blurt out her confession anyway when one of the ladies, her eyes on the fan in her lap, said, "We saw a leaflet this morning. Normally I wouldn't read such things, but the servants were in a fervor. We wish to give you the benefit of the doubt, Lady Britta, and so we came in person to allow you to explain."

"Explain?" said Britta. Her face drained of color.

The woman nodded. "Surely the claims in the leaflet were not true."

Miri wished the palace would come down over her own head and bury her alive.

"I have little explanation and no excuse," said Britta. "Some of the things written were, in fact, true."

"Some?" asked a woman with an arch of her eyebrow.

Britta's ruddy cheeks deepened into a painful red. "I did go to Mount Eskel. I did claim to be an orphan and attend the princess academy."

"I see. And what do you think about that, Lady Miri of Mount Eskel?" asked the woman.

Miri sat on her hands, then remembered her Poise lessons and folded them on her lap. "I think . . . I think that Britta is my friend. And maybe whoever wrote that leaflet didn't mean any harm. And I don't think Britta meant any harm, going up to Mount Eskel. And I didn't want to be the princess anyway."

Miri winced. Master Filippus would have given a sad shake of his head at the way she'd shambled around the rules of Rhetoric. Confusion and even amusement crossed the ladies' faces. Britta looked lost.

The ladies reminded Miri of the hungry fish she had seen in the ocean, swimming beneath the fishing boats and waiting for the cast-off entrails of gutted fish. Knowing that Britta's "dearest friend" had written the leaflet would only give them more fodder for gossip. She excused herself.

In the girls' chamber, Miri could not meet anyone's eyes. They'd been right—she *had* written "The Mountain Girl's Lament," or at least most of it. But how could she explain without implicating Timon? Sisela's husband had been executed for as much.

Miri wrapped a cloak around her scholar robes and went outside.

Night had fallen over Asland, flames fizzing in the kerosene lamps like fallen stars. The lamplight drained the color out of the painted houses, making the world as black and white as the starred sky.

In Lady Sisela's part of the city, the flower beds overflowed with heaps of crocuses and daffodils. Soon wagons would lumber up to Mount Eskel for spring trading. The thought gave Miri a shiver. Though she had written a dozen letters to Marda, she could no longer imagine sending any of them. What could she say of the tribute and the cruel poverty that threatened them? How could she fix anything in time?

She entered the Salon, and all the faces turned, their eyes brightening at the sight of her. She tightened her fists, wanting to hold on to her anger.

"Miri!" said Sisela, rising to take her hand and kiss her cheek.

Clemen played a few bars of a popular song, changing the words for Miri.

*Goodness knows she is so fierce and true*
*Our warrior girl slays giants with words*

He pounded out the final notes, and the room applauded—not for Clemen but for Miri.

"I read 'The Mountain Girl's Lament,'" said Sisela, "and I understand you better than I ever have before. My sweet, lovely girl, how I adore and admire you!"

"Don't, please. I didn't want this. I didn't mean to betray my friend."

Sisela tilted her head to the side. "I respect your

loyalty, but Miri, this girl tricked Mount Eskel out of the right to have one of your own on the throne."

"Britta and Steffan are in love . . ."

"It makes a pretty story," said Sisela. "But consider it logically. Is this wedding good for *all* of Danland?"

Miri did not answer.

"It is difficult to find a soul in this city who supports Britta," said Sisela. "Yet I suppose she'll be princess whether they want her or not."

"And that, too, is getting people to think," said Timon. "I know she is your friend, Miri, and I *am* sorry, but people are finally speaking out. The heat of the revolution is spreading!"

He offered her a strip of blue cloth. She took it, not understanding, and then saw they all had tied strips around their upper arms.

"For you, our lady of the revolution," Clemen said with a bow, "Asland is draped in blue."

Timon smiled at her quizzical look. "You don't know your own power, do you? In 'The Mountain Girl's Lament,' you talk of Mount Eskel wrapped about by blue sky. Your words resonated across the capital, and all of like mind are wearing blue bands. The color of the coming change!"

Miri sat heavily on the sofa, letting the blue strip go.

It rippled as it fell, reminding Miri of a living thing—an undulating caterpillar, a snake.

"You shouldn't have taken my words." She glared up at Timon. "You shouldn't have used them that way."

"I know you, Miri," he said. "You wouldn't sacrifice the good of all the people for one entitled girl. Please, I'm sorry."

"I can't let Timon take the blame." Sisela sat beside Miri and put a hand on her back. "This is my fault. I encouraged him to print the leaflet. You have fit into our group so easily, you seemed a sister to the cause from the beginning."

"I am," said Miri, straightening. "I really am. I think." Her voice dropped lower. "I don't know what to do."

The anger was straining out of her, her hands relaxing. Timon and the rest had grown up in a huge city, reading books and talking in Salons, while she'd been tending goats. Surely they knew better than she did.

Sisela smoothed a lock of hair off Miri's forehead.

"My poor girl, you're too hard on yourself," she said. "Why should you have the burden of doing everything?"

It was true. None of the other girls had come to Asland with so much responsibility. They could relax, enjoy the city, develop interests. But Miri was expected to "go and learn for all of us," as Britta had said. Miri felt tired just thinking about it. It was a relief when Sisela lay Miri's head against her shoulder.

"I don't know what to do," Miri whispered again.

"You don't have to do anything," Sisela answered. "Just let things happen. Everything will happen as it should."

"In three or four weeks, officials will go to Mount Eskel and demand tribute," Miri said. "The families are finishing off their winter food supply and counting what coins they have saved, anticipating buying enough food for the season, and perhaps a comfortable chair for a grandmother or new blankets for a baby, spoons and pots, boots and buckets. Instead they'll give their saved coins to the king—and likely lose their goats besides. They'll be . . . they'll be devastated . . . *ruined* . . . and they'll wonder if there wasn't something we could have . . . *I* could have done. . . ."

Tears stole away her words. She looked at the floor and in the silence felt the compassion of those around her. They, like her, had faced the brutalizing injustice of kings and nobles or they would not be here. She could not sell them out to the king, as Katar suggested, not even to save Mount Eskel. There had to be another way.

Sisela said, "A few weeks can change the world, Miri. I will do all I can. I promise."

Miri closed her eyes. She wanted to believe so badly,

her muscles tensed. Clemen was playing a sweet melody, and the notes softened the edges of everything. The room smelled of lavender and beeswax candles. The music and hum of conversation sounded as familiar to her now as the bleating of goats.

Her stomach still felt tight as a fist, but Sisela's hand was on her head, motherly, comforting.

*She knows best*, Miri told herself. *She is smart and wise.*

Miri squeezed her eyes shut tighter.

Palace of Stone

*Winter Week Thirteen*

*Dear Marda,*

*I do not know what to write. I stare at this blank paper and wish words wrote themselves, words to tell me how to feel and think and what to do.*

*There will be a tribute demanded of you all. You and Pa and everyone thought I was so smart to figure out how to trade linder for fair value. But soon you will know that I am useless. Nothing I changed lasted. Everything is falling apart.*

*I am so sorry about the two gold coins in mother's shawl. I had imagined them for you when you wed, to fix up your own house with a door and windows, a table and chair, a pot and spoons and such. Gone. And our goats! My heart aches for our goats.*

*I honestly believed that we would not have to go hungry anymore.*

*Britta's wedding is near, at least. I wish she were safely the princess already and that no one could try to stop it. I want change, but I want Britta to be happy too. Why is that impossible?*

*I cannot stop the tribute. I cannot do anything. Except maybe be Britta's friend. And your sister,*

*Miri*

# Chapter Fourteen

※❦※

*Loan me your lace of yellow, sister*
*Lend me your fine kid gloves*
*Tonight is the bridal ball, sister*
*Tonight I'll meet my love*

*Present me a sash of blue, sister*
*Gift me a ribbon of white*
*My love awaits me below, sister*
*I am a bride tonight*

Britta finished Miri's hair by pinning a white hothouse rose at the back. It was the night of the bridal ball, the first of three ceremonies that would bind Steffan and Britta as husband and wife. By this time tomorrow, they would be wed. The Queen's Castle was on hiatus for the week, so Miri had been free to help Britta practice the ball dances and her part in the coming formalities, as well as to make her laugh during her final dress fittings.

It was so easy to be with Britta, there were moments Miri forgot why her insides felt like a twisted rope.

Then she would remember—the leaflet, the tribute, the revolution. Sisela believed the commoners would rise soon, and Miri was not as happy as she thought she should be. She had decided to put it out of her mind for the wedding and focus on Britta.

"Tradition holds that single young women who attend a bridal ball will marry one of their dance partners," said Britta. "Steffan says every girl in the city has probably been checking daily for an invitation!"

"Who gets to attend, Britta? Just the noble girls of Asland? Any commoners?"

"I never thought to ask." Britta rubbed a rose petal against her chin. "You see, this is why you would be a better princess."

Miri remembered Sisela declaring the same thing. The truth of the leaflet was heavy on Miri's tongue. She would not spoil Britta's wedding with her confession, not before she could figure out how to fix everything. She hoped Britta did not realize how many Aslandians opposed her marriage. *Just one more day, and Britta will be Steffan's wife.*

Servants came to ready Britta, but she sent them away.

"I want to do my own hair tonight and put on the dress of my choosing," she told Miri. "Maybe that's silly, but I want to look *myself*, not what the palace has made me. Steffan is still distant. Maybe he's just busy, or else he always acts stiffer in Asland than he would in Lonway. But if he's the tiniest bit hesitant . . . well, when I walk into that ball, I want to be sure he knows I'm just me, no flounces or pearls to distract him."

Britta had asked to borrow the silver-and-pink dress Miri had worn at the academy ball and lowered the hem. In turn she lent Miri one of her new ball gowns, a deeper blue than the open-sky robes, with full skirts over layers of tulle.

"I saw a crocus this color, working its way up between cobblestones," Miri said, letting her hand slide down the tight middle and over the exploding skirts. "Exactly this color."

Miri wore a pair of Britta's heeled shoes so her skirts would not drag too much.

"You look so . . ." Britta smiled shyly. "I'm going to keep track of everyone who asks you to dance tonight."

*But Peder won't be there*, Miri thought, and then quickly shrugged the worry away. It was just an old wives' tale that the bridal ball paired girls with their future husbands. She need not take it seriously.

Britta would enter the ball later, so Miri walked with the girls into the linder grandeur of the king's wing.

"Why is it, Miri, that you always try to be the fanciest?" Liana asked, looking over her royal gown.

"If I looked like you, I wouldn't have to try." Miri said

it smiling, but Liana answered the compliment with a glare.

"She thinks you're trying to outshine her," Esa whispered. The palace seamstresses had added a pocket to Esa's gown so she could tuck her limp arm away. In bright pink silk, she looked like a princess herself.

"Liana spent *three hours* putting all those tiny curls into her hair and a week fixing up that gown," said Gerti, running her fingers through her own wavy hair that never grew past her shoulders.

"And she looks pretty," said Miri. "She always does. I don't know why she has to be the *prettiest.*"

They arrived at the ballroom doors and gave their names. Miri had attended a ball at the princess academy and thought she knew what to expect. This time, she was determined not to gawk like a coarse mountain girl.

And then she entered the palace ballroom and gawked as she had not since first arriving in Asland.

She had never seen so large a room. There were countless candles lit and sparkling in massive chandeliers. Hundreds of people resplendent in gowns and suits of silk spoke and laughed, moving fluidly as if aware of their own beauty. An orchestra played sounds so sweet and resonant, Miri felt herself reduced to sand, swept up and flying.

"You look beautiful."

Miri opened her eyes to find that she was not actually sand blowing about on the music but a mountain girl in a ball gown, and Timon was looking at her.

"I meant, you *are* beautiful," he said.

She wanted to shake her head but managed to say "thank you," because a rule of Poise stated that one should always accept a compliment. "I didn't know you'd be here."

"Commoners can attend, for a price. My father is always willing to pay for a chance to rub shoulders with nobility." Timon smiled, and she realized how tense he looked, afraid even. Of her? "For once my father and I agree on something—you."

"Me?"

"He approves of my courting you because I told him you are a noble. But *I* know you would throw off your title in a moment if that would help release others from the shackles of poverty."

She smiled to show he was correct, but it slid off her lips too quickly.

"Do you forgive me?" he asked. "Will you forgive me and dance with me?" He bowed over her hand. His eyes were blue as mountain ice.

She nodded. Though her insides were still as knotty and worried as ever, she could not muster any more anger. He closed his eyes and kissed her hand. Heat ran from that kiss up her arm and into her cheeks till she suspected she looked more apple than girl.

Timon put his other hand on her lower back and guided her into the center of the dance floor.

She had never danced like this, one body in the swirl of many bodies, spinning so fast she seemed part of everything and Timon too. The room spun. The world spun. And Miri was at the center of it.

The orchestra played another song, and Miri and Timon danced on. She worried at the unfamiliar tune, but he led her easily through the steps. She whirled. She skipped. She lifted her head and smiled. In her extravagant gown at an Aslandian ball in the arms of a scholar, she did not feel a bit like the girl from Mount Eskel.

At that moment, she did not miss it. At that moment, she did not care if she ever returned. She skipped. She swayed. She spun.

The music thrummed out of the dance tune and into a march of state. At the head of the room, the king and queen arose from their chairs, Gummonth beside them as he almost always seemed to be. Golden doors opened, and Britta entered alone. She'd plaited her hair in two braids as she had often worn it on Mount Eskel and tied them with ribbon. Her braid loops and ankle-length skirt made her look very young. At the academy ball, Miri had thought the silver-and-pink dress as royal as diamonds, but in the palace, it looked humble, a poor girl's dream of royalty.

All eyes were on the hopeful princess. Britta clenched her skirts, and Miri wanted to go to her and hold her hand. She made a wish on the flower in her hair that Britta could be happy tonight.

The dancers parted as a procession, led by Steffan, crossed the ballroom. Despite Britta's fears, Steffan went straight to his intended bride, bowed, and offered his hand. Britta took it. The crowd applauded politely. The music began again, and Britta and Steffan danced.

"And so ends the first act of marriage," Timon said. "Britta has become Steffan's partner on the dance floor, a symbol that they intend to be partners for life."

Miri exhaled, one knot inside her relaxing. "So they're almost married."

"Until they complete both the chapel ceremony and the presentation on the Green, nothing is official," said Timon. "Britta need not be the princess."

"But she will."

"Logically, is Britta the best choice?"

"Yes, she is. I'll write a Rhetoric paper on the subject and get back to you, Master Timon."

He smiled. "Sorry. I know I sound like an old man. I have a tendency to feel things too strongly, and I've worked hard to *think* instead." He was holding her gloved hand, feeling her fingers beneath it. "I love to think about things with you, Miri. But sometimes when I'm with you, all I can do is *feel*."

Miri could not find her breath to respond, but she did not need to. They were dancing again, her crocus-blue skirts swishing. Timon held her waist so that her feet seemed to barely touch the ground. They leaped and whirled, and Miri imagined wings on her back. Her breath was fast. Timon's hand was warm.

They danced for hours, it seemed, and Miri did not ever want to stop. But at last Timon offered his elbow to escort her from the floor to the refreshment room, where she drank cucumber-scented water and ate cups of red currant pudding drizzled with browned butter and crunchy sugar. He kept his arm around her waist to hold her close in the crowd, and they whispered about recent protests.

It was not until she saw Peder that Miri recalled what Britta had said about the bridal ball.

Peder was wearing his nicest clothes. Miri knew his mother had scavenged the best bits of cloth she could and carefully stitched each piece of the trousers, shirt, and vest. How grand they had looked on the mountain. Miri's chest pinched.

"Excuse me," Miri said to Timon, and hurried away.

Peder was looking around as if unsure how he'd

arrived in this place. His gaze stopped on Miri, but he stared at her for several moments before seeming to recognize her underneath all the tulle and silk and roses.

"Peder!" she said. "You came!"

"Britta sent an invitation, but Gus let me go only now." Lifting a cautious finger, he poked at her skirts. "How do they stick out so big?"

"It's all padding for show. For some reason, huge hips on a girl are supposed to be pretty."

"Huh. I don't think I'll ever understand lowlanders." He smoothed out his frown and offered his arm. "I mean, you look pretty."

"Even though my hips are as wide as a wagon?"

"Even though."

She took his arm and pulled him toward the music.

"I feel like I haven't seen you in weeks," she said.

"I'm sorry. It's your fault, you know," he said with his teasing smile.

"Oh really?"

"Absolutely. You think I'm so amazing and talented."

"I do, do I?"

"Uh-huh, and so I'm forced to prove you right by working like a dog."

"Because it would be horribly impolite of you to prove me wrong."

"And if I was ever rude to a girl, you know what my ma would do to me."

"Hang you by your ankles on the clothesline and whack you like a rug?"

"Or make me sleep on the floor of the goats' pen."

"So that's why you used to smell like a dung heap. And I thought you'd just dabbed on some lowlander cologne."

He jostled her with his shoulder, a playful nudge, and she caught a whiff of his clothes. He must not have worn them since leaving the mountain because they still carried the smell of Doter's homemade soap. As if the scent were a quarry-shout in the linder palace, the memory of home became vivid. She imagined they were tending goats on a hilltop, looking out at the eternal chain of mountains. The dazzle of candlelight was just the sun sparkling off Mount Eskel's snowy head. The music was the sensation of her heart beating.

"That's funny," Miri breathed. "All winter I haven't been able to remember home clearly. Not till just now. Here, smell."

She lifted the corner of his vest, and he breathed in His smile was softer but just as real.

"Every day I finish up my chores and stay awake as long as I can to practice carving, and then I fall into my cot, too tired to take off my shoes. But even then, all I want to do, more than sleep even, is talk to you. Talk like we used to when we tended the goats or hiked to the summit." He shifted, looking at his shoes. "The longer we stay here, the more you seem to belong, and the more I miss home."

The conductor announced the final number of the night, "Rose of Asland," and as the music began, panic charged into Miri's throat. She took Peder's hand and pulled him onto the floor.

"Come on, quick. We have to dance."

"Why?"

Because she had looked into Timon's eyes and felt wonderful in his arms. Because it was the bridal ball, and what if the old wives' tale was true after all? Because she had made a thousand wishes on a thousand miri flowers that she and Peder would one day hold hands as they entered the carved chapel doors on Mount Eskel and stand together under the stone lintel to swear devotion, and hear the cheers of their families and friends and receive gifts of goat kids and blankets and a wooden chair to put in their own little stone house.

But she had danced with Timon at the bridal ball, and the world was spinning so fast she did not know where her feet stood or where her heart lodged. Perhaps it would be her last dance with the love of her childhood, or perhaps it would be her first ball with the boy she would marry. Either way, she needed to dance.

But all she said to Peder was, "Please."

He took her hands. And they danced.

It was a simple dance to follow. All the dancers spun in a wide circle around the floor, the pace gallop-quick, the exercise jovial and breathless.

Peder's arms did not hold her as securely as Timon's had. She did not float, did not feel wings on her back. Peder's turns were sharper, and he looked more at his feet than into her eyes. They barely made it around the room one time before the other couples went zooming past. Was everyone staring? Did they look like the most backward, ham-fisted, lame-footed, provincial dancers Asland had ever witnessed? Miri felt tired and embarrassed, and she almost groaned. But as the groan rose up in her chest, she decided to turn it into a laugh. And when she laughed, Peder laughed.

They danced a little faster, and laughed a little louder, clomping their way over polished linder stones in the palace of the king.

*Spring Week One*

*Dear Marda,*

It is late. I danced at a ball tonight with two different partners. I still feel dizzy from spinning, and I suspect that feeling will not go away anytime soon.

Britta and Steffan danced, and it was as if he had chosen her all over again. Tomorrow is the chapel ceremony. I have failed Britta in ways I will tell you about one day. I do not think I can undo what I have done. But I can see her wed, at least. And I can be happy for her.

Miri

# Chapter Fifteen

*We stand up for the farmers*
*Who can't keep enough to eat*
*We walk out for the workers*
*Who don't know the taste of meat*
*We run forward for the children*
*With no shoes upon their feet*
*We will march this kingdom down*
*We will break the golden crown*

The next morning, the sun seemed a little closer, the air almost mountain-fresh after a night rain. Spring pulsed green and golden. The palace courtyard filled with the courtiers and ladies of the princess, their clothing fine though more subdued than their ball attire, and their eyes showing evidence of a late night dancing.

"Brutally early," muttered a man with a green-feathered cap and heavy fur coat. Liana was on his arm.

"*Must* the chapel ceremony take place the *very* morning after the ball?" she said. Miri had not realized that Eskelites spoke with an accent until she noticed how much Liana sounded like an Aslandian. Miri wondered if Liana had practiced long to work the accents of home off her tongue.

Liana would marry this noble, so whispered Bena. If she returned to Mount Eskel, it would be to visit, not stay. Such a future was possible—for Liana at least. And for Miri?

The murmuring stopped when Britta and the royal family emerged. Everyone curtsied or bowed. Britta wore a white dress, tight in the waist, lace over silk that spilled to the ground. Her head was wreathed in daffodils, her cheeks reddish-purple. She did not smile.

*Just nerves?* Miri wondered. *Or is Britta having second thoughts?* Perhaps Steffan's aloofness had finally worn her out and she would not go through with the ceremony. Some part of Miri hoped that were true. Changing Danland would be less complicated if Britta were not tangled up with royalty.

Courtiers began climbing into the carriages, hiding yawns behind hands. An official directed Miri, Katar, and the other Mount Eskel girls to the front carriage. Britta came toward them, running as if she feared she were late. Her slippers fell off. She paused to put them back on, and an official directed her to a nearer carriage.

The caravan began at a leisurely pace through the quiet streets.

"What is wrong with this city?" said Katar. "The chapel ceremony isn't open to the people like the presentation on the Green, but still, it's been over twenty years since the last royal marriage."

"You'd expect people lining the route of the procession," said Esa.

"Exactly," said Katar. "I know many are angry that Britta isn't an Eskelite, but she's still the prince's choice. Besides, I like her."

"You like someone?" said Miri. "That *is* saying something."

Katar yawned hugely, as if to show how little she cared about Miri's jest.

They turned a corner, and Miri could hear singing. At first she thought it some Aslandian celebration song, but then she recognized the tune and the words: *We will march this kingdom down, we will break the golden crown.*

It was "The Shoeless March." Perhaps her Salon friends were in the crowd. Miri looked out the window. Hundreds, maybe thousands of people surrounded the chapel and spilled into the street. They were not waving handkerchiefs and cheering. They were forming a barricade. As the carriages neared, yelling replaced the singing.

Katar leaned out the window and cried, "Don't stop!" at the driver, who was already whipping the horses faster.

SHANNON HALE

The mob rushed forward, pushing at the carriages, their faces twisted with anger.

". . . not *our* princess!" Miri heard one man shout as he hurled himself at their carriage door.

"Well, I'm not your princess either!" Frid yelled back. He yanked at the door, but she shook it until the man fell off.

The carriages crawled on, tilting and jolting as people banged on the doors and threw stones. Miri gripped the seat. They hit something, and with a bounce Miri and the girls fell onto the floor of the carriage, knocking heads. A moment later there was a cracking sound, so loud Miri's ears buzzed. The glass pane of the carriage window was fractured, a neat hole in the middle. Miri started to get up, but Katar pulled her back down.

"They've got muskets, Miri. They're firing at us!"

Miri could not have stood up then if she wanted to. Her legs felt wooden, her feet useless.

"Why us?" she asked.

"Maybe they think Britta's in here?" said Katar.

Until that moment, Miri had not believed, could not have imagined, that the people who yearned for change in Danland also wanted Britta dead.

The air stung with another shot, but the horses were running now. Miri could hear the carriage straining against the motion, wood creaking, nails pulling. She put her arms over her head and waited for whatever was happening to be over. She hated waiting. She wished for a mallet or a hammer, a needle and thread, a pen and paper—something she could *do*.

She did not look out again until the carriage stopped. Through the cracked glass she recognized the palace courtyard and leaped free, her legs shaking under her as if solid ground were still a carriage in motion, the whole world on the run.

The rest of the caravan was pulling in, with clatters and shouts and the brays of worried horses.

Britta spilled out of a carriage, her feet lost in her long skirts. She started toward Steffan, who looked equally dazed, but members of the royal guard surrounded her and led her away. Beside tall and striking Gummonth dressed in brilliant green, the king looked pale and weak. Miri had no trouble imagining him as a small prince locked all day in a closet.

"They should be hanged for this!" Gummonth was shouting.

"Now is not the time for aggression," said another official. "You need to placate the people, sire, console them, promise them peace and prosperity."

"Are you insane?" said Gummonth. "Now is *precisely* the time for aggression. I warned you, sire, if you did not punish the provinces after their insolence at the gift giving, the people would think you weak, easy to topple."

"You did, Gummonth," said the king. His hands shook as he pointed. "You warned me."

"Sire, you must act swiftly and decidedly," said Gummonth. "Round up as many protesters as you can, and have a public execution on the Green as a warning to others. You will prove to them that you are the king. If we show any weakness, they will attack again."

"That's right," said the king. "The people *must* recognize the absolute power of the crown. They *will* fear me."

"Please, Your Majesty," Miri said. "I think the other official was right. If we—"

"You may not speak," Gummonth interrupted her. "The king has not asked you to speak."

"But I know some of those people, and if you want peace—"

"You *know* them?" said Gummonth. "You sneaky little Eskelite rat. You're a part of this!"

"No! Well, I . . . I mean . . ."

"Get her out of my palace," said the king. "Out!"

Miri was scarcely aware of anything but hands on her arms. Two soldiers pulled her so quickly she managed to take only a step or two of her own on the way to the courtyard gate. The gatekeeper unlocked it, and the guards pushed Miri out. By the time she turned around, they had locked the gate against her.

She peered through the bars. The group was going into the palace, and Esa and Frid looked back.

Miri hurried into the street. She did not want them to speak up for her or do anything that would get them in trouble. Miri felt she deserved this, and worse too.

She wished for wings to take her back to her mountain. No wings appeared. So she walked. At first headed for Peder, she changed her mind.

She had never been to Sisela's house by daylight. The facade was painted the same red as the brick of the Queen's Castle. Patches were flaking off, revealing gray wood beneath. The crocuses and daffodils in the front garden were weedy and sparse, springing up defiantly.

Miri knocked at the door. Sisela herself answered.

"Oh! Hello. My . . . servants are off this morning," she mumbled, straightening her shawl and patting her uncombed curls. The black paint that outlined her eyes was smudged and made her look tired. "I wasn't expecting . . ." She laughed lightly. "I must be a sight! Never mind, come in, sister, dear."

Sisela led her into the Salon, the room lifeless without lamplight. She opened one of the drapes and let a slice of hard sunlight enter. Rather than bring color into the room, the high contrast made everything look black and white.

It felt odd to sit casually, just the two of them, in that formal and spacious chamber. Surely in a house that size there would be a smaller reception room?

Miri remembered something she had not thought of in weeks. The night soldiers had come, Miri and Timon fled through the house, dark room after dark room, each empty of furniture. Why would Sisela's house be mostly vacant?

The lady reclined on her lounge in her house robe, the slab of sunlight illuminating her from knees to brow. She looked bloodless.

"I would offer you refreshment, but as I said, the servants . . ." She shrugged prettily.

"I read a lot about the king recently," said Miri. "I can't help thinking differently of him, knowing that he was once a little boy tormented by his big brother."

"Sweyn tormented Bjorn? Yes, I can believe it. He still is just a poor little boy, isn't he? I used to be a courtier, you know—a noble who lives at court—until I couldn't bear to witness Bjorn, his queen, and their useless little lives any longer. I wonder if Bjorn realizes how close he is to losing his crown. . . ." Her voice quieted. "I wonder if he thinks about how different his life would be if he'd chosen me."

There was an impatient knock at the front door. Miri sprang to her feet, remembering the officials and soldiers, but Timon entered.

"Sisi—"

"Timon, dear!" Sisela said. "First Miri calls unexpectedly, and now my lamb Timon. I am popular today."

He squinted into the room. "Miri, are you all right? I heard that guns were fired at the royal carriages."

"A bullet went right over my head."

"No!" said Timon. "Miri, you have to stay away from the princess. She's marked for death."

"What do you mean—"

"He means the people are angry at her," Sisela interrupted.

"Yes, they made that pretty clear," said Miri. "They were shouting that they will *kill* Britta before allowing her to marry the prince. You didn't know that stupid leaflet would cause all this. Did you?"

Timon hesitated, putting his hands in his pockets, taking them out again.

"Miri, I know you understand that the greater good outweighs the cares of one person," said Sisela. "We must make sacrifices in order to realize our goals."

Miri's legs felt cold. "What *exactly* are those goals?"

"Ultimately, to rid this kingdom of the infestation of royalty and nobility."

SHANNON HALE

"I thought we were fighting for change, for a country where everyone has fair treatment and the hope of prosperity."

"Well, yes, of course," said Sisela. "And that will be possible once the royals and nobles are gone."

"Gone where?" Miri asked.

Timon paced to the window. Sisela smiled at Miri and patted the lounge beside her. Miri stayed standing. Sisela pressed her lips together.

"I have studied the history of many kingdoms. Whenever a people overthrow a king but allow him or his family to live, those royals eventually return, usually with foreign support, and reclaim the throne through war. Miri, my precious one, we must not make the mistakes of the past. Peace will set us back. I know it sounds harsh, but sometimes we must kill to prevent more killing."

Sisela paused, and Miri felt disconcerted by the silence. On Salon nights, Clemen played stirring marches behind Sisela's words, the notes rousing people into an ovation. Now, only the soft creak of the empty house punctuated her speech.

*Music creates mood, directs feeling*, Master Filippus had taught. Miri now wondered how much of what she had felt in the Salon had been created by Clemen's music.

In the hush, Miri remembered one of the rules of

Diplomacy she had learned at the academy: *The best solutions don't come through force.* Was that always true? Or could Sisela be right? Miri hoped not, but she was not certain.

The room felt airless. She wanted to feel stone under her feet and see sky above her, the same sky that covered Pa and Marda.

"I should go," said Miri.

Timon stepped forward and watched her as if waiting for an invitation to follow. She shut the door behind her.

The day was bright, the streets strangely calm after the terror at the chapel. Miri believed Britta ought to leave Asland. She could return home to Lonway or even Mount Eskel. It would not be so bad if Britta were not the princess. She seemed so lonely at the palace. Perhaps she would be happier if she could give it up. That was the simplest solution, and Miri hoped for it in a giddy, foolish way. Couldn't she have a fair world *and* her friend?

She pictured the way Britta's eyes widened whenever she spoke of Steffan, and despair sank back into her chest.

Miri found Master Filippus alone in their classroom, reading an unfurled scroll. He smiled when he saw her.

"Not many seek the enlightenment of books and old men when offered a free day and sunshine."

"You're here too," she said.

He moaned and patted his cheek. "I have fair skin. I burn easily." He set down the parchment. "You have questions. You may ask."

"Some of my friends seek change in Danland."

He nodded. "Examine not only an idea but the people behind it. What do they have to gain?"

"Timon Skarpson—"

"Son of wealthy merchants. His parents have donated gold to the crown in hopes of claiming a noble title."

"Lady Sisela—"

"—is a *lady* no longer. Years ago she published leaflets condemning the king. When they were traced back to her, her husband claimed them to save her life. He was declared a traitor and stripped of his title before execution."

Miri blew air out through her lips.

"Did you guess I was such a gossip?" Master Filippus said slyly.

"They're willing to risk everything for the cause. I believe they really do care about the shoeless."

"Perhaps," he said.

How could Miri know what was the truth? She shook her head.

"Master Filippus, what happened in Rilamark after they killed their queen?"

"The rebels . . . mmm . . . executed her family. And her friends. And her supporters. That wasn't enough, so they executed as many nobles as they could get their hands on. The ax fell daily for weeks. And now the rebels look about themselves and wonder what to do next. Those who were fond of the old way fight the new leaders, and the killing continues. Few of their trade ships sail, and when trade stops, people starve."

"The very people that the rebels were trying to help," she said.

Master Filippus shrugged in agreement.

"You are a master scholar, so you know the harder subjects, like Ethics."

"That is true."

"Tell me what to do. I need to know what's right and what's wrong."

"A question every scholar wrestles with. Let us use the question of the painting and the prisoner as an example. What do you think of the painting?"

"It is not good or evil. It is only what a person sees in it."

"Exactly," he said. "It has no capacity for evil. It is safe. A man who has killed might kill again. He is not safe."

"But what if the murderer was sorry?" she asked.

And what if he had kind eyes? What if he made a

joke at his own expense that made Miri laugh? What if he'd been many years in the dungeon with no window and all he longed for was to gaze into a pure blue sky? The painting was beautiful. But the painting could not sit under the sky, look up, and smile. The painting could not admire the waning moon and think how much it looked like a face half turned away from the light. The painting had lasted many years longer than any person might, but it did not care. It did not fear the fire.

"So you would choose the murderer," said Master Filippus.

"But I love the painting. I don't want to have to choose."

"And so you choose nothing. You let both the painting and the murderer burn. Which is worse—acting in the wrong or not acting at all? Let us look at another example—"

"No more examples. I have a real question. There are changes brewing. And there is a girl. The change is about what's best for people like my own family, which apparently includes preventing the girl from marrying the boy she loves, and possibly even killing her. But the girl is my friend."

"An interesting dilemma. As you study History, you discover a pattern of revolutionary thought that invariably fails to meet its goals."

Miri was pacing now. "Everyone keeps saying history has proven this or that. But it seems like people look only at the parts of history that agree with them and ignore all the rest."

"A valid point. Perhaps if you study the philosophies of Mikkel—"

"Just tell me what to do!"

"I can't," he said. "That is the sad truth you seek, Lady Miri. I don't know everything. No one does."

"Then what good is all this?" She slapped at the table, knocking a parchment onto the floor.

Master Filippus sat back, groaning like a tree branch pushed about by wind. His slow gaze took in the spilled parchment and then returned to her face. She had never realized before that he was quite old.

His voice creaked. "We study, Miss Miri, we read and ponder and examine every side, so when it comes time to make a choice, we have hope of a good one. But I don't know which choice is good for you. Ethics happens here"—he pointed to his chest—"as much as here." He pointed to his head.

"I wish everything was easier," she whispered.

"So do I," he said.

She exhaled heavily and felt a tightness in her throat that meant she could cry if she wanted. She carefully rolled the fallen parchment and placed it on the table.

Master Filippus rested his head on his hand, his cheek wrinkling, and looked out the window. He could not have been more opposite the young girl in the painting, and yet, Miri noticed, their expressions were identical. But the master was as real as his wrinkles, while the girl was nothing more than color on canvas. Miri hoped that if a building caught fire, she herself would be worth coming back for. Just then, she was not sure that was true.

*We are what we do,* Timon had said.

Miri sat beside Master Filippus. "Will you show me the philosophies of Mikkel?"

He nodded, and his wrinkles turned up slightly to admit a smile.

Miri arrived at Gus's very late. She had sat with Master Filippus all day, debating many ideas and finding no easy answers. Gus's gate was locked. She felt too tired to knock and leaned against it, nearly asleep upright.

Peder came from the direction of the street. "Miri! I was looking for you. Britta sent me a note about what happened."

He unlocked the gate to let them in, and they settled on the pile of straw. Miri felt like a fire burned down, embers barely pulsing orange. But she talked, Peder listened, and a kind of quiet heat flickered in her that promised not to burn out yet. She told him about "The Mountain Girl's Lament" and Timon, Gummonth and the tributes, Sisela's empty house, the gunshot in the carriage, the painting in the classroom.

"I don't know," said Peder. "Why do you have to choose between the painting and the prisoner?"

"Because there isn't time and the fire is raging."

Peder rubbed his eyes and lay his head on his arm. "But there isn't actually a fire, right?"

"Well, no."

"Then isn't it kind of a stupid question?"

"But if there *were* a real fire—"

"I'm too tired to think about pretend fires," he said.

"I know. Me too. I just wish . . . I want ethics to tell me what to do."

"I'm going to sleep here. You take my bed. There are some oats in the bucket. . . . The horse is so pretty. . . ."

Miri squinted at him. "What are you talking about— horses and oats?"

Peder snorted and opened his eyes. "What?"

"You were falling asleep."

"No, I wasn't. Maybe for just a second."

Miri laughed. "I'm in crisis about Britta and musket shots and tributes, and you're falling asleep and dreaming about pretty horses!"

"Don't laugh," he whined, "or you'll make me laugh and I'm too tired."

He covered his face with his arm and snored once.

Miri sat on his low bed beside Gus's fire. She stared at the wall, her gaze sleepy, her thoughts chasing one another like a dog after its own tail. She wrapped a blanket around her shoulders. It smelled like Peder.

He was sound asleep on the straw and did not twitch when she lay the blanket over him.

# Chapter Sixteen

*Bury the embers, extinguish the spark*
*We plunge ourselves in the well of the dark*
*Far from voices that trouble and chatter*
*Down, deep down where worries don't matter*
*Our minds all teem with the unseen thing*
*But night is a blink, and sleep but a dream*
*Wake, wake, see things as they seem*

In the morning, Miri drew a bucket of water from the well to wash up and drink. Her stomach gurgled, protesting against nothing but water for breakfast. She tried to be quiet as she left, but the gate squeaked.

Peder ran out, his hair full of straw and sticking straight up on one side.

"Are you going to the Queen's Castle?" he asked, his voice dry from sleep.

"We're on break. But I have to go out there and try to do *something*, you know?"

"Wait a moment."

He returned quickly, wearing his jacket, his hair wet, his face red from washing with cold water.

"I asked Gus for leave. I want to go with you." He locked the gate behind them and paused. "It feels as if today is important."

She was about to protest—this was her mess, and cleaning it up might prove dangerous. But he took her hand and smiled that confident smile of his that lifted higher on one side. She smiled back and believed perhaps for the first time since coming to Asland that somehow everything might work out.

They passed through the alley and into a snowfall.

Clumps of snowflakes hovered and bumped along the breeze like fat bumblebees. Miri held out her hand, a place for snow to land. A flake settled onto her palm, its presence just a prick of coldness, a melting. It felt like a gift. She breathed in through her nose and shut her eyes.

"Smells like home," said Peder.

The snow was too light to stay, the ground too warm to keep it. And the strange spring snow fell only in that golden moment of dawn, the turning of the page between night and day. Miri caught one of the last flakes on a fingertip and let it disappear on her tongue.

The streets were quiet, just slow-moving delivery wagons and servants walking to work. Peder and Miri made their way to the palace, taking the route past the great wooden chapel.

Without speaking of it, they both climbed the chapel steps and stood before the doors, so huge Miri wondered if they had been built by giants. The same scene of the creator god first speaking to humans graced Mount Eskel's own humble chapel doors. Miri's neck hurt, leaning back to look up so high.

"They're big," Peder said.

"Big," Miri agreed.

"They look a lot like ours, but bigger."

"Big, big, big."

"Massive." Peder scrunched his nose. "It seems kind of unnecessary, doors that big."

"Maybe Aslandians used to be four times as tall."

"That would make sense. Only it doesn't."

"Exactly." She touched the wood. It was not as polished and well oiled as the Mount Eskel chapel doors. And perhaps not as well loved. With so many things to look at in Asland, who cared enough to love these doors?

"Britta and Steffan were supposed to exchange vows here yesterday. And after, they would have climbed the bridal edifice in the Green and been presented to the people as husband and wife." She turned, scanning the grassy park across the main avenue from the palace. "I watched them build the bridal edifice from a palace window. It's a huge wooden platform, topped with banners and . . . That's funny, we should be able to see . . ."

There was no edifice on the Green, but there were piles of lumber and colorful banners torn apart and scattered across the grass.

"They destroyed it," Miri whispered. Her stomach felt sick.

A small boy affixed a paper to the chapel wall. He lowered his cap over his eyes when he noticed them and hurried away.

"I've never seen so many leaflets," Peder said.

There were always some leaflets in the city. Timon said that since it was illegal for anyone but the king's officials to print news journals, leaflets were the people's way to speak out. The abundance of leaflets that morning felt like a shout.

Miri scanned the one the boy had just tacked to the chapel.

This titled girl named Britta is not content to merely live in luxury while the shoeless labor for her silks, but she must steal a crown from them as well. She will lie, she will cheat, she will rob to wed the prince. But we the people will not allow a thief in the palace. We will cut off her hair and sell it for thread. We will strip her skin for ribbons.

Miri read no further, crumpling it up and tossing it as far as she could. She scanned another leaflet and another, dozens of different authors saying about the same thing. One sounded a good deal like Sisela.

Peace will set us back. If you are hungry, if you labor without rest, look no further for blame than this robber princess. The first to cut out her heart will be the hero of Danland.

Miri fled down the chapel stairs toward the palace. "It's my fault this is happening."

"It's not your fault," Peder said, racing down the street beside her.

"I was careless and boastful when I wrote that Rhetoric paper. My words helped start it, and I have to undo it."

"My ma says *You can't unspill a stew.*"

"She also says *Undoing a wrong is greater than doing a right.*"

"You know, Ma is very good at saying two things at once."

They neared the tree where Miri met Timon on the way to the Queen's Castle in the mornings. She stopped running when she saw his figure pace around the corner. His pale hair was stressed and lying every which way.

"That's that boy you danced with at the ball," said Peder.

Miri did not know that Peder had seen.

"Timon!" she said. "What are you doing here?"

"I . . . I was hoping to see you." Timon noticed Peder and his expression stiffened into a frown.

"What's going on?" Miri asked.

"You need to stay away from the princess," said Timon. "For a few days at least, all right?"

"Why?" she asked, her eyes narrowing.

"Just listen to me and do it."

"No," she said. "Tell me why."

"Miri—"

"Tell me why, Timon."

Timon looked about. The few people in the street were not near enough to hear.

"Some of us . . . Sisi . . . well . . ."

"Just spit it out, *Timon*," Peder said.

Timon glared, but he turned back to Miri and took a deep breath.

"Sisi heard that the rebels in Rilamark hired an assassin to 'take care' of their queen. She found him and wrote to him, asking him to do the same here. I . . . we . . . some of us—those of the group with money—we paid the fee."

"I don't understand," Miri said, though she was afraid that she actually did.

"This was three months ago. We never heard back.

I figured our letter went astray, or perhaps it was just a hoax. But yesterday Sisi received a letter from the assassin. He claimed he is in Asland now and helped agitate the mob at the chapel. And that was just a precursor. And . . . and . . ." Timon's voice was so low now, Miri had to lean closer to hear. "He guaranteed the princess would be dead by midnight tonight, if not by a mob, then by his own hand."

"He's going to kill Britta? No! Why would you do that? Stop the assassin. Stop it from happening!" She realized she was gripping his shirtfront and forced herself to let go.

Timon rubbed his hair and face with both of his hands. "I don't know who he is. I don't know what he looks like or where he is staying. I don't know anything, Miri. He said he would contact us for the second half of the payment *after* he finished the job. His target is the robber princess, but he promised he would take care of any other royals as well if circumstances permit. I don't know how to stop it. I don't think anyone can."

Peder went at Timon, shoving him hard in the chest. Timon stumbled backward.

"You're trying to get Britta killed?" Peder said. "You're the reason someone shot at Miri. She could be dead!"

Peder shoved again. Though Timon was taller, Peder was a mountain boy, who cut and hefted stone all day.

Miri was afraid he might really hurt Timon. A small part of her wanted to let him try. But she put out a hand and stepped between them. Peder bounced on the balls of his feet as if ready to swing a punch at any moment.

"It was bound to happen with or without me," Timon said, his voice hot. He brushed off his jacket, glowering at Peder. "All over the continent, people are speaking out against royalty. Nobility will follow, and then freedom. But revolution doesn't happen all at once. The strike must start somewhere."

"And so you all put your scholarly little heads together and decided Britta's death would be the spark to ignite the bonfire."

"I know she was your friend," Timon said. "I just wanted to warn you to stay away. Please. Stay away from her so you don't get hurt."

*I know she was your friend*, he'd said. Dread made the day seem dark, and nothing mattered but getting to Britta's side. Miri grabbed Peder's arm and pulled him into a run.

Miri was going over in her mind what she would say to get into the palace courtyard, but the guards at the outer gate did not ask for a password and let her through. Perhaps the king's banishment order had not traveled that far. She was not certain she would be so lucky at the entrance to the palace itself.

They ran through a walled garden toward the south wing.

"If they refuse me," Miri said, "they might still let you in. Go first to Britta's chamber and—"

Miri stopped. The entrance was entirely unguarded.

"Should we be able to walk in like this?" Peder asked.

"Definitely not," said Miri.

They creaked open the door. The foyer was empty. Miri felt cold.

On the way to Britta's apartment, they passed two royal guards in silver breastplates and tall hats.

"No one was at the entrance," Miri said to them. "Is the royal family all right?"

"Of course," said one. "The guard is protecting them. Excuse us, we're called away."

Miri frowned but continued on.

The palace was as quiet as the early-morning street, just servants moving through the corridors. Their pace was quick, their faces unhappy. Miri wondered if they had read the latest leaflets.

She took a deep breath at Britta's door and decided she could not tell her about the assassin. Britta would be too frightened. But somehow she had to get her out of the palace.

"Keep watch," Miri whispered to Peder. She knocked and went in.

Britta was still in her white lace marriage gown, sitting on the floor with her legs tucked under her. The curls in her hair were droopy and loose. Morning light glinted on her wet cheeks.

"Miri! I'm so sorry. I told the king that of course you had no part in what those people at the chapel did. After all, they shot at you! But he won't listen to me. Sometimes I feel as if when I speak no sound comes out at all. . . ."

Tears spilled down her face.

"Britta, don't cry for me. Please."

"I can't stop. I've been crying all night like a baby, though it's not just for you. I'm far more selfish than you give me credit for, Miri. It just feels as if everything is coming apart."

"Where's Steffan?"

"That's the heart of it," Britta said with a sad smile. "They have him in the king's wing. Keeping us separate. I waited all night for someone to fetch me, but no one's come. Not even a servant with supper. I knocked at the girls' chamber a few times. I don't think they slept there last night."

Miri did not think the assassin would target Mount Eskel girls, but her unease quickened.

"Perhaps everyone's forgotten me," Britta said. "Or perhaps it's been decided Steffan and I will not wed."

Miri poured Britta a glass of water from a pitcher.

"Might it be for the best?" said Miri. "There are worse things that could happen."

"I can't imagine."

Miri thought of the shattered glass in the carriage window, the axes falling in Rilamark. She gave Britta the water and watched her drink it down, her toes curling and uncurling with impatience.

"Things are getting dangerous out there. We should leave Asland for the time being."

Britta shook her head, confused. "Not without Steffan. Where would I go anyway?"

Miri glanced at the door. "Home to Lonway?"

Britta shuddered. She'd stopped crying, but her eyes were red and swollen.

"I'll never go back. The day my father put me on a wagon to Mount Eskel, I watched the house grow smaller and smaller, and I swore it would stay like that in my mind—tiny and harmless, sized for a mouse."

Miri thought of her own wagon ride away from home, her village swallowed by the mountain, her promise to return.

"Was home so horrible?" she asked, gathering some of Britta's clothing into a bundle.

"Perhaps not. I'm probably just being dramatic." She tried to smile, but the attempt was piteous. "I'm much younger than my siblings. They were all married before I was five. And my parents preferred to spend a great deal of time at court, attending plays and concerts. They said their house in Asland was too small to bring me along. It had ten bedrooms, but it was too small for a girl . . . like a mouse house, maybe."

Not a sunrise passed that Miri did not put her arms around herself and remember that her mother had refused to put down her new baby even for a moment in the week before she died. It was a sadness that ran under everything, like the low notes of a horn in an orchestra's song. But it made Miri feel stronger too. She had this secret, this fierce love from her mother, that was always hers.

How much worse to have a mother who lived and simply did not care. Miri hugged the bundle of clothing to her chest.

"When my parents were in Asland," Britta was saying, "I stayed in Lonway with the servants. My father forbade me to play with commoners, so I played alone. Except when Steffan stayed at the Summer Castle. I didn't understand why my father encouraged this one friendship. All I knew then was I had a friend! We invented games and stayed outside from breakfast till the crickets sang. He was the first person to shout out my name when he saw me coming, as if for pure happiness. The first who made me feel like more than a piece of furniture—like a girl." She blushed. "He was my *only* friend, Miri, until you. I cannot imagine life without him. I can't imagine."

"I'm sorry," Miri said. And with those words, the weight of what she'd done collapsed over her. She felt her mistakes like an avalanche, and the grinding pain of regret broke into sobs.

"Miri? What's the matter?"

"I'm sorry, I'm sorry, I'm so sorry, Britta. . . ." She felt Britta rub her back and shook her head. "I don't deserve your comfort. I've wanted to be a part of the changes so badly—for Mount Eskel, but for me too . . . though I knew it might hurt you . . . I was so afraid the king's tributes would crush our village, would make everything so hard again . . . harder even . . . but I wanted to help make things good everywhere . . . and . . . and I didn't mean to lie at first, but I never told you . . . when I found out . . . that the words were mine. 'The Mountain Girl's Lament.' I wrote it. Most of it anyway."

She could feel Britta's hand on her back freeze.

"That's not true," Britta whispered.

"Timon suggested I write about the academy for a Rhetoric paper. I didn't write that last part, of course! Timon added his own words and had it printed. When you asked me about it, I didn't know. But I should have told you when I found out, I should have written a different leaflet explaining, I should have done *something* . . .

but Sisela said to let it be and I believed her—she's so smart—so I did nothing, I'm sorry . . ."

Britta stood and went to the window. Her back was tense. Miri held her breath, unshed sobs straining in her throat, and waited for Britta to send her away as the king had done.

"I wondered. You were gone so many evenings. Gummonth told us about all that happened in Rilamark and said there was dangerous talk in Aslandian Salons. But I never imagined that you—" She took a shuddering breath. "I can't think about this right now, Miri."

"That's all right." Miri sniffed and wiped her nose on a handkerchief. "You don't have to forgive me—or not forgive me—or anything. But you need to get out of here, Britta. The palace guards are gone from their stations."

Britta's hands clutched together. "Gone?"

"We need to go somewhere safe. Please."

"I don't . . . I don't know where to go," Britta whispered.

Miri felt a hopeless panic rising up on a sob in her chest. She shoved it back down. *We learn and talk and think so that when it's time to act, we know what to do.*

What to do? She thought of History, Ethics, and Diplomacy, as well as Peder and Esa's ma, who said *Truth is when your gut and your mind agree.*

Miri took Britta's hand and said, "Stay with me."

# Chapter Seventeen

When thoughts aren't sticking, are thicker than stew
What is true? What to do?
When strife is looming, naught brewing for you
Ask anew, what to do?

Peder was waiting outside Britta's door.

"Hello, Britta," he said, taking the clothing bundle from Miri.

"Good morning, Peder. You're out early."

"Being friends with Miri has consequences."

He followed the girls to the king's wing. It too stood unguarded.

"Something is definitely wrong," Miri said.

Down the corridor, Steffan and his father were in their sleep clothes, speaking hurriedly. Britta called out to Steffan. He ran to her and they embraced. Britta's shoulders heaved as she sobbed, her fingers gripping his shirt.

"The bridal edifice in the Green was torn down," Miri told Steffan. "I'm worried for Britta."

"There are some pretty threatening leaflets out this morning," Peder said.

The king pointed a hard finger at Miri. "How did you get in here?"

"The guards are not at their posts, sire," she said.

"I noticed," he said, gesturing to the emptiness beside his door. "At the palace entrance?"

Miri shook her head.

"This is unconscionable! The royal guard would not abandon me."

Miri wondered if somehow the assassin had maneuvered the guards away. If so, the battleground had moved from the streets of Asland into the palace itself.

"We have reason to believe a mob might be forming today in Asland," Miri said. "We need to keep you all safe, and right now this palace is not feeling safe."

The king glared. "I do not trust anything you say, you who consort with murderers."

"I do know some of those who seek change, but I swear to you, I never imagined any of my friends might consider violence—"

"Get out!" said the king.

"No, wait, please. There is a man who arranged the fate of Rilamark's queen. This assassin is here in Asland, paid in gold to . . ."

Miri could not bear to continue. She glanced at Steffan.

"They want to kill the prince heir, do they?" said Steffan.

"Not exactly," Miri whispered.

He seemed confused and then his eyes widened with real fear.

"It's me, isn't it?" Britta asked, seeming a little tired. "The assassin is here for me."

"No," said Steffan. "No." He moved between Britta and the open corridor.

"In Rilamark, he got a mob to do his work for him," said Miri. "I imagine that's his plan here."

"I will not be trapped in my own house," said the king.

"We can go to the Summer Castle," Steffan said. "Surely the servants and soldiers there are loyal. Besides, it's smaller."

He did not say "and easier to defend," but Miri heard the idea in the silence. Rilamark's queen had been dragged from her palace into the street. Miri wondered if there was a girl somewhere in Rilamark who would have saved an unpopular queen and let a painting burn.

"Perhaps if we bring a priest with us," said Steffan, "Britta and I could be married in Lonway?"

"You cannot wed her now," said his father.

SHANNON HALE

*No*, Miri wanted to protest. But she did not speak out, too afraid the king would send her away again. She wondered if Britta would weep, but she just clung to Steffan's arm.

The king sent a servant to prepare a carriage. Steffan and his father dressed, then fetched the queen and their personal servants, as well as, Miri was sorry to see, the chief official. Gummonth's eyes darted about as if expecting danger from every shadow.

The group made their way through the eerily quiet palace. When they passed an open window, Miri could hear shouting outside. She grabbed Peder's hand. They would be safer if they left Britta and the royals behind. Miri knew this. Peder surely knew this as well. But he did not suggest it either.

Every time they turned a corner, Miri's pulse quickened. But the corridors were empty.

The group hurried outside to the courtyard, where a few months before, Katar had presented the king with Mount Eskel's carved mantelpiece. A faithful groom had a carriage with six horses ready. It stood not fifty paces ahead, but to Miri, it seemed an unreachable distance.

A mob had gathered.

Held back by the high iron gates that separated the courtyard from the city street, the crowd pressed against the bars, yelling. Every arm bore a blue band. The noise was overwhelming, like the crash of a mountain rockfall. Out of the cacophony, the word "princess" seemed to lift on the wind. Some held muskets and pistols in the air, waving them about like flags. Some pointed them at the royal party. A few fired, too far away to strike anything but the cobbled ground, sending puffs of dust and rock chips into the air.

The queen made a horrible sound in her throat, a choked cry like an animal in pain. Her eyes and mouth were wide open and wet.

"Back inside," Steffan ordered.

So many people pressed against the gate, there was no way to escape. The hope of the castle in Lonway was dashed.

The shouts and musket shots were spooking the carriage horses. They pranced and shook their manes. The groom let go of the lead horse's bridle and fled for the palace. The horses tossed their heads, and the carriage rocked.

Miri turned back to the palace with the others. She did not realize that Britta had not until Steffan shouted her name.

Britta was running straight for the gate. Steffan started after her but his father grabbed him and held him back.

"Don't. They will kill you," said the king.

"Britta!" Steffan shouted in a blind panic, thrashing to get away. "Britta!"

Miri did not shout. She did not go after Britta. She did not seem able to do anything except watch her friend run toward the muskets, holding the long white skirts of her marriage gown in both hands so she could get there even faster.

Did Britta think that by sacrificing herself she could save the rest of them? This mob's anger would not be sated by Britta's blood alone. They would demand the king and queen and Steffan too, and would it stop there? Or would every feathered cap in Danland fall?

The moment seemed slowed. Miri's hands covered her face, her eyes peering through her fingers—too afraid to look, too afraid not to. A shot would fire and Britta would fall. Would a shocked silence follow, or howls of triumph? The moment was agonizingly long, all of them watching each stride that took Britta closer to the mob, closer to the muskets, dozens of them poking through the bars of the gate, all pointed now at the running princess.

They did not fire yet, as if the shooters, like Miri, were too astonished to act. What was this princess in white running *to*?

And then Miri noticed what she had not before. A boy, perhaps two years old, was standing in the courtyard, his head tilted up as he stared at the palace. His back was to the carriage. The horses pranced and shook, and the jolting carriage was backing up, its metal-rimmed wheels now inches from the child.

In full run, Britta grabbed the boy, and they tumbled onto the stones, rolling away from the carriage. The next moment its wheels lurched over the spot where he'd been.

The crowd stopped shouting. Miri was certain that they, like her, had not noticed the child before. The only sound now was one wailing voice. Miri looked for the source—a woman, her arms extended through the bars toward the child. His mother, surely. Perhaps she'd been screaming for help all along, Miri realized; only who could hear the cries of a mother above the calls of a mob?

Britta stood slowly, as if her fall had hurt and she was testing her limbs. The boy seemed dazed as Britta patted his arms and legs, searching for injury. He did not cry, but his eyes were wide and his chin tense, his breathing visibly rattling his chest. She picked him up and took him to the gate, where he fit back through the bars he must have climbed through. He reached for his mother, and she held him and buried his face in her neck. In the silence, Miri could hear the exhausted sobs of the woman as she said, "Thank you, thank you."

The crowd parted for her, and the woman carried her son away.

All now was silent. Britta stood alone in her marriage

gown, touching distance from an armed mob who'd threatened to cut her skin into ribbons. It would be useless to run, Miri knew. If they wished to kill Britta, they could.

Britta faced them, her hands clasped behind her back, her shoulders rising and falling as she breathed.

"They'll shoot her," Steffan said, his voice raspy.

"Wait," Miri whispered. *Offer silence*, she thought.

Britta met the gaze of the crowd. The crowd looked back. A couple of the muskets lowered.

"Why doesn't she come back?" Steffan said.

"She's too scared to move," Miri said, and her heart ached.

Steffan started, but the king held him still. Miri put a staying hand on Steffan's arm.

"Not you," she said. "Not yet."

Miri took a step forward.

"Miri," said Peder.

"I can do this," she said.

The walk seemed eternal. How had Britta run this length so quickly? Miri's breath tangled in her chest, and she could manage only short gasps. The horses had calmed in the silence, but Miri skirted the carriage just in case. There was something on the ground up ahead, and as she drew nearer she recognized Britta's gray slippers. They must have fallen off as she ran. Miri picked them up.

She joined Britta at the gate. The fall had shredded some of the lace of her gown and dusted her with dirt. Miri pried one of Britta's hands loose from the other and held her cold fingers. She could feel Britta shaking.

*Fix this, Miri,* she thought.

She straightened her shoulders and lifted her head.

"I am Miri of Mount Eskel," she said in a loud, clear voice. "I wrote 'The Mountain Girl's Lament.'" *Or most of it,* she thought. She wanted to explain that she had not written that final paragraph, and to tell them how she loved Britta, and that it was not merely chance that Britta had noticed the boy when no one else had because she always saw, really *saw* people, and cared about them sincerely, and why a girl was more important than a painting. But the crowd was large and deep. Her voice could not reach them all.

*Be as succinct as possible,* Master Filippus had taught of Rhetoric.

She needed to say something that carried great meaning in only a few words. Like a song. Like a poem.

She still had Britta's slippers. She held them aloft and shouted, "Look! The princess is shoeless!"

The crowd stirred. Some pointed to Britta's bare, dusty foot peeking from beneath the hem of her dress.

"The princess is shoeless," a woman repeated.

Others picked up the phrase. And though they had just been shouting for her death, the mob tossed the phrase around with awe and excitement: *the princess is shoeless, the princess is shoeless.* . . . Miri shivered with the sound.

"Come on, Britta," she whispered. "I'll walk you back."

Squeezing her hand, Miri walked and Britta followed. The return seemed even longer. All it would take was one musket, one pistol, one person who did not care that Britta had saved that child, or perhaps had been too far back in the crowd to see. One bullet would end this. But neither ran, and when they reached the royal group, no shot had fired.

Steffan rushed forward to meet them, pulling Britta into his arms.

"You are so brave," he whispered. "Too brave."

She shook her head but did not let go.

"Inside," said the king.

The group followed him through the door and down the wide central corridor. It was deserted.

"Your Majesty," Miri said, trying to keep pace beside him. "Please don't cancel their wedding. Every person who was at that gate feels differently toward Britta now.

And those people will talk. People always talk. Word of what happened will pass around the city—"

"Perhaps. But what of the rest of us? The *shoed?*" he added fiercely. "Curse the lot. Gummonth was right. I should have sent troops into each province after their disrespectful gifts. I should have raised tributes and doubled the army. They will feel the wrath of the crown."

Miri was not so sure it was a terrific peacemaking idea but did not dare point that out.

Far down the corridor, the Mount Eskel girls rushed by. Miri called to them and they hurried over.

"Where have you been?" she asked.

"We slept in the library last night," said Gerti. "It was Liana's idea."

Liana flushed and mumbled that she had thought it would be fun. It seemed like a strange suggestion to Miri but she did not have time to think it over.

"There are people in the south wing," said Katar. "They broke some windows."

Not everyone had seen Britta's actions in the courtyard. Miri believed the news would spread, but only if it had time.

In the distance, shouts echoed against stone.

The king directed them all to a chamber in the center of the palace. There were no windows—just four solid linder walls and one thick wooden door, reinforced with metal bands.

Peder and Frid shut the door behind them and lowered the heavy locking bars.

"Wait, where are we?" Liana said.

"A refuge room," said Steffan.

"I'm not supposed to be in here," she said, pacing near the door.

Miri thought it an odd comment but supposed Liana was just in a panic. Miri helped Britta and Steffan light the kerosene lamps around the room, filling the space with a twitching brightness. The queen slumped down on one of the many chairs. The academy girls began sorting through crates of supplies—jugs of water, blankets, jars of kerosene, tins of sailor biscuits.

Bena sniffed one of the hard biscuits that were made to last weeks at sea. "Just how long are we planning to stay here?"

"No longer than necessary," said the king. "The royal guard will rally and free us."

Britta was backing toward the far corner, where a doorless closet waited, so deep Miri could not see past its first shadow. Miri wondered if it held more food storage or perhaps a privy. She glanced back at the door just in time to see Liana trying to lift one of the bars.

"Don't you dare open that door, Liana," said Miri.

"I'm not!" she said angrily, and then mumbled, "The bars are too heavy anyway."

Miri forgot the closet and watched the door instead, as if her vigilance alone would keep danger out. The threat seemed to lurk outside, so she never thought to turn and look behind her. Not until she heard Britta's strangled scream.

# Chapter Eighteen

*When the mountain quaked*
*Like an elbow's nudge*
*Like a shout that something is wrong*
*The people woke and*
*Knew, yes, knew, that bandits had come*

Three men stormed out of the closet, each holding a musket or pistol with a spare tucked in his belt. The scuffle was quick. A bearded man grabbed Britta. A second moved toward Steffan and the king. Frid was there, and she punched him in the face. The man fell backward, his pistol firing at the ceiling. Frid, Steffan, and Peder started toward Britta.

The third shouted, "Hold or we shoot!"

Everyone stopped. The bearded man was pressing a pistol to Britta's temple.

"Hear us out, ignoble king," he said. "Hear us or the robber princess dies! Death to all who grind the shoeless into the dirt. Now is the time for the people to take power."

On he shouted, eager to share his ideas about a new age for the kingdom. His audience was captive. His captive was trembling. His friends were armed, and the royal party was powerless to do anything but listen. He was clearly a shoeless Aslandian, and not the assassin from Rilamark.

Britta did not cry, just bowed her head as if resigned.

"Reason with them," Miri whispered to the king. "Please. If they were here for blood alone, they would have shot her immediately. Perhaps they only want to be heard."

"They will not listen to me." The king gestured wildly. "I've never felt so much hate."

The queen nodded, a hand pressed to her stomach.

Miri frowned. It was easy to assume such people hated royalty, but the king sounded so sure. And then Steffan, tense and shaking, said, "He's going to shoot her. He feels no remorse. He's . . . no, please—"

Steffan did not seem able to stop himself. He lurched for Britta and the bearded man, but the second man, recovered from his blow, got in the way. He struck Steffan with the butt of a musket. The prince fell. The rebel held him down, the musket pressing against Steffan's neck.

Britta jolted as if to go to him, but the bearded man held her tight and continued talking. She gripped his arms, too weak to pull them away. She looked up, her lip trembling as if she were preparing for the moment her soul would leave her body and drift into the heavens. Then she closed her eyes. With a sharp *click*, the bearded man paused his rant to cock the pistol.

*No*, Miri quarry-spoke, almost without thinking.

It was one fierce, defined, powerful idea. It was the mathematical concept of "not true" formed into emotion. She was not conscious of any particular memory that drove that idea down into the linder. The word was enough on its own. Mount Eskel's linder understood *no*. She detected the faintest shift under her feet, and remembered Esa's violent quarry-shouts from the palace library and how the stone had vibrated then.

Those of Mount Eskel looked Miri's way, hearing her quarry-speech. The bearded man lectured on, his finger twitching on the pistol's trigger. He was going to kill Britta, Miri now had no doubt. She had once been caught and held by such a man, a bandit who wanted her dead. Miri's pa, big as a boulder and strong as a bear, had come to help her. Britta's father would not come.

*He doesn't matter*, Miri thought. *Britta is one of us now. We're her ladies.*

Miri quarry-spoke the memory of becoming ladies of the princess, a moment all the girls shared. They turned to Miri, understanding, coming in closer. They were Britta's ladies. They would stand beside her.

All came but Liana, who stayed crouched behind a

sofa. Though they shared the memory, Liana's feelings about it must have been quite different. She felt no attachment to Britta, only bitterness that she had not been chosen herself.

*Just like Sisela*, Miri realized.

The man was still shouting. Miri quarry-spoke the memory of that frightening night in winter when bandits had come to the academy. Of standing by the window, looking out toward the faraway village, and hoping that their families would know they were in trouble and come to help. With the memory she hoped to communicate *When there is danger, the people of Mount Eskel hear.*

And then she spoke aloud. "We of Mount Eskel—" Her mouth was as dry as a fallen leaf. She swallowed nothing and tried again. "We Eskelites have something to say."

The ranting went on, so she repeated herself, louder this time. The man quieted.

"We girls want a chance to speak before justice is decided. We who were chosen by divination to attend the sacred academy. We who took Britta in, not knowing who she was. We want to speak."

The bearded man nodded, and the man beside him said, "Speak, little sister."

"Don't shoot anyone yet. Please give us a chance to make our case first."

"Speak the crimes of the false princess," said the bearded man. "We'll give her a trial here and now."

Miri took a shuddering breath. If she said the wrong thing, Britta would be shot. And perhaps the royal family as well, or even she herself. If she told them that Britta was kind and patient and loving, would that be enough?

The queen was beside her. She touched Miri's arm and whispered, "I think they are afraid. They hate, but they fear too."

Miri nodded. A rule of Rhetoric advised: *Speak in a language the listener understands.* These men were too angry just then to hear pleas for compassion, but fear they would understand. Despite their bravado, they must have hoped to escape with their lives. So she would tell them the story.

"There is a tale we repeat each year during our spring holiday," said Miri. "One lifetime ago bandits came to Mount Eskel."

Katar smiled, her dimples making a rare appearance. She took a turn with the telling, as was the custom on Mount Eskel. "They thought to sack such a small village easily enough. They thought they could steal, burn, and be gone before the sun saw their deeds. But they were ignorant, tiny men. They did not know Mount Eskel's secrets."

"The mountain knows the feel of an outsider's boot, and the mountain will not support its weight," said Esa. She moved ahead to the middle of the story, just as she had two years before when they'd told this story to the bandits who'd come to their academy. Only this time her voice did not quaver.

"The bandits came nearer and nearer, and the mountain groaned in the night," said Bena in her bright, confident voice. "It groaned, and the villagers heard and awoke. They were waiting—with mallets and chisels and levers, they waited."

Miri noticed Frid lift her head as if to speak, then stop herself. Given her fist's recent encounter with a rebel's face, Miri thought her wise to keep silent.

Gerti's voice was soft, but her words flowed like the music of her lute. "That night, the quarriers stood taller than trees, taller than mountains, and they struck like lightning. When the first bandits fell, the rest ran. They ran like hares from a hawk."

"Mount Eskel feels the boots of outsiders," Miri said, speaking the final words of the story. The other girls joined in unison. "Mount Eskel won't bear their weight."

There was not a sound in the chamber. Every face watched the girls.

"We told this story to the bandits who claimed the

princess academy as their plunder," said Miri. "They were afraid, but not enough to let us go."

"In the end," said Katar, "they learned what it costs to ignore villagers who live on that ancient mountain."

Gerti sang a line from a song—"Mount Eskel, My Lady." The tune made Miri's throat tighten with emotion, and for a moment she could not speak. Esa spoke for her.

"My ma says a rock lasts forever, but people don't, and that's what makes them more precious."

*That's true*, Miri thought, and wondered why she had never come across the idea in Master Filippus's books.

She reclaimed her voice and continued. "Mount Eskel is older than any kingdom. This palace is built of linder cut from the slopes of our home. Mount Eskel remembers its own. And we of Mount Eskel claim Britta as one of our own."

Silence followed. The bearded rebel tilted his head, as if that was not the ending he'd been expecting.

Miri repeated herself. "We claim Britta as our own. She no longer belongs to Lonway or her dishonorable father. A person belongs to those she loves and those who love her back. She belongs to *us*. And she did not steal from us the right to be princess." Miri made eye contact with the other Eskelites around her to include them in her words, and then turned back to again face the man with the pistol. "We gave it to her."

Britta's body was trembling as if every part of her was profoundly aware of that pistol to her head. But her eyes met Miri's and her lips managed a small, grateful smile.

The bearded man was shaking his head. He seemed confused that Miri did not agree with him.

"Death to the robber princess," he said, his voice less sure now yet edged with anger.

He adjusted his hold on the pistol, his finger pressing lightly on the trigger. White-hot panic charged through Miri.

"You will not harm her!" she shouted.

"My son is sick, my children hungry," said the man. "And she's to blame, the lying wench!"

Miri wrestled calmness into her voice. "I'm sorry, but you *cannot* harm Britta. Her mountain will not stand for it."

She did not know quite what she meant, only that it felt true.

"I will do as I like," said the man, his voice hard as a bullet.

Miri felt that word rush through her again—*no*.

She stamped her foot in the rhythm of a quarry work song, speaking *no, no* in time. The other girls and Peder took up the quarry-spoken chant, their voices weaving together, strong as an iron lever.

*No.* Miri let that word pound out of her, through the stone, toward the bearded man with the gun. There was a sound like a faraway shriek, and the floor started to crack. Some of those in the room startled or gasped, but the Eskelites kept working the quarry-speech into the stone.

*No.* She spoke not through but *to* the very stone. She sang memories of high windy peaks, of quakes that rose up from deep in the earth, of the hammering of mallets and the sweaty blows of the quarry workers. The stone remembered. And the stone rumbled in reply.

*No!* The floor stones split as if the word were a mallet. The room quaked.

The bearded man's hand tightened on the pistol, and Miri knew just before it happened that he would pull the trigger. *No!* came her quarry-shout, and as the pistol fired, the stone beneath the man's feet cracked so violently he fell one way and Britta the other, the bullet striking the wall above her head.

*No!* The room gave one more shake. The rebels turned about, gripping their muskets, but there was no attacker to fire upon.

Britta curled up on the ground, her arms over her face just a heap of ragged, dirtied lace. The bearded man unsteadily recovered his feet. He turned to Miri, a second gun from his belt aimed at her.

"What are you doing?" he asked.

Miri turned up her empty hands. She hoped he did not notice how hard they shook. "Only talking. Just words."

"You made the room quake," he said.

"You give me too much credit. I'm telling you, this room was cut out of Mount Eskel. I've seen entire mountainsides tumble down. If you hurt one of Mount Eskel, this room will tear apart and bury you in it. You should leave."

The rebels looked at each other.

"She said you should leave!" Frid shouted.

The bearded man took a step back, and the broken floor stones beneath him shifted. He gasped and ran for the door.

The royal party moved away as the rebels threw aside the bars, seized the door, and fled into the corridor.

Steffan was the first to Britta. He crouched beside her, putting his arms around her shoulders.

"Are you hurt?" he asked.

Britta shook her head but touched the red mark on Steffan's neck where a musket had pressed him down.

"Shut the door," Miri said.

Liana ran out just before the king helped Peder close the massive door and lower the bars back in place.

There were some light laughs, the others in the mood

to celebrate. Miri peered into the closet to make certain no one else lingered. Her neck muscles felt as fraught as her stomach. Someone had orchestrated all of it—calling the royal guard away, leaving the palace unguarded, leading the attackers to the very chamber where the king would await rescue.

The assassin. He was out there somewhere. Perhaps in the palace. The day was not yet over, and Britta was still alive.

# Chapter Nineteen

*She's as fetching as brown hair done up with ribbons blue*
*The mountain, my lady*
*She's as sweet as pink flowers made bright with morning*
*    dew*
*Mount Eskel, my lady*

Miri felt tense as an icicle, easy to shatter. She paced till she found herself standing beside Peder. He put his arm around her, and she forced herself to relax against him. His nearness eased her some, warmed the ice of her core. She had a sudden desire to rub her head against his neck, like an affectionate nanny goat. Miri snorted a laugh. Peder raised his eyebrows, a question.

"Goat humor," she whispered back.

He shook his head. "Rocks tearing apart around you, and you're thinking up nanny jokes."

A fissure ran through the floor stones from the point where she and the other Eskelites had stood all the way to the closet. The walls and ceiling were intact, but the floor cracks were impressive.

"The guard *will* rally," the king was saying. "My supporters will come forward."

"What just occurred in here?" asked the queen.

"Mount Eskel got really mad," said Frid, and the girls laughed.

"Did you know that would happen?" Peder asked.

"Not exactly," said Miri. "But I had a . . . a feeling."

Esa nodded in agreement. Miri met her eyes and wondered if Esa too had felt a flicker of invitation, a whisper of strength. The rock was not living—it had no mind, no thought. But it had responded to their quarry-speech like a goat to the call of its herder. She imagined that the power of generations of quarry-worker blows had lain dormant inside the rock and had moved at the sound of their quarry-shouts. The linder was a kind of history, Miri realized. Memories soaked up in the stone, ready to erupt.

The king kicked at a loose shard and shook his head. "Perhaps you could refrain from encouraging the rocks to split in the future? Linder is expensive to replace."

Peder mumbled under his breath, "If you think it's hard to replace a few floor stones, you should try cutting them out of a mountain."

Steffan was bruised but not seriously hurt. Britta sat beside him, and they talked quietly, their foreheads pressed together. The other academy girls and servants took to the sofas and floor. Miri could only pace.

Peder was pacing his own path alongside the fissure.

"You think the assassin is still out there?" Miri whispered to Peder.

He glanced at the door and nodded.

Miri shivered. Waiting was a bitter game. She needed something to do. The king and queen sat on chairs, as rigid as ship masts. Miri crouched beside them.

"Your Majesty," she said to the queen, "you knew how the rebels were feeling. Your advice helped me know what to say."

The queen shook her head. "I was just guessing."

"It may have seemed so," said Miri, "but I think it was more than a guess."

"Impertinence," said Gummonth. "Stand back, girl."

"Please, Your Highness, just talk with me a moment. I have reason to believe that the royal family is capable of sensing more than others can."

Steffan and Britta had come closer.

"Like quarry-speech?" Britta asked.

"Sort of. Quarry-speech runs through linder. I think that only those exposed to raw linder over time can do it."

"What are you talking about, *quarry-speech?*" said the king.

"It's just . . . just something Eskelites can do, something the linder makes possible," said Miri. "But I think what you can do is a little different. Have you read your father's diary in the library? He referred to a secret—he called it 'linder wisdom.' I believe it's the root of the tradition that only the royal family may live in the king's wing, the only building in the world built entirely from linder. Over the years, being so surrounded by linder changes you somehow. And the kings of the past must have wanted to keep that advantage to their own families. Does any of this sound familiar?"

"Your Highness—" Gummonth began.

The king held up a hand to silence him and looked at Miri, an invitation to continue.

"I'm going to quarry-speak now," Miri said, and she silently sang of the time the academy girls stood up to their strict tutor and fled the academy.

On hearing her quarry-speech, many of the Eskelites stood up.

"What is it, Miri?" Esa asked from across the room.

"Nothing, just ignore me, sorry," said Miri. She turned back to the king. "If you had quarry-speaking ability, what I just said would have nudged a similar memory in you, perhaps inspiring you to stand up. But you can't quarry-speak. On the mountain we're inhaling linder dust and drinking from a stream white with it. Linder flows in our blood and coats our bones, while you're encircled by it."

The linder was *outside* for the royals, not *inside*. It must simply amplify the thoughts of those around them. . . . No, not thoughts exactly. Miri realized their linder wisdom would be less complicated than communicating in memories—less thought, more emotion.

Instead she tried to *feel* something the king might understand. She chose the time the princess academy tutor had punished Miri's insubordination by locking her in a dark closet—the agony of being trapped, her terror of the rat in the dark, the fear and uncertainty. She quarry-spoke it to help herself experience the event all over again, making her emotions as loud inside her as a musket shot.

"How do you feel?" Miri asked, shivering at the memory. "Could you sense how I was feeling?"

"No . . . ," said the king.

His hesitation made her wonder. He too had spent time in a dark closet, locked in alone, afraid.

"I was recalling a time I was abandoned in a closet," she said. "I wondered if . . . if the way I felt reminded you of your own experience. With your brother."

The king's chin trembled under his beard. "Just because we are trapped in this room does not mean you may speak this way to your sovereign."

"But I may never get another chance. Sire, you

understand the rebels better than they could know—and not only because of your linder wisdom. Was it fair that just because he was born first, your brother could do whatever he liked? That because of his selfishness and cruelty, you and your mother were sent away?"

The king's face reddened.

"I don't understand what is happening," said the queen.

"Some of your ancestors wrote of sensing what others felt," said Miri. "Linder amplifies thought . . . and emotion too, I think. Because of the years you spend surrounded by linder, you three absorb that. Past kings were taught by their parents about this ability and how to use it. I believe King Bjorn's parents and brother died before they could teach him of it."

Gummonth made a sound of exasperation in his throat. "This is ridiculous—"

"Just a moment, Gummonth," Steffan interrupted. "What Miri suggests . . . It's true that when I'm home in this palace, I feel cramped by all the people. . . ."

"And their emotions?" said Miri.

"Perhaps that's it. Whenever I'm here, I must . . ." He frowned.

"You close off," said Britta. "You become a stone column."

"So I don't have to feel so much." Steffan put a hand

on Britta's shoulder, and his expression seemed a kind of apology.

"Those ridiculous plays!" The king slammed his fist on a table. "That's why I can't stand them. I'm constantly flabbergasted by how some can watch and sigh and cry as if they almost believed it real, while I feel nauseated by the obvious disparity between the actor and the false emotions he expresses. Turn the theater into storage for all I care."

"But the plays are so beautiful!" said Miri.

"Don't you feel the same way, Miri?" asked Steffan.

"No. Quarry-speech is different. We can speak—or more like sing or think—memories through the linder to others. You are simply bombarded by the feelings of those around you. But maybe . . . if you know what linder does to you, you could pay more attention to it and hone your ability to listen. Or even block it. I imagine such a skill was helpful to past kings when weeding out liars and traitors."

The king's eyebrows raised.

"You could try right now," said Miri. "What do you feel from the people in this room?"

The queen rubbed her arms. "I don't know, but I do not like this room. It's not safe."

"I don't think the stones will break—" Miri started.

The queen shook her head. "It's as if . . . someone feels too much like that man who held a pistol to Britta's head. It hurts my stomach."

Steffan straightened and looked around.

"Who?" asked Miri.

"Over there." The queen gestured vaguely.

Miri was surprised—and just a little disappointed—that she had not indicated Gummonth. The only other people in the room were the royal family, a few servants, Britta, Peder, and the academy girls—except Liana, who, strangely, had fled the safety of the room.

Miri leaned in closer to the queen and king. "Would any of these servants here have known you would come to this room when threatened?"

"Certainly," said the queen.

"These are our personal servants, Miri," said Steffan. "They wouldn't betray us."

Miri recalled reading in the history books that the royal family had a knack for selecting the most trustworthy servants and guards. Perhaps that had to do with the linder wisdom. She glanced at Gummonth, whose lips were stuck in a permanent snarl. If the king trusted him, he must be loyal, but that did not make him any more pleasant.

"Someone riled up that mob at the gate to keep you

in the palace," said Miri. "Someone told those rebels to hide in this room. And now that they're gone, someone is still wishing you dead. Who?"

The royal family fell silent, as if straining for a sound just beyond hearing.

The queen stood, looking toward a cluttered corner full of barrels and crates. After a moment, the king's eyes rested there as well. Steffan leaned forward.

"Is . . . is someone over there?" he asked.

Miri found herself squinting at the corner, as though narrowing her eyes would allow her to see through wood. It was too late by the time she realized that if the assassin was hidden there, he might be able to see them. He would know he was discovered. And he would act before being taken by surprise.

"Wait—" Miri started to whisper. *Wait, don't look, pretend you don't know—*

She was too slow. A lid was flung off a tall crate. A man rose up. He was dark haired with a stiff, pointy beard, and wore a long coat. As he stepped out of the crate, his coat swept back, and Miri could see he had at least a dozen pistols strapped to his chest and stuck in his belt.

Even as he climbed from the barrel, he lifted one pistol and aimed.

*Britta.*

Action without thought gave Miri speed, and she flung herself toward Britta, her arms out to push her away. But Peder was fast as well.

"Miri!" he said.

The crack of gunfire shattered the moment. Miri pushed Britta, and they slammed into the wall.

Peder was still standing. His expression showed utter shock. His hand was pressed to his middle, and through his fingers blood trickled. He sat down hard on the floor.

"Peder!"

On her first day in Asland, Miri had seen the king's guards throw themselves in the path of danger, one taking a lead ball for his sovereign. Miri had marveled. What did they feel for the king that they would die for him?

Peder had put himself between Miri and the bullet.

A loud clatter tore her attention away. The assassin had tossed the spent pistol onto the stone floor. But he had plenty of others. He raised a second, aiming again at Britta.

Steffan was on his feet, running at the assassin. So was Frid, and perhaps others too. But no one was faster than a pistol ball. They would not stop him before he pulled the trigger. Nothing would stop him. He would shoot them all—Steffan, Frid, Esa, and Miri too, just as he had shot Peder. He would kill as many as he needed till he got to Britta.

Miri screamed. "No!"

Even as she screamed with her real voice, she screamed in quarry-speech. *No!* She did not quarry-speak a single memory but a lifetime of them, and not just her own. She filled that word with every story she'd heard of her father, of her grandparents, stories from Peder's ma, Doter, and especially stories of *her* ma—the week she held baby Miri in her arms, the hazy memories Marda still kept, anecdotes the villagers told her alongside details Miri had just imagined. Stories true and made-up, songs and wishes and everything she knew of her family and Mount Eskel, the history of her home that no one had yet written down—all of it went into that one word.

At the same time, Miri became aware of the entire palace, as if it were her own body. She felt the weight of its stone, history running through the pink veins and silver, the green and the blue, the white stone embracing it all. The stone vibrated with her memories, her song, her scream. Her palace, her mountain, her body. She lifted her hands.

Her quarry-speech moved through the rock, and where it went, rock tore apart. A second fissure erupted from where she stood, traveling with the speed of one spoken word across the room, up the wall, tearing through the ceiling.

The assassin looked up.

The ceiling fell.

A puff of dust and debris filled the room. Miri rushed through it to Peder, placing her hand on his, getting wet with blood. His breathing was labored, his eyes wide open.

When she glanced back where the assassin had stood, all she saw was a pile of broken linder. A lifetime near a quarry made her certain that no one could survive the weight of that much stone.

Katar and Frid flung aside the door's bars and fled the room, quarry-speaking as they ran that they would get help. The king locked the door behind them. Miri thought it wise. As much as she wanted to get Peder out of that room, there could be other rebels in the palace, others with muskets, waiting their turn. Though if someone wanted to get in, Miri thought, they could simply go upstairs and lower themselves through the carriage-size gap in the ceiling.

*I made that*, Miri thought vaguely. But that massive hole felt a million times less important than the tiny one in Peder's middle.

Esa went to her brother, gently pushing Miri aside. Miri sat on the floor. Her defiance was spent, her body tired of fighting, and she cried. But Esa was calm as she inspected Peder.

"The ball went clean through," Esa said. "That's good, Peder."

"Ow! It doesn't *feel* good," he said.

Esa pressed a cloth to his wound, instructing others to wrap him and keep him warm.

"Don't everybody fuss," he whispered. "I'm all right."

"You will be," said Esa.

"It doesn't even hurt that much." He tried to sit up.

"Stop showing off for Miri," said his sister. "You will let us take care of you, Peder Doterson, or I'll tell Ma all about it, so lie still."

He lay still.

They waited in the ruins of the room for the royal guard to rescue them. Everyone gathered in a circle around Peder, away from the fissures and the hole where white dust shifted like snowflakes. They sat on the smooth places between the cracked and jutting stone. They whispered questions that no one answered.

"Are we safe yet?"

"Is Peder all right?"

"What just happened?"

Miri was silent. She held Peder's hand.

There was an old story of a princess who wept tears of pure love over her fallen prince, healing his injuries and letting him live again. It was just a story. Miri knew it was not true. But just then, she felt capable of a love so huge it would break the entire palace. Maybe outside of stories, holding Peder's hand and loving him fit to crack her heart like a linder stone could not heal him. But then again, it could not hurt to try.

She scooted nearer. She leaned her head against his. She squeezed his hand.

Just in case feeling was not enough, just in case such a magic needed powerful words spoken, she whispered, "I love you." And then she quarry-spoke memory after memory—the time he had carved a linder hawk for her; the night she was captured by the bandits and he heard her far-off quarry-speech; when they laughed and danced at the ball; that perfect afternoon in Asland when they kissed in the straw-dusty shed. And those memories also said *I love you, I love you.*

She did not know what personal memories her own nudged in Esa, Gerti, and Bena, but Esa smiled, Gerti sighed, and Bena rested her chin on her knees. The queen sat beside the king and took his hand. He leaned against her and kissed the top of her head. Miri guessed they must feel what she was feeling, and perhaps they remembered loving each other too.

Britta sat behind Miri and touched her hair, as a friend would. Until that moment, Miri had not considered that she herself might need a little bit of healing.

By her boot lay a shard of linder. It had recognized her voice; it had responded to the quarry-shout. Hundreds of years it lay as a floor stone in a palace, far from the mountain, yet it was *still* of Mount Eskel. How could just a few months in the city transform *her* entirely?

She clutched the shard in her fist. They had been in need, and the stone had remembered, the mountain had heard. Britta might have been felled beside Peder, and perhaps Esa and Frid, Steffan and Miri too. It was hard to feel anything but anxiety for Peder, but once she opened herself to a tiny bit of gratitude, it swelled till her chest ached with it. She started to sing the song Gerti had begun, an anthem to Mount Eskel, a love song. Esa and Gerti picked it up. Britta and Steffan joined in the second time around. They sang it for the stone, for their mountain and home, and for Peder. The stone chamber held all the voices, bouncing them back again till it seemed hundreds of unseen singers joined in. The room sang.

# Chapter Twenty

*Sweet girls are sighing*
*Young boys are pining*
*Eskel is skying*

*Hammer is beating*
*Daylight is fleeting*
*Eskel sends greeting*

It did not take the royal guardsmen long to realize they
had been tricked away from their posts. A traitorous
chief guard had sent groups to points all over the city,
supposedly to quell protests that never occurred. Within
the hour they'd returned, driven all intruders from the
palace, and freed the party from the refuge room.
The plan to assassinate Britta and spark the revolution
had failed. Miri imagined the mood was gray in political
Salons across the city. She wondered how many of those
passionate scholars and talkers, facing Britta, could
have pulled the trigger themselves.

Miri spent the night beside Peder's bed in the palace

infirmary. The physician stitched up his wound and said it looked clean, but as morning drew near Peder's skin fevered.

"Infection," said the physician. "This kind will heal on its own or it won't."

He sent everyone away except Esa, who, as Peder's sister and a physician's assistant, had a right to stay.

Miri was too tired to sleep. She walked outside, her mind so full of prayers that for a moment she fancied they had turned into white birds that flapped on the breeze. Leaflets, not birds, covered posts and windows, shuffled loose on the ground, and lifted on the wind. Miri caught them like butterflies and read parts. Nearly all retold Britta's actions in the courtyard.

### How a Pure Heart Saved Danland

The princess lifted her fair hand, her tear-filled eyes beseeching the heavens on behalf of the young inno-cent. Although she was clad in the finest garments of the land, her feet knew her heart and would not abide slippers, for Princess Britta's heart was ever with the shoeless.

### The Princess and the Mob

Those of us in the crowd did not even notice the boy until she had pulled him away from the carriage. After she returned him to his mother, she stood before us. No guards. No words. She had saved him. But she did not know if we would save her.

**What I Saw**

Someone put a musket in my hand. The girl came running at us. I was angry. I do not have enough coin to buy bread. I thought about shooting her. She saved that boy. I did not want to shoot her anymore.

Most mentioned that the "Mountain Girl" herself had voiced support of the shoeless princess. One was even titled "The Mountain Girl Laments No More."

A warmth pulsed through Miri, and she forgot her exhaustion. She found a cobbler she'd heard about, whose secret press had printed many a Salon's leaflet. Miri asked him if he'd print hers as well.

"For coin I will," he said, his browned skin as smooth as the leather he was working over a knob. "Where is your leaflet?"

Miri bit her lip. "Um, can I borrow quill and paper?"

A rule of Rhetoric suggested offering stories, not lectures. Miri sat on his floor and wrote.

### The Robber Princess

Theirs was a love forbidden by tradition. A childhood friendship deepened until neither could bear to live without the other. Though heir to castle and crown, Steffan was helpless to choose his true love as his bride. He could not seek her, so she must seek him, all the way to the princess academy.

Britta climbed the highest mountain in the land. She threw off her silks and slippers and donned rough woolens. She spurned the name of her cruel and noble father, labored in a quarry, became a mountain girl. She risked everything. And if Steffan rejected her, she determined she would stay on Mount Eskel forever. She was Lady Britta no more.

Britta awaited Steffan's arrival with a fearful heart. After a year and a half's separation, perhaps his love had dimmed. Would he scorn her? Would he have her thrown in prison?

Miri watched the cobbler place the tiny metal letters in the press with a speed and deftness that reminded her of a blackbird building a nest. He brushed them with ink, lowered the press, and her few hundred words stained the white paper.

Britta does not care about being a princess. She loves Steffan, not the prince heir, and is perhaps the only one in the world who sees him truly.

This is how their story begins. The people will decide how it ends. I, Miri of Mount Eskel, do not like tragedies. I am hoping for a wedding.

The cobbler gave her a wedge of wax to rub on the corners of the papers so she could stick them to posts. The last of her allowance purchased only a slim stack, and a few dozen windows and lampposts later, she had just one left.

She'd arrived at the Green, the ruins of the bridal edifice strewn across the grass. The fever of energy still burned in her. She discovered a hammer in the wreckage and tried nailing two pieces of wood together. They stuck at an odd angle, not quite square. She scavenged some more wood about the same size.

By the time the sun was high enough to heat the part in her hair, Miri had a rough square frame as high as her knee, several splinters, and one bruised thumb.

*If I work all day*, she thought, *I won't be able to remake the stairs let alone the platform and the rest. It's useless.*

She picked up another piece of wood.

She was nearly finished with a second square frame when she realized she was not alone.

There was a man, tall and lean, wearing a featherless cap. He stood with hands in pockets, the blue band around his arm clearly visible.

"You're one of the Mount Eskel girls, aren't you?" he asked. "I saw you in the palace courtyard."

She nodded. Her eyes flicked to his belt to make sure he was not carrying a pistol.

"What are you trying to do?" he asked.

"Rebuild the edifice."

His brows twitched in surprise. "And what have you got so far?"

She held up her two pieces.

"That much, huh?"

His smile made her want to smile.

"They're going to be a step," she said. "See how cleverly I nailed the wood together to almost form a square?"

"I do indeed."

"A square is a lot harder than it looks. Why, a square is perhaps the most difficult shape in all the world."

He laughed and put on worn leather gloves. "Lady Mount Eskel, what I need is a sorter. You think you could arrange wood in piles by size?"

Miri's grin felt good against her cheeks. "I think I have the potential to be the most amazing sorter you've ever seen."

She worked till she was sweating, sorting wood, piling loose nails. The lonely sound of the man's single hammer multiplied, and she knew others had joined them. Hammer and nail, saw and ax, the *snap* of fabric and the *creak* of joints—the noise of work was loud and merry as a festival. She did not rest. All that mattered was the speed of her own two hands. If she kept working, perhaps she could help Peder, and Britta and Steffan, Mount Eskel, and all of Danland too. If she just worked hard enough.

Soon she was singing as she worked, a Mount Eskel habit. Her third time through a work song, other voices joined in, picking up the words.

She felt dazed by her sleepless night and too focused to pay attention to anything beyond her own hands, so by the time she stood up, stretched, and looked, the Green had collected a mob.

She saw feathered and flat caps, blue-bannered and bare arms, the solid black of servant attire beside the colorful skirts of merchants' daughters and the silk trousers of noble sons. All were rebuilding the edifice. It was not the same edifice as before; it was lower and longer, cobbled together and a little rough. But it stood. She stuck the last copy of "The Robber Princess" to its front.

The lean man called to her from the platform and pointed up. He'd nailed her misshapen squares to the tallest pole like a banner, its colors the blue sky beyond.

"It's been two days, and the rebuilt edifice is still on the Green," Miri told Peder, though she was not certain he was awake. He slept most of the time, moaning when Esa changed his bandages or swabbed his face. "The first day, soldiers guarded it through the night, but the king called them away. I think he's testing Asland, letting them decide if Steffan and Britta should wed. If they tear it back down . . ."

Esa put a hand on Miri's shoulder, letting her know the visit was over. Peder's little sister looked as tired as Miri felt, darkness under her eyes.

Miri went in search of Britta, hoping at last to talk to her alone, but before she reached Britta, Inga found her. Miri was commanded to see the king.

Miri joined him in the throne room, where he sat grandly on his gilded wooden chair in a cavernous linder hall. She remembered the proper curtsy for such an occasion and performed it with only a small trip. Gummonth, beside the king as usual, did not hide his smirk.

"You were brave," said the king.

She nodded. She did not feel particularly brave, but she did not want to argue with a king—at least, not about that.

"You were also too familiar."

She nodded again.

"You may go," he said.

She blinked in surprise and turned away.

"You're welcome," she said under her breath.

"What was that?"

She came back. "I said 'you're welcome,' because I think you brought me here to say a thank-you of sorts, and it's not your fault if no one ever taught you those words. But that's no reason for me not to be polite and say 'you're welcome' as I ought to."

His eyes widened, but they wrinkled slightly too, as if he was amused. Now she did indeed feel brave, if a bit embarrassed. But she was too worried and tired to care about angering a king.

"Sire, I'm going to be overfamiliar for a few moments more. You should know that every time you take tributes of food, food prices go up, and people starve."

The king made a noise of surprise and indignation. "Starve? Don't be ridiculous."

"Go out into your kingdom and see for yourself. There are poor everywhere, except Mount Eskel this year, because for the first time we have enough to eat.

But that will change when you demand Gummonth's high tribute of us too. A lot is changing in Danland, and none for the better."

He straightened, his chin flexed, whiskers bristling. "My officials assure me I may take as I please. I am king."

"Exactly! You're a *king*, not a bandit. Don't let them bully you into being one."

"Enough insolence!" said Gummonth. He started forward as if to physically remove Miri from the room.

"Wait," said the king. He considered them both, then said to Gummonth, "Step outside, sir, if you please."

Miri resisted sticking out her tongue at Gummonth, but only barely. Gummonth's face turned a fierce red, but he bowed and left.

The king looked at Miri.

She looked at him.

He smiled. She could not remember seeing him smile before.

Too curious to be quiet any longer, she asked, "Is it easier to sense what I'm feeling when we're alone?"

He nodded. "I am beginning to realize just how strongly my chief official *feels* things, and how easy it is to feel as he does whenever he is near."

"Which is often," she said.

He nodded again. And smiled again. She smiled back. And then the king did something that surprised

Miri more than a musket shot—he laughed. A dozen lines wrinkled out from the corners of his eyes, and Miri thought he looked the better for it.

"You have a good sense about you, don't you?" he said. "I like it."

"I like you too," she said, and was happy to believe it.

They talked longer, about linder and quarry-speech, and even the pleasures of a roast duck. But when Miri suggested he listen to the revolution's concerns and consider making changes, his smile dimmed and his look returned to stern.

"My duty," he said, "my entire reason for existence, is to protect the power of the crown. I will never budge on that."

But he did not seem angry, and when Gummonth came back, the king declared Miri would find his next meeting interesting and bid her accompany him. Gummonth impressed Miri with his ability to look like the nastiest, orneriest billy goat she could imagine.

"With all that has occurred, sire," said Gummonth as they made their way to a receiving room, "I must insist that you further enlarge your royal guard."

Miri pressed her fingernails into her palms to keep from shouting her opinion on the matter. Just outside the door, the king halted.

"No, not this time, Gummonth. I know you mean to protect me, but not at the expense of those who pay for it. Train them properly and those we have will suffice."

Miri smiled. She stood by the door, letting the king and Gummonth go in first.

Gummonth turned back to whisper, "No one ever wants to pay the tribute, but they always do."

Miri's mood sank. But as she walked into the room, she was comforted by Steffan's smile. He motioned for her to sit beside him at the round table of officials, where the Justice Official presented a suspects list.

A chief guard had already confessed to accepting a bribe from the assassin to misdirect the other guards and leave the royal family unprotected.

"This chief guard ignored the mandate to stay no more than eight hours each day in the king's wing," said Steffan. "For years, he secretly slept in the linder-walled guardroom instead of the barracks."

Steffan looked at Miri, and she nodded slightly to show that she understood—this guard must have developed linder wisdom, and so was able to sift the disloyal from the rest to choose his coconspirators.

Before his execution, the chief guard had written the names of all who had played a part in the scheme.

Miri peered at Steffan's copy of the list. She was not

surprised to see Sisela's name, but the rest of her Salon, including Timon, had escaped notice.

*So did Liana*, Miri thought, just now realizing what must be true: Liana had been part of the conspiracy. She knew about the danger in the refuge room and so fled it when she had a chance. The thought that someone from Mount Eskel would have tried to get Britta killed made Miri so angry she could have chewed rocks to dust.

"The law is clear," said Gummonth. "Treason is a capital offense."

"Your Highness?" Miri said.

Gummonth groaned, and other officials started whispering to one another, as if to question Miri's presence at all. But the king gestured at her, allowing her to speak.

"I recently read about an old Danlandian custom. Past kings often heard grievances in their linder halls and pronounced judgment themselves."

Knowing now the royal secret about linder, Miri wondered if the tradition was a chance for the king to sense the truth in a person before pronouncing judgment. Even though the people on the list had conspired to kill her friend, Miri felt sick looking over the long list and imagining them all called to the Green. So many names, so many lives.

The king announced he would meet the first few

prisoners personally the next day. Gummonth would not join him.

Miri had not truly believed her suggestion would change anything. However, the very next morning the royal news journal listed the rebels' names but declared no more would face execution.

A kingdom at war with itself will not long stand. Let us wash the blood from our hands and start anew.

Miri laughed out loud with relief. She wondered what Sisela would make of that!

But mistake not this pardon for unlimited lenience. Any new crimes of treason will be punished swiftly and justly. The so-called revolution ends now, or the executioner's ax will fall.

Though many lives would be spared, Miri was not completely at rest. She discovered from Bena where Liana was now staying, and she went alone to the opulent inn.

"You heard that I'm getting married?" Liana said, inviting Miri to sit on the white velvet sofa in her suite.

She looked more beautiful than ever in a pink silk dress, her hair pinned up as the Aslandian women did. "My betrothed is paying for my private accommodations here. He keeps a country home in Elsby *and* a town home in Asland, and employs twenty-eight servants, not including his tenant farmers, of course. He owns a gem mine and paid fifteen gold for my trousseau, which includes two velvet travel dresses, three garden party dresses, five—"

"I know you betrayed Britta," Miri said.

Liana's mouth was still open from speaking. She snapped it shut. Then, batting her eyes, she said, "Pardon me?"

"Yes, the king *pardoned* all of you, didn't he?" said Miri, holding up the news journal. "That faithless guard saw the bitterness you harbored against Britta and Steffan and knew you'd be willing to help. Was your part to keep the Mount Eskel girls away from Britta so she would be alone and vulnerable? You might as well have tied up a goat and left her on a hill for the wolves. I suppose you thought *you* should have been chosen as the princess. I have made a lot of mistakes—we all do—but what you did was way beyond *wrong*."

"Really, Miri—" Liana started, but Miri was not done. She'd seen Britta almost killed, and Peder was so fevered her own skin ached just to think of it. She was in no mood to worry about the rules of Rhetoric.

"The king pardoned all of you," said Miri, "and so I'll try to as well. But if you do or say anything against Britta again—make no mistake—I will tell your parents."

Liana stared, and Miri expected her to deny everything. But then she laughed. "You're going to *tattle* on me?"

"For all you're so eager to leave Mount Eskel, I know you care about them. Just imagine the look on your parents' faces if I told them you tried to get our Britta murdered."

Liana was not laughing anymore.

"Don't worry, I won't tattle if you're good," Miri said, rising to go. "But I do think Britta and Steffan should know what you did. I doubt you will be welcome in their court." *If they marry*, Miri thought. "I understand nobles who aren't courtiers are often scorned by other nobles in Asland. I hope you enjoy Elsby, because that's where you'll be spending the rest of your life."

She was stepping out the door when Liana spoke again.

"Britta knew what the lowlands were like," Liana said. "She *knew* about the food and servants and furs and feather beds, the concerts and the carriages and the way the noble ladies dress. You know why she never told us how wonderful it is? Because she didn't want any of us to get between her and the fancy linder palace."

"You're wrong. Her lowlander life was not wonderful, no matter what she ate or wore."

"Don't imagine for a moment she would have given up this life to freeze half the year and work in a quarry."

"Steffan chose her, Liana. It's over."

"She had no right!" Liana's beautiful face turned a beautiful shade of purple. "She's a liar! If she hadn't been there—"

"Then Steffan would have chosen me!" Miri shouted back. She'd never allowed herself to think it, let alone say it, but she knew it was true. "So it's *my* choice to make, and I say Britta is more of Mount Eskel than you are, and I give her to Steffan. Liana, you *never* would have been the princess."

Liana leaned back as if she'd been struck. She blinked rapidly and then stammered, "It-it-it's not over, you know. The revolution has already started. The people won't just let it go."

Miri let Liana have the last word and quietly shut the door.

Gerti was waiting for Miri back at the palace entrance.

"They want you in the physician's chamber."

Miri ran. Her heart pounded harder than her feet against the floor. Fear pricked sweat on her forehead.

*Don't be dead, Peder, don't . . .*

She slammed open the door. Esa and the physician

were standing beside the bed. Esa turned to Miri. She was smiling.

"There you are," said Peder. "I'm sick of this bed and they won't let me out. Make me laugh?"

Miri stared at Peder. She looked at Esa, who nodded happily. Miri looked back at Peder. She stuck out her tongue.

He shrugged. "Not your best."

"Just give me a moment to realize you're not going to die, will you?" she said.

He nodded.

She stuck out her tongue *and* crossed her eyes.

Peder laughed.

# Chapter Twenty-one

*She wore white heirloom lace about her throat*
*And in her hair a bright golden feather*
*A pearl like a plum hung ripe from her neck*
*But her smile fetched ten gold together*

Peder's fever had broken. A kind of stupor that had lain over the palace broke as well. Steffan asked, the king agreed, and Steffan and Britta held a private ceremony in the palace chapel. The second ceremony of the royal marriage completed, there remained only the presentation on the Green.

Gummonth warned there were rebels too angry to be placated by the story of a small boy and a carriage wheel. But Britta and Steffan declared they would rather risk their necks than wait any longer.

In a move Miri thought surprisingly wise, the king revoked Britta's family's title. Miri read of it in the news journal as she rode in a carriage to the Green.

In punishment for conspiring to undermine the sacred academy, His Royal Majesty King Bjorn strikes down Pawel Storason of Lonway and his immediate family. They are reduced to commoner status, and all their lands are hereby the property of the crown. The former Lord Pawel is the father of Britta Paweldaughter of Lonway, betrothed of Prince Steffan. For her part, Britta will also remain a commoner for life. However, the king, the prince, and the priests of the creator god accept Britta as the lawful and dignified betrothed to the prince. She will hereafter be known as Britta of Mount Eskel. She will marry the prince as a commoner.

*They got a commoner princess after all,* Miri thought.

Britta and Steffan rode from the palace in an open vehicle for two, Steffan at the reins. Miri could not stop thinking about how the Green served as the place of executions as well as royal marriages, praying that today it would not be both. The copy of "The Robber Princess" was still stuck to the edifice, its corners curled from rain.

Britta was wearing a simpler dress than her lace marriage gown—peach silk gathered in folds around her hips and back, then falling to a hem short enough that her bare feet were visible as she climbed the edifice steps.

Traditionally a bride's family stood beside her, but Britta had asked the Mount Eskel girls to take that place of honor. Liana was not present, of course, and Bena was too afraid of muskets to climb the stairs, but Miri, Frid, Esa, Gerti, and Katar held bouquets of tulips and daffodils and smiled at the crowd. The priest wore a robe of brown with a white cap on his head, reminding Miri of Mount Eskel, forever topped with snow.

The wood of the edifice creaked beneath Miri's feet, but it did not collapse. The sun was setting. The empty frames of Miri's square banners faded from blue into rust and gold. The priest spoke the sealing words. Britta kissed her prince. And the crowd cheered.

Miri did not see Britta for a few days, while she and Steffan vacationed at the Summer Castle. She knew Britta must be happy and perhaps did not have the time to think of her friend. Perhaps Miri would never know if she was forgiven.

One morning on the way to the Queen's Castle, Miri passed Sisela's house. The windows were bare of drapes. She could see into the Salon, now empty. Even the chandelier had been removed from the ceiling.

The door opened, and the elderly servant limped out, startling when he saw Miri.

"Lady Sisela . . . er, she is . . ."

"I know she isn't a lady anymore," Miri said.

The man nodded, his shoulders relaxing. "I suppose there's no point in protecting her any longer. I warned her she could not pretend to be a wealthy noble forever, but she begged me to come on Salon nights."

"Where did she go?"

"I don't know, but it looks like she's sold the rest of the furniture, even dug out the linder tiles from the entry. Maybe she made enough to get her to Rilamark." He shook his head, his thin gray hair wagging. "I used to work in her family's home till my hip gave out. She was such a sweet little girl. . . ."

At the Queen's Castle, Miri inquired after Timon, who had not come to classes since the assassination attempts.

"I've had no word from him," Master Filippus said. "Perhaps there was a problem with his endowment."

"His what?"

"His *endowment*," said the master. "All who become scholars here write over a parcel of land or equivalent to the Castle. I imagine Timon endowed one of his father's ships."

"But I don't have any ships or land or anything," said Miri.

"Mmm? Perhaps someone gifted land in your name."

That evening, Miri hurried with her questions straight to Britta's old chamber and almost knocked before

SHANNON HALE

remembering she no longer lived in the south wing. Miri went to the king's wing, passing over the linder threshold with an exhale. Britta and Steffan had returned to Asland, but Miri did not have the password to go farther.

*Britta,* she called in quarry-speech, using a memory of the first time the two of them had talked at the academy.

From down the hall Miri could hear the soft slaps of bare feet running.

"Miri!" said Britta. "I thought you were here. I was sure . . . almost really sure . . ."

"You did hear me," said Miri. "You see? You are one of us."

"Some official tried to tell me I couldn't come find you, and I thought, why not? They always act the tyrant to me, and I've let them, but no more. If I want to see my friend, then I shall!"

Miri was going to ask if she was forgiven, but Britta hooked her arm and smiled, and all was as it had been.

They walked into the garden. The night air lay against Miri's skin, wet and cool as well water. She leaned into Britta.

"Are you happy?" Miri asked.

"I'm happy," said Britta, her smile pushing dimples into her cheeks. "So happy. Whatever this linder palace does to Steffan, it went away as soon as we did. And now that we're back . . . well, I think he's figuring it out."

"I'm trying to figure something out myself. What are bridal lands?"

Britta flinched. "What?"

"I heard a story about Queen Gertrud and how she donated her bridal lands for a school."

"Oh that. Well, when a noble girl gets betrothed, her father allots her some land that will always belong to her. It's a safeguard, so if her husband treats her cruelly or abandons her, she'll have land of her own and an income from its farms and rents."

"So women tend to hold on to their bridal lands," said Miri.

Britta nodded.

"And it would mean a lot if a bride were to give them away for some reason—as Queen Gertrud did."

Britta nodded again.

"Britta, how did you gain me admittance to the Queen's Castle?"

She squeezed her eyes shut.

"Britta, you didn't . . ."

"You see? This is why I didn't tell you. Because you would make a bigger deal of it than it is. They were my bridal lands and I could do with them whatever I wanted, and what I wanted was for you to go to the Queen's Castle and learn everything you wanted to know so you could be as happy as I am. But my father did not give me much, and so I could only get you into the Queen's Castle, and not Esa or Bena or anyone else, and I'm so sorry, Miri. . . ."

Miri laughed. "Yes, by all means, apologize for giving away your most valuable possession for my sake."

"Stop that. Besides, they'd have been lost to me anyway, since the king claimed my family's lands. You realize that I'm a commoner now. How the tables have turned, my lady!" She smiled slyly. "The income is only enough for one scholar at a time, but you could stay on for as many years as the farmland produces crops."

"I could?"

Britta nodded, her smile easy. "I saw a copy of 'The Robber Princess,' by the way. Thank you. I was thinking about how I'm going to end up as one of those names in lists of kings and queens. Isn't that strange? And I don't want the sum of my life to just be that I feared my father and lied, even if it was for love."

"Your history isn't written yet," said Miri.

Lately she marveled at how her own history was constantly shifting. Two years before, she would have written: *Laren of Mount Eskel was disappointed in his daughter Miri. She was so slight and weak, he forbade her from so much as stepping foot inside the quarry.*

Just the past year, Miri had learned the truth. Her ma had been injured in the quarry and died a week after

Miri's birth, and so great was her father's love and sorrow he would not risk his baby girl in that place. What other truths would one day be revealed about old stories? History was as hard to hold as a wet fish.

Britta's silence felt mournful, and Miri pulled her closer.

"What *do* you want history to say of you?"

"That I did things," she said. "Helped people. But I'm not very good at figuring those things out. I hope you stay, Miri, and help me be a good princess—and one day, a good queen."

"I . . . I would like to. . . ." Could Miri's home be Asland? The thought made her stomach feel like a beehive shaken. "Um, how are your parents handling the loss of their lands?"

"They're livid, of course." Britta picked a blossom from a tree and twirled it in her fingers. "The king left them the smaller house in Asland, though they will pay tribute for it and will have to work to earn income. It won't kill them to work a little, and maybe having them closer won't be all bad."

Miri folded her arms. "I won't let your father anywhere near you."

Britta's fingers worried at the blossom till the stem bruised and stooped. "He mostly ignored me, you know. He wasn't terribly cruel until . . . until he first told me to go to Mount Eskel and I refused. I ran from him and hid, and he made everyone leave the house so no one could help me, and he hunted me out, and . . ." She briefly closed her eyes. "I've never been so afraid, Miri. If I never see him again, that would be all right." She watched the blossom's petals drift to the ground. "But my mother . . . Perhaps we would like each other. If we knew each other. I'm willing to try again."

There was movement in the shadow, and Miri jumped.

"Don't worry, it's just a couple of heavily armed, scary-looking men," Britta said, looking over her shoulder. "They follow me everywhere now, by Steffan's command. I think he's overreacting, but he just can't forget what almost happened."

Britta's words stayed with Miri as she kissed her good night and headed back to the girls' chamber. *Steffan can't forget.* No one could. Liana had predicted that. Miri had hoped that everyone was so enamored of the shoeless princess, there would be no more violence. But it was a foolish hope. Nothing had changed for the shoeless of Danland, and tributes would soon strike Mount Eskel.

The girls looked up at the sound of Miri locking the door.

"Hello, girls. It's been a long time since we had a Salon night," Miri said. "Do you think we could have one now?"

She confessed to writing most of "The Mountain Girl's Lament" and disclosed some of the dangerous talk from Sisela's Salon. While she spoke, Katar checked the door three times to make sure it was locked.

"The rebels lost," said Bena. "Britta and Steffan are married. It's over."

Miri shook her head. "An idea is like a fire under ice. You can try to put out the fire, but the melting has already begun."

"Who made up that saying?" Frid asked. "Doter?"

"Um, no," said Miri. "Just me."

"It's pretty good," Frid said, squinting. "But I don't understand why there would be fire under ice. And Doter's sayings are shorter."

"Anyway," said Miri, "those ideas are out there, and the people are not going to forget. If things don't change, the people will turn to violence. In the palace library I read about charters—a group of laws that protects a people's rights. We could write a charter in favor of the commoners. Katar can take it before the delegation and the king—"

"You have something against my head, Miri?" said Katar. "If they don't chop it off, at the very least they'll throw me out of the delegation, and then Mount Eskel won't have any chance for fair treatment. The delegates are all nobles; they won't vote against themselves."

"And no one but nobles can create new laws," said Miri. "It's an impossible situation! We're the *only* nobles who have been commoners and understand the shoeless. It's our responsibility to make change. If we're convincing, the delegation will agree for the good of the country—commoners and nobles alike."

"Even if I thought we had a chance, I can't," said Katar. "A member of court must sponsor any new laws."

A member of court? Miri had not realized. She slumped in her chair.

"Surely Britta would do it for us," said Esa.

Miri shook her head. "She lost her noble title when her parents did, and the king said he won't raise her back up. I think he realizes that the people are happy calling her the commoner princess."

"Would Prince Steffan do it?" asked Esa.

"He can't," said Katar. "The king and the prince heir oversee the delegation and cannot sponsor new laws."

Miri was still wearing her scholar robes. She ran her fingers over the embroidered emblem on her chest: a crown and an open door. The sign of the queen.

# Chapter Twenty-two

The army slew a thousand and showed little pity
The king ordered fealty from the conquered city
The prince charmed its people with words wise and witty
And the queen sat on a couch, looking very pretty

The hours Miri spent at the Queen's Castle the next day seemed agonizingly slow, the sun barely scraping along in the sky, the droning of the master scholar like the heavy buzzing of a summer bee. The moment class ended, she was on her feet and out the door, clutching a first draft of the charter she and the girls had finished that dawn. By the light of day, it seemed impossibly ambitious. For one thing, the delegates would never vote to abolish all noble titles.

*But perhaps they will compromise on land ownership. . . .*

Miri was full of thoughts and walking straight into the hot yellow sunset, so she did not notice Timon until he called her name.

He was waiting at their corner near the palace, his hands in his pockets.

"You haven't been to the Castle in weeks," she said. "But I guess completing another open-sky year was never your intention."

He shook his head.

"You knew about Britta," she said. "You knew she could be the key to incite revolution, and you used me to put her story to the people—well, the part of her story that made her look bad. A shame you didn't meet Liana instead of me. She would have *loved* writing a leaflet condemning Britta."

"I never knew I was a coward until these past weeks." He kept his gaze on the tips of his shoes. "I couldn't face you."

"Well, now you have. Congratulations." She started to walk again. He kept pace with her.

"Years from now," he said, "Britta will be just a name in a book. And so I thought, when compared to the entire nation, what does she matter? Names mean nothing—lady or lord, or Skarpson for that matter."

*How far apart we are*, Miri thought. Timon was working so hard to turn away from his birth and background. Miri looked north and felt a yearning for home. And yet those twisting feelings inside reminded her again of all she'd have to give up in Asland if she returned to Mount Eskel.

"I know you think me a thug," he said, "but I did what I thought was best."

She threw up her hands. "What do you want from me, Timon?"

"You don't need to be curt, Miri. I'm doing you a favor. I came to give you fair warning."

"That change is still brewing?"

"If you're not among the blue-banded, then you are the enemy. And this time there won't be a lone musket shooting through a carriage window. Groups across the city have come together. There will be thousands united."

Miri shivered. "Not yet. We have some ideas, and if they work, nobody has to die. Just give us more time."

"It's not up to me, Lady Miri." Her title on his lips sounded like an insult. "The revolution isn't a bridled horse anyone can stop with a yank of the reins. The robber princess married her prince, but commoners are still paying tributes they can't afford. There *will* be an uprising."

"Against Britta?"

"No. She's a commoner now, and frankly, the people are taken with her and her *adorable* habit of flinging off her shoes."

"Then who will be attacked?" she asked. "When?"

"I can't tell you. I've said enough."

She tried to argue it out of him, but he would not budge.

"I *am* sorry, you know." He smiled a little, and his

tired eyes brightened. "I learned of you long before I met you. Traders who worked with my father talked of changes on Mount Eskel, led by the academy girls. Your academy's tutor spoke with other scholars about one girl in particular. I used to imagine giving you books and a house in Asland, and sailing beside you to see the world. Then we met and everything I had dreamed seemed possible. I believed I would see your face every day for the rest of my life."

She supposed her face looked a lot like his just then, tired after her night up, a little sad, but resigned too.

"Not everything that we imagine comes to pass," she said. "But thank you for the warning. And the books."

She smiled at him and left.

When she was a block away, she thought about looking back but realized that she did not care if she saw Timon—then or ever again.

Miri went straight to Peder's recovery room at the palace and rewrote the charter at his bedside. Nervous energy made her letters too large, her lines crooked.

"It's good, Miri," he said. "If they're smart, they'll see that."

"I'm not sure intelligence is a requirement for being a delegate."

The girls had to wait until Inga left for the night, and so debated and made changes straight through till morning. Delegates could introduce new laws only on the first of the month, when the king was in attendance. They had two more days to prepare, or they would have to wait another month.

"And that might be too late." Miri took a big breath. "Are we ready to woo our sponsor?"

Bena had arranged for the girls to have an audience with Queen Sabet in her chambers.

"I don't know how to play a lute or forge a sword," Bena had said, "but believe me, I know how to set up lunch with a member of court."

Miri had practiced her speech several times, but even so, once they were actually facing the queen, her voice quavered.

The queen petted her little white dog as Miri read the charter. It started with simpler ideas, such as commoners having the right to a rest day each week, and allowing news journals freedom to publish without court approval. And then it built up to land ownership being open to everyone, not just nobles, as well as to commoner representation in the delegation.

"Commoners from each province will vote one of their own as a delegate. The combined commoner and noble delegates must approve all royal tributes. In addition—"

The queen rose to her feet and started to leave.

"I can't . . . I can't listen to this. Bjorn would be so angry."

"Please," Miri said, rushing to her side. "Please, don't go. We can't afford to wait until mobs storm the palace or nobles are murdered in their houses. Nobles and royals need to make an offering to the commoners. It's a step forward for the entire kingdom. And *you* are the only person who can make it possible."

The queen stared at her, the line of her mouth stiff. "You well know that I have no power. Do not mock me."

Miri was silenced. The queen was turning again to go when Gerti quarry-spoke.

*Queen Gertrud*, she said. The memory was of the girls' first Salon night, when Miri returned from the Queen's Castle and recounted the story of its origin.

"Your Majesty, forgive me," said Miri, "but do you know of Queen Gertrud?"

The queen paused on the threshold. "Gertrud, wife of Jorgan, sixteenth king of Danland," she recited.

"Yes, but do you know her story?" Miri asked.

The queen blinked, not understanding the question.

"Gertrud was from Hindrick province," said Miri. "There was no school for girls in Hindrick at the time. She attended the princess academy and became the first girl in her family to learn to read. Jorgan chose her, and when she left for Asland, she dedicated her bridal lands for a school."

Gerti took up the story. "King Jorgan began construction of a new palace built of linder. During his reign, much of the king's wing of this palace was completed."

"The old castle on the river isle was going to be a prison," said Frid. She smiled as if that detail was her favorite.

Miri continued. "Queen Gertrud approached the king and the delegation on the day the old castle was to be given over to the Justice Official. She said—"

*"My king, you have never given me a wedding present,"* Esa said in a high voice, and then in a low voice for the king, *"I am thirty years late!"*

"It was written that when crowned, the new king should bestow a gift upon his bride," said Miri.

"She'd never asked him for anything before," Esa said, "so he dared her to name a gift of her choosing and swore it would be hers."

"She asked for the castle!" said Frid and Gerti, talking over each other.

"The Justice Official was outraged at losing his prize," said Miri, "but the king was true to his oath. The old castle became known as the Queen's Castle."

"There she started the first academy for teachers," Katar continued. "Over the years it became the center of Danlander scholarship. Scholars who train at the Queen's Castle become tutors all over the kingdom, preserve history, promote the arts and science, make discoveries and inventions. Queen Gertrud's legacy is powerful. So will be yours."

When Katar stopped, Miri wanted to speak quickly, present logical arguments, beg for the queen's aid. But she reminded herself of the last rule of Rhetoric: *Offer silence.*

After a time, the queen spoke.

"My husband gave me a wedding gift. A small house on the shore. We used to spend two weeks there every winter. Then one year, we stopped. I left my favorite set of teacups in the kitchen."

"You should go back," said Gerti.

"Yes, I should send someone for the teacups," said the queen.

"But *you* should go," said Gerti. "With the king. It sounds like you miss it. The way you talk about it, that's how I feel about Mount Eskel."

The queen considered Gerti. "I can feel your longing."

Miri wondered if the queen could sense a longing in her as well, one strong enough to pull her away from Asland. She did not dare ask.

"Your Majesty," said Miri, "if the nobles and royals don't take the next step, the commoners will. They believe they can claim power only through violence.

Even if they don't succeed, think how many will die trying."

The queen studied Miri's face and then held her hand out for the charter. She sat and read for long, aching minutes before giving it back.

"I will see you at the next session of the delegation," she said, and then left. Her servants followed.

The girls stood there, looking at one another.

"So . . . did she just agree to sponsor the charter?" asked Katar.

"I think so," Miri whispered.

"You *think* so?" Katar grabbed the paper from Miri. "If I present this in session and the queen doesn't offer her sponsorship, 'I think so' isn't going to save my head."

"Your head will be fine," said Miri. "It's your neck you should worry about."

"Miri!"

They started back to their chamber. Katar trudged behind as if dragging stones, and Miri slowed to walk beside her.

"I'll hand copies to the delegates myself," said Miri. "I'll stand beside you, Katar."

Katar grimaced, but she nodded. "Thanks. I thought . . ." She pressed her lips together. "I thought when I wrote you that letter last spring that you'd know what to do."

Miri nodded, unsure what to say.

"Though it took you *ages* to figure it out," said Katar.

Miri knocked her with her shoulder, Katar knocked her back, and Miri wondered at what moment she and Katar had become friends.

*This very moment*, Miri thought. *Just now.*

*Spring Week Three*

Dear Marda,

If you receive these letters along with a note advising you of my execution, please do not be too sad. Someday you might even laugh about it! "Oh that Miri. She <u>would</u> go off to Asland and drum up trouble. Remember when she forgot to tie up the billy goat, and he ate two shoes and a blanket? Such a prankster!"

If you have a funeral for me, sing loudly and let the goats attend. They love a rousing ditty.

Your troublesome baby sister,

Miri

# Chapter Twenty-three

Oh land of farms and green hills mild
Once formed by giants rough and wild
With massive paws they gripped and tore
With one great rip they formed the shore

Where heavy boots left prints so deep
Blue lakes remain 'tween summits steep
The giants fought beneath our skies
And from their bones our mountains rise

The night before facing the delegation, the girls smuggled Peder from his sickbed into their chamber. Miri felt fragile and afraid, and yearned to keep all she loved near. Accustomed to late nights debating the charter, and too nervous to sleep, they all talked into the dark hours, not of laws but of home. Miri could almost hear the sleepy mumbling of goats, sense the ice-tipped winds coming off the peak, smell snow melting and miri flowers blooming, and feel spring as it is on the mountain—full of promise.

In the morning they dressed and pretended to eat breakfast.

"No matter that we could be beheaded for this," said Esa. "Heads are overrated."

"Yes, they are *so* unfashionable," said Miri, imitating an Aslandian accent. "This spring, ladies of style are wearing their feathers in their necks."

They laughed, but not for too long. Gerti rubbed her own neck.

"Katar and I can do it alone, if you'd like," Miri said.

But when Katar rose to go to the door, even Bena followed.

Miri left last, pausing to look back at Peder, lying on Liana's old bed.

"Get some rest. I'll send news as soon as there is any."

"Just make sure it's good news," he said. "If you happen to be killed, I'd rather hear it from your own lips."

"Absolutely. I'll roll my decapitated head back here to bring you word."

Peder's teasing smile faltered. "Please be careful."

She nodded and left but returned a moment later to give him a last quick kiss on his lips. He touched her hair.

The Delegate House waited on the other side of the Green from the palace. Hordes of people were gathered around the yellow-brick building, the murmurs tense.

"Quite a crowd," Katar said.

"Unusual?" asked Miri.

Katar nodded.

The procession of the king's carriage and his attendants stopped, the road clogged with people. The royal guard yelled for passage, and very slowly the people edged backward. Their gazes were somber. Miri rubbed her arms to dispel the chills. As she squeezed through the crowd, she was grateful she wore her scholar robes, free from the mark of nobility.

The entire building was a huge open chamber. The floor was linder, but the walls were yellow brick, leading to a domed ceiling, painted with a starred sky. The round delegation table took up the center of the chamber and was surrounded by sixteen high-backed chairs, one for each province's delegate. Miri noted that the table was large enough to add sixteen more chairs for the commoner delegates. If the charter passed.

Three galleries opened off the central chamber. The king sat upon a dais facing the delegates, the Court Gallery behind him. The Mount Eskel girls climbed the stairs to claim seats in the Noble Gallery, which was half empty. Opposite, the Commoner Gallery overflowed.

Miri handed Katar the couple dozen handwritten copies of their charter. Katar wore her reddish hair in a bun, perhaps imagining it made her look older. But beside two white-haired delegates, Miri thought she looked like a child who had sneaked into a meeting of the village council.

"She's here, at least," Katar whispered.

Queen Sabet waited in the Court Gallery. Her face was in shadow, and if she noticed Miri, she made no signal of greeting. Britta sat beside Steffan. It seemed she tried to smile at Miri, but her expression was taut. She had thought the charter a wonderful idea, though she had not been able to hide the fear in her eyes.

"It's not too late—" Miri started.

"I'll do it," said Katar. "Someone has to."

Miri tried to think of a hopeful thing to say, but her stomach hurt with worry.

"Your face is making me even more nervous." Katar put her hands on Miri's shoulders and turned her away. "Go where I can't see you."

Miri found a seat with the girls. Esa held out her hand and squeezed Miri's.

"I'd rather face bandits," Miri whispered.

The session opened with the singing of Danland's anthem. The first verses told of giants fighting, the fall of their bodies pounding out Asland's valley, their kicks pushing the trees together to make the forests. Miri did not believe it was real history, but she liked the idea of it. She had felt part of a giant once, on the docks protesting the oil tribute. *Any group united creates a giant,* she thought. Could their little group actually reshape Danland?

The chief delegate acknowledged the king's presence and introduced extremely boring laws for debate. An hour went by. Then two. In Miri's mind anxiety warred against drowsiness. When would Katar speak?

Miri's gaze wandered over the Commoner Gallery. No one she recognized, but all wore blue bands on their arms. Messengers were constantly coming and going, perhaps carrying news of the debate to the crowds outside and returning with messages they whispered in ears.

The building was full of nobles and court members, not to mention the king, queen, and prince.

Drowsiness drained out of Miri with a chill that washed from her head through her legs.

"What if they mean to attack here today?" she whispered to Esa.

The royal guard had searched commoners for weapons before allowing them into the Delegate House, but there were enough commoners outside to qualify as an army.

"Speak to the guards," Esa whispered back.

Miri nodded. She was making her way out of the Noble Gallery when she heard Katar's voice pierce the dome of the chamber.

"Mount Eskel wishes to speak."

The chief delegate acknowledged her.

Miri froze where she was, her body iced with anticipation.

Katar walked around the table while speaking on the need for change, handing each delegate a copy of the charter. When she passed one up to the king, Miri could see her hand shook. But her voice was steady.

When she returned to her seat, the delegates and the king were absorbed in reading the charter. Katar opened her mouth, then shut it. She handed extra copies into the galleries and then stood, waiting for them to finish, her heels quietly bouncing. Whispers noised around the hall like the flap of bats.

"You are of Mount Eskel," the king said slowly, "and I have reason to favor your province of late. So I will ask you politely. Who sponsors this charter?"

Katar looked into the Court Gallery. There was no movement.

The king swung around. "Who dared this yearling to present such a betrayal? Who challenges the power of the crown? Who?"

The members of court all seemed to have loose threads on their cuffs or pieces of fluff on their skirts that required immediate examining.

The queen stood. She was up behind the king, and

with the members of court occupied with threads and fluff, no one saw her.

*Speak*, Miri quarry-spoke. The word traveled through the stone, slick as a fish in water, and though Miri knew the queen would not understand, perhaps she could feel the rumblings of support through the linder at her feet.

*Speak*, said Esa, with an image of the time Miri spoke up to the village council.

*Speak*, said Frid, and Gerti and Katar too.

*Speak*, came the soundless voices of the academy girls. It was a word of encouragement—a mother bird chirping to her young to flap their wings; a child impatient at a window, wishing for spring.

Miri saw Britta silently mouth the word. *Speak*.

The queen took one step forward.

"I do," she said, as quiet as a feather lands.

"What?" The king whirled in his chair to face her. "Did you say something in my Delegate House?"

His wife flinched. She glanced up at something on the wall that Miri could not see, but it appeared to give her courage. Her shoulders straightened, and she nodded.

"I sponsor this charter."

The king looked about as if for something to hit. Queen Sabet descended the steps and grabbed his hand, holding it between both of hers. Miri noticed for the first time just how beautiful the queen was. She wore a deep purple dress, embroidered along the hems and sleeves with white flowers. Her black hair was up, also stuck with white flowers and a graceful plume. Gems sparkled at her ears and throat. Even in that crowded room, she stood out. And Miri realized that she must have chosen her attire with that intention. She had not come to the Delegate House to be forgotten in the corner. She had come to speak.

"It's for you," the queen said in a whisper, perhaps believing no one else could hear. But the rotunda picked up the sound and trilled the echo to the entire chamber. "Because I love Danland, and you are Danland. Because I love you, Bjorn."

The king stared at her. The room was silent.

"Do you wish to voice displeasure?" the chief delegate asked the king.

Katar had said that if the king voiced displeasure for any motion and the delegation's vote was not unanimous, the king had the right to remove the motion entirely.

"No," he said, and leaned back heavily in his chair.

*He knows*, Miri thought. *In order to preserve the monarchy, he must bend.*

So the delegation debate began. It was not slow and accommodating as before. It was choppy and violent as a river thrashing white against rocks. Miri could barely follow the debate. It became noise to her, just cries in the air. The strain of waiting almost hurt, and she wished they would just vote.

Every person in the Commoner Gallery was standing up, many on tiptoe. The copies of the charter were passed from one to the next with a hungry urgency. The crowd seethed with energy and anticipation, their power like that of an ax raised up, poised to fall.

What would happen if the vote failed? Miri moved again toward the royal guards by the door. If she warned them, perhaps they could defend the Delegate House from an outside attack.

Messengers were sprinting now between the Commoner Gallery and outside. The leaders of the blue-banded would wait till the vote, Miri hoped. Moments after the charter failed, the thousands of commoners outside would know, and the delegates might as well throw a firebrand onto a heap of straw.

*This is the spark*, Miri thought. She had created the spark for the revolution after all—the commoners would be enraged at the nobles for voting down the charter and so decidedly denying them rights. War would begin. And it would begin with killing, just as Sisela had predicted.

Miri reached the nearest guard.

"Sir," she whispered, "I'm worried the crowds will turn violent."

He tilted his head, meaning he could not hear her.

"Sir," she said more loudly.

He shook his head and put a finger to his lips, and his attention returned to the delegates. She realized the guard must be a commoner and as eager to follow the debate as any.

"Please," she said. "It will be a massacre. They'll kill the king and the delegates and—"

"A vote!" the chief delegate cried. "A vote. Lords and ladies, rise if you support this charter."

Not yet! Miri was not ready. Nothing was ready. She saw Katar stand and raise her hand to vote. Another female delegate followed, and a man with white at his temples. Three. Three of sixteen. That was nowhere near a majority! Miri stumbled forward, hoping to reach Britta and warn her to get Steffan away. Walking through the chamber was like trying to run underwater. The press of bodies was hot and tight, and she could no longer see the delegation table or the Court Gallery. Suddenly the noise level rose with shouts of surprise and alarm.

"Britta!" she cried, but the clamor doused any sound from her mouth.

The doors from outside flung open, and more blue-banded commoners pressed into the chamber. Miri choked back a scream. She pushed harder through the people and the noise that echoed off the rotunda in an ear-shattering shriek. The bedlam made her feel tipsy, as if she were on a ship. The shouts were high and tense, like the call of gulls. The shoves tore at her like wind.

She squeezed between two large men who were yelling with fists pumping the air, and suddenly the delegation table was before her. None of the delegates had been killed yet. She counted—sixteen, all standing there.

Sixteen. Standing.

Miri looked again. Yes, they were standing, each with the right hand raised in unanimous vote. Many of them were smiling. The shouts from the Commoner Gallery wound up the walls like smoke, and she recognized now the tones not of terror but of jubilation. They deepened, heightened, cheers rolling over cheers.

The chief delegate was speaking to the king, who nodded solemnly. The nobility in the Court Gallery looked stunned, even angry. But the delegates—nobles themselves—seemed relieved. Miri wondered if they had considered such a charter in the past, but had not dared.

Katar broke from the table and ran straight to Miri.

"It passed?" Miri asked, yearning for it to be true but too afraid to believe.

Katar nodded, her smile huge and dimpled. She clenched Miri in an embrace so tight Miri coughed for lack of breath. *She just needs practice,* Miri thought. Miri squeezed her back.

As if by some signal, the cheering slowed and then silenced. The building was full to bursting, hundreds of blue-banded commoners filling the floor and entrance. A commoner near the king bowed. Then he turned to face the queen and lowered one knee to the floor. In silence, hundreds of commoners did likewise—a bow to the king, a knee to the queen.

The queen's hand rose to her mouth, her eyes wet. She looked back up at the wall.

Miri was close enough now to glimpse what the queen was seeing. It was a portrait of Queen Gertrud.

# Chapter Twenty-four

*Mud in the stream*
*And earth in the air*
*Clay in my ears*
*And stone in my stare*

*I'm on the mountain*
*But the mount's in me*
*I can't shake the dust*
*I won't wash it free*

The charter, it seemed, was the only possible topic of conversation in Asland, and most especially in the Queen's Castle. Some seemed terrified of the changes, some confused, but most could not stop exclaiming with wonder and delight.

The latest news caused a stir in Master Filippus's class: Britta's family's lands, seized by the crown when they lost their noble titles, were being put to immediate use. Queen Sabet had ordered the property sold and the proceeds used to build schools in Asland. Children who attended would be fed two meals during the school day, to encourage their parents to send them to studies instead of work.

But the change that most often brought an unbidden smile to Miri's lips was the release from current tributes. Each province would elect a commoner to the delegation, and Miri felt hopeful that whatever tributes the new delegation approved would be fair.

Her eyes lifted to the painting on the classroom wall. Since their course on Art, Miri understood how remarkable it was that the painter had chosen a commoner girl as a worthy subject for a masterwork. Why had Miri ever assumed the girl felt trapped? She seemed content now, pouring milk in her little house. Couldn't a girl just admire a moon from time to time?

Master Filippus was saying again how the Danlandian charter was unprecedented, that there was no correlation in history. That they were *making* history.

Miri wished he would ask that ethics question again. *Which would you save, the murderer or the painting?* She knew her answer now: both. She would find a way. *Which do you choose, the princess or the revolution?* Both. Who says it has to be one or the other?

*Where will you live, Asland or home?*

Miri took the long way through the palace grounds to stop by the forge.

"Frid!" she called. The noise was as deafening as in a quarry. She tried quarry-speech, doubting it would carry with no linder underfoot. But whether she heard or not, Frid stopped pounding on a red-hot metal bar and looked up.

"Hello, Miri." She stuck the bar in a bucket of water with a fizzle and a puff of steam, and then held it up. "Like my sword?"

One of the men working near her laughed.

"If that's a sword, mountain sister, then you're the princess," he said.

A strapping boy dropped his tongs and stalked over to the man, his chest puffed up. "Frid's work is better than your sloppy denting."

"That's right," said another boy. "She's . . . she's perfect!" And he blushed.

"Ease up, you bunch of lumps," Frid said sweetly.

She took off her leather apron and walked with Miri to get away from the noise. Miri glanced back and noticed several of the forge boys still watching Frid.

"A nice group?" Miri asked.

"Nice as they come. A couple keep giving me flowers." Frid laughed as if it were an excellent joke.

"I just heard the trader wagons are leaving in the morning," said Miri. "Bena has decided to go back with them. I think she's annoyed that Liana is getting married but no one has asked for her hand. Get Bena any letters before she goes."

Miri had a stack of letters for Marda written over the past months, but still not one she felt good about sending. How could she explain all that had happened? How could she comfort them that she would be home soon when she was not certain herself?

"I can't believe the year's half over already," Frid said, wiping her sweaty face with a handkerchief gray with use. "Remember how we sat up in our room at first, afraid to go outside and get run over by a carriage? Asland's a lot tamer than a mountain, if you ask me. No wolves, no she-cats, no bandits, no rocks falling on your head—unless you're an assassin."

"Naturally. Asland is downright dangerous if you're an assassin." Miri's smile broke. "Frid, will you stay here?"

"Tonight? Don't be silly. I like the forge well enough but I'm not going to sleep in it. I'll be back before bedtime."

"No, I meant in the fall when we . . . when the rest of the girls return to Mount Eskel. Will you stay in Asland?"

The original invitation had been for only the one year, but Miri knew Britta would welcome her friends to stay indefinitely.

Frid's wide-open eyes opened a little wider. "Why would I do that?"

SHANNON HALE

"Well, you seem so happy working in the forge. With your new friends."

"Sure, I like the boys well enough. We have some laughs. But Mount Eskel is home."

Miri nodded.

"And just think, if I set up a forge on the mountain," said Frid, "we could make and fix our own tools!"

Her mouth opened with the happy thought, and she forgot to say good-bye before returning to her anvil.

When Miri arrived at the girls' chamber, Esa and Gerti were gathering letters and gifts for their families and pressing Bena with instructions to deliver love and hugs and kisses.

"I'll take your letters," said Bena, "but I'm *not* kissing anyone." She paused. "Except Frid's brothers. The younger ones. And only if they beg. If you're all so home-sick, why not just come with me?"

"I'm not quite ready yet," Gerti said, plucking a lute string.

Esa put her hand on her hip. "You realize lowlanders have known for *centuries* how to care for the sick? Centuries! You think I'm going to leave before I learn as much as I can? When I think of it, my blood just *boils*. . . ."

"Great, there she goes again," Bena whispered.

"*You* set her off," Gerti whispered back.

Miri sat down for the fifth time that week to write

another letter home, but her thoughts were a snarl too thick to unpick. She was not ready yet either—to go home or not to go home. She needed to find her words.

It was late when she entered Gus's courtyard. Peder was leaning against a stone as white as the moon. It could only be linder. He was reading a sheet of paper, his brow furrowed. She did not want to startle away the line between his eyes, the way his lips slowly moved as if sounding out the words of his thoughts. So she stood and watched him for a few moments.

Then she lay her hand on the linder and quarry-spoke the memory of the first time she had come to see him. *I am here.*

He looked up. As much as she'd enjoyed his thoughtful expression, it got even better when he saw her. His eyes took up his smile.

"Hello," he said.

"Hello. How are you feeling?"

"What, this old thing?" he said, lifting his shirt partway to reveal the pink scar on his middle. "I only got it to look manly. We warriors call them 'manly marks.'"

"You let a lead ball go through your belly so you could look tough, did you?"

"But of course. Why else would I leap in front of a shooting musket?"

Miri hoped she knew why, but the words were too precious to speak aloud.

"What were you reading?" she asked instead.

"A letter to home. I've rewritten it a dozen times already. It's a tricky thing to express nearly six months in one letter. It's hard to know what to say—"

"And what not to say."

"Exactly."

They sat on the linder block and stared at the moon. She knew from her Astronomy studies that the moon was a huge ball of rock that reflected the sun's light. Marda would see that exact moon tonight. Miri knew she would not think about rock and reflected light but about a little sister who was far away and yet under the same moon.

"Timon told me how sailors navigate by the stars," Miri said. "I'm glad to know it, though I'd rather not be reminded of him every time I look at the night sky."

"Did you like him?"

Miri was surprised by the question, but she tried to answer honestly. "There were moments when I thought about it."

Timon's touch, his kiss, had felt good, and that goodness made her believe her feelings had been true.

"But when he wasn't around, I didn't talk to him in my head, like I do with you. For a few weeks, I wasn't sure what I felt. But now everything seems so clear, I can't believe I was ever unsure."

Peder did not say anything. Miri hesitated, then chose her words carefully.

"I'm sure about you," Miri said. "But I'm not sure . . . not sure if *you're* sure about me."

Peder tilted his head to the side. "Of course I am."

"You are? But . . . so often here you've been distant with me."

He twisted a rag in his hands. "I have been anxious about using my time well. You're the only person who cares if I become a sculptor, and I don't want to disappoint you."

"I'm sorry, Peder," she said, a sting of loneliness in her chest. "I didn't want to burden you with expectation. I know how that feels."

"I do want to be good at carving, Miri," he said. "For you, but for me too. When I'm carving, I feel more like myself than ever, more like I matter. When I'm carving *and* when I'm with you. I assumed you knew that."

Miri laughed, mostly from nerves. "Boys need to talk more. Boys need to say things and not assume things. You and my pa and Steffan and everyone, you're going to make us girls insane!"

"No more insane than you already make us," he said.

"Fair enough." She looked down, running her finger

over a silver vein in the linder. "I am of age for betrothal, you know."

"Oh?" he said, polishing the stone with a cloth.

She sighed in exasperation. "I'm of age, and you haven't asked me to be your betrothed."

He looked up, his eyes wide. "You want to get married right now? In Asland?"

"No! No, but you know that when a girl and boy are fond enough of each other that they might want to wed one day, they make promises. Then they have to wait at least a year to test those promises and make certain they mean them before they marry—at least a year, though they can wait as long as they like—but the promises are customary, and . . . you're looking at me as if I'm speaking in ancient Rilamarkian. You can't possibly not know this."

"Maybe I did. I never really thought about it."

He was the oldest child in his family, and no one close to him had ever wed. Perhaps he had never cared enough about weddings and betrothals to pay any attention.

She sighed again, this time with slightly less exasperation. "Peder, I like you better than anyone I've ever known. Someday I want to have a house with you. I want to teach in the village school and gather the stories of Mount Eskel and then come home to you in the evening and see what you've carved and talk about the day. In other words, I want to marry you, Peder. Eventually. In the meantime, I promise to be faithful, to always tell you the truth, and to share my heart with you alone. Will you accept my betrothal?"

Peder was on his feet. "Whoa! Did we just get betrothed?"

"No. For one thing, you haven't accepted."

Peder forced himself to sit back down. Miri felt sick, but she waited, counting the loud beats of her heart. Ten. Twenty. Thirty. How much silence would she have to bear? When could she run away?

Peder looked at his shaking hands and laughed, holding them out for Miri to see. "When we go back home, don't tell Jans and Almond that I got so nervous. They'll make fun of me till I'm gray haired, I know they will."

He looked at her, shook his head incredulously, and started polishing the stone again.

Miri was pretty well done with silence.

"Peder, you have to answer me before my heart dies in my chest and plops onto the ground!"

"Answer you? About . . . Oh, I have to say yes? Well, yes, of course. And I promise the same things back to you." He smiled in his way, one side of his mouth pulling higher. "That wasn't so bad. I think my hands have stopped shaking."

He lifted them again. She took hold.

"Isn't someone supposed to witness the vows or something?" he asked.

"Our fathers. The head of the village council can stand in for a father, and so can a priest or . . ." She'd looked up this detail in the Queen's Castle library, though she decided to omit that confession. "Or the king."

"We could ask the king," said Peder. "He sort of owes you his life."

"Perhaps. . . ." Now that she knew Peder's thoughts, the rush fell away. "But it might be nice to wait."

"Let our fathers do it at home," he said.

"Exactly."

"All right, we'll make it official in the fall." Peder grinned. "It feels like a big deal, doesn't it?"

"It is a big deal. But I'm certain about it. About you. Even if I'm a little scared too. We don't have to get married for years and years if we don't want, you know. You'll have time to change your mind."

"I won't."

"But you could—"

"I won't," he said again.

Miri's eyes stung, but she did not feel the need to look away.

"Miri, I want to live on Mount Eskel. Is that what you want?"

"Yes." As she said it, she held the stone beneath her, just in case that word split the linder in two and dumped them on the ground. *Yes* felt mighty. *Yes* was the most powerful idea in the world.

"I believe you," he said. "And yet, it doesn't seem fair. You want to keep studying at the Queen's Castle."

"And you want to keep learning from Gus. Mount Eskel is home, but I don't want to have to choose only one or the other forever."

"Are we supposed to talk about this stuff out loud?" he said. "I thought, you know, *relationships* or whatever can't be planned. They just happen or they don't, like a laugh. Or a kiss."

Miri smiled, because she guessed that he said "kiss" because it was on his mind, and sure enough, he leaned forward and kissed her. She still felt a little nervous along with the glee, and that was all right. Her hand was on his chest, and she could feel his own heart beating even harder than hers. It made her smile.

"I can't kiss you when you're smiling," he said. "It makes me want to laugh."

She giggled and then controlled herself, because she did want to kiss him. Kisses were like words, she thought. They meant many things, their meanings fickle, dangerous even. Kisses could be lies, or they could be promises. She could feel the truth of Peder's kiss in her ribs, in her heart, in the breath held in her lungs. She believed his kisses.

It was later than late when he offered to walk her back. The palace waited to the north, the same direction as Mount Eskel. Miri turned toward it and, smiling, breathed in the night. She did not want to sleep yet. She still had a letter to write. She would not take it lightly. From all she'd seen in the libraries, letters and diaries preserved history. And her letter to home would be one of the very first written pieces of history in all of Mount Eskel.

Timon was wrong; history was more than names on a page. History was stories, like Queen Gertrud and the Castle, Dan and the Blackbird, the Princess's Ladies and the Charter. And stories were as plentiful on Mount Eskel as rubble rock—both true and fanciful, told and sung. She wanted to listen to the stories and memories of the villagers and write them down. To be a keeper of memories, like the linder itself. A writer of history. What a wonder.

Would she go home or stay? *Both.*

*A person can be more than one thing*, she thought, and wondered how she had not thought of it before. She could be a historian, a scholar, and a teacher. A daughter, a sister, and a friend. A princess's lady and the betrothed of an apprentice stone carver. A citizen of Asland and a girl of Mount Eskel. She need not decide every moment of her life now. There would be years and years to learn and act and make mistakes, to travel and to stay. She did not know all the future, but she knew what to do next. She took Peder's hand and walked toward home.

*Spring Week Four*

Dear Pa and Marda,

It makes me happy imagining you two inside our little house. Marda is sitting at the table, reading this aloud. Pa is standing by the window, looking out while he listens. And now Marda is smiling, because I have described the moment just right.

None of the letters I wrote these past months seem true anymore, but I will send them anyway. I no longer feel like the lost girl who wrote them, but I was her once. Perhaps you will like to see where I was and where I am now.

I worry that reading my words will make you sad because you miss me. And I miss you too. A lot. The ache of the missing fills my chest, yet it does not hurt. It almost feels good, because it reminds me I have a family I love and that I will see you again.

Yes, Pa, I will come home in the fall. Asland is more wonderful than I could have imagined, but it is not home. Esa has learned doctoring, Frid can make an iron lever, Gerti's lute plays like springtime formed into sound, Peder's carvings are as beautiful as mountains, and my own head is full of questions, numbers, and words. All these things we learned, what would they matter if we do not return?

Some say we are what we do, not where we come from. I say we are both, because I will always be a Mount Eskel girl. I want to milk the goats, teach in the village school, have you accept my betrothal to Peder, and write our province's first history. Someday other Eskelites will study at the Queen's Castle, and I want them to find a book about home in the library. Maybe I will even be there to show it to them.

Because I will return to Asland, so I can be a friend to Britta and Katar and continue to study. I hope you will still love your girl now that I am of two places. Whenever I leave, I promise I will always come home again. Home will always be Mount Eskel. And I will always be

your Miri

# Acknowledgments

Many people supported and inspired this novel, including Dean Hale, Victoria Wells Arms and the wondrous folk at Bloomsbury, Barry Goldblatt, Kindra Johnson, Kayla Huff, Bonnie Bryner, Max Hale, Kira Janke, Hannah Wengersky, and my childhood friend Molly Orange Richardson, who first introduced me to ethics.

While doing research for this novel, I particularly enjoyed *The Days of the French Revolution* by Christopher Hibbert.

Writing this story made me even more aware of how many people in this world cannot meet their basic needs. My family and I decided to donate a portion of the proceeds from this book to LDS Humanitarian Services to aid their millions of projects worldwide, such as clean-water access, immunizations, neonatal care, and food production.

A hearty thank-you to the many readers of *Princess Academy* who wanted to hear what happened next. I'm the luckiest writer in the world. You are a joy to write for.

# THE ROYAL TABLES ARE TURNED . . . AND THE STUDENT BECOMES THE TEACHER!

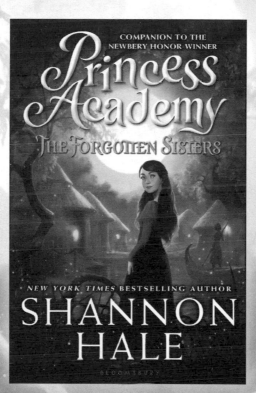

Just when Miri thinks she's finished with princess life, she's called upon for a brand-new task. She must journey to a distant swamp to start her very own princess academy for three sisters, cousins of the royal family. But to help them, she'll need to unravel a big mystery . . .

READ ON FOR AN EXCERPT FROM SHANNON HALE'S ENCHANTING THIRD VOLUME IN THE *PRINCESS ACADEMY* SERIES.

*The god of creation broke me from stone*
*The mountain's the only ma I've known*
*My pa is the blue sky sheltering me*
*So stone I am and sky I'll be*

M iri woke to the rustle of a feather-stuffed quilt.
She stretched, her muscles humming. Warm yellow light poured through the glass windows, filling the chamber with morning. For a moment she was not sure why her breath felt ticklish in her chest, as if she were at chapel and trying to hold in a laugh. Then she remembered. She was going home.

"Today," said Miri, her voice creaky with sleep.

Her roommates were awake too. A year ago, six Mount Eskel girls had come to Asland, Danland's capital city, for their friend Britta's marriage to Prince Steffan. Now four remained at the palace.

Esa dressed slowly, expertly using her right hand to pull her dress over her lame arm. Frid tore off her night things and stuffed her broad shoulders into a travel dress. Gerti, the youngest, just sat on the edge of her bed, her feet dangling.

"Today," said Gerti, and the word was both mournful and glad.

Their bags were already packed and fat with presents for their families. With her allowance as a lady of the princess, Miri had purchased a set of chapel clothes, paper and ink, and chocolates for her sister, Marda. For Pa she had boots, honeyed nuts, and a new mallet. For the village school, an entire box of precious books.

Palace servants offered to carry their bags, leaving the four girls free to hold hands as they walked through the grand corridors, perhaps for the last time.

"It's kind of like home now," Gerti said. A servant was carrying her lute, and Miri thought Gerti looked small and vulnerable without the instrument strapped in its usual place over her chest. "It's strange, isn't it? How we're leaving home to go home?"

"The boys at the forge tried to make me swear I'd come back." Frid laughed. "Asland is all right for a visit, but I'm a Mount Eskel girl."

"I think I'll visit again, one day," said Esa. As they passed the infirmary, she waved to the palace physicians who had spent the past months training her in their science.

Miri did not admit to the girls that she was already

planning to return next spring. After all, even her pa and her sister did not know yet. But she and Peder had agreed that there was too much to do and learn in Asland to say farewell forever.

Miri took in a deep breath, memorizing the smells of the palace—sunlight warming the oil and lemon polish, the lavender soap used on the linens, and the hard scent she associated with metal. Miri smiled. But at the moment, she yearned for linder dust, warm goats, the wind against the autumn grasses. All the welcome smells of home.

"First thing when we get to Mount Eskel," Frid said, "I'm going to throw a rock into the Great Crevasse."

"A big rock, no doubt," said Esa.

"As big a rock as I can lift. Ha! I can't wait."

Frid marched first out the doors and into the palace courtyard. Miri was last but hesitated only a moment before passing into the sunlight.

The traders' wagons were loaded with food and other supplies to sell to the families on Mount Eskel. One empty wagon waited for the girls. Peder was sharing the bench with the driver.

Beyond the palace gates, beyond the sea of green park, the colorful buildings of Asland rose like a range of mountains. Autumn had softened the heat of summer, but the buildings were painted bright—red, yellow, blue,

white, rust, green—as if in the capital spring was endless, always blooming, never cold.

The princess Britta, Miri's best friend, was waiting to
see them off, standing beside her new husband, Prince
Steffan. Britta lifted a hand to wave at Miri but wiped a
tear instead. Her cheeks were bright red as always, that
merry feature contrasting with her wet brown eyes.

Though they had spent every day of the past week
together and already said good-bye in a hundred ways,
Miri hugged Britta again. Britta's back shuddered with a
small sob.

"Remember, Britta—" Miri started, trying to think of
something funny to dull the sadness, but a man's voice
interrupted.

"Miri Larendaughter?"

Miri turned. A royal guard in a shiny silver breast-
plate and tall fur hat was striding across the courtyard.

"I'm Miri."

"The king requests your presence," he said.

Miri laughed nervously. "Right now? We're just
leaving."

"The king requests your presence," the royal guard
said again.

"What is this about?" asked Steffan. He stiffened to
his full height, and his manner reminded Miri that a boy
who grows up in a palace probably never truly relaxes.

The guard bowed, noticing the prince for the first time. "I don't know, Your Highness, but the king has also sent for you."

Britta hooked Miri's arm. "Fine, we'll see what's going on and be back in a few minutes."

"You'll wait for me?" Miri asked Enrik, their wagon driver.

He lifted his thin nose and sniffed, as if he could tell the time of day by smell. "If we want to reach the first camp before night, we have to go now."

Miri's middle felt yanked.

"On horseback you can easily catch up to a caravan of wagons," said Britta.

"That's right," said Steffan. "Even if my father delays you for a couple of hours, I could get you to the camp by tonight."

Peder jumped down from the wagon. "Then I'll stay with you."

The sun behind him, Peder's curly hair looked pale gold. This past year's apprenticeship with a stone carver had broadened his shoulders. His face and arms were brown from the summer, and to Miri, he looked as handsome as morning.

"But what if . . ." Miri cleared her throat. "What if I'm delayed longer?"

"All the more reason I should stay."

"You promised your pa you'd be home after a year. If you aren't on the first wagon, he'll be—"

"Grumpier than a hungry billy goat," finished Esa, Peder's sister.

"I don't want him mad at us, not now," said Miri. As soon as she and Peder got home to Mount Eskel, they were going to ask their parents to approve their betrothal.

Peder scowled, but he did not disagree.

"I'll find out what's happening," said Miri, "and then I'll catch up on a fast horse, like Britta said."

"I don't know about that," Peder said, "I have never actually seen you ride a fast horse."

"Steffan can strap me to the horse's rump like a sack of wheat."

Peder smiled. "These lowlanders sure know how to have fun."

Miri leaned in to hug him farewell, but Peder stopped her with a kiss.

Frid, Esa, and Gerti exclaimed and hooted. Miri's and Peder's affection for each other was not a secret, but they'd never announced their intentions to become betrothed and certainly never kissed in front of others. Miri's face burned forge-fire hot, but feeling stubborn, she put her arms around his neck and kissed him back.

"See you tonight," he said, still holding her.

She let go and felt colder without his arms. The cold creeped into her heart and pinched there, a sharp, unexpected loneliness.

She scolded herself for being silly. After all, surely she would see him by end of day.

Peder and the girls sat in the wagon backward, their faces turned toward Miri. She watched until their wagon had passed through the gate and disappeared into the streets of Asland.

"Now, if you please," said the royal guard.

As they made their way to the royal breakfast chamber, Miri's sadness simmered into anger, her hands tightening into fists. She prepared herself to be bold and speak frankly with the king about her sudden summons. But then she entered the chamber and breathed in the icy, tense mood. With the king sat all thirty-two delegates, an elected noble and a commoner from each province in the kingdom. Three priests of the creator god stood along the wall in their brown tunics and white caps. Everyone wore equally grave expressions. The queen's gaze found Miri, and her smile seemed relieved.

"Your Highness," Britta said after the guard formally announced them, "Lady Miri was about to return to Mount Eskel when your summons prevented her."

"And is my summons not good enough anymore?"

The king's beard shook as his chin trembled. "Does the wish of the king mean nothing?"

Britta blushed, her entire face turning as red as her mottled cheeks. For the first time that morning, Miri thought to be afraid.

"Father—" Steffan began.

The king waved his hand dismissively and gestured to the chief delegate, a thin man with a small, pointed beard.

"Early this morning, traders sailed from the commonwealth of Eris with news," said the chief delegate. "The kingdom of Stora has invaded Eris. The battle lasted only three days. Eris surrendered."

Steffan leaned forward to grip a chair back. Britta reached out for Miri's hand. Stora was the largest kingdom on the continent. Miri imagined its vast army pouring into tiny Eris like all the sands of a beach trying to fill a single jar. And Eris bordered Danland.

"Danland can no longer take for granted our longstanding peace with Stora," the chief delegate continued. "We must secure an unbreakable alliance. Stora's King Fader is a widower. The delegation has decided to offer King Fader a royal daughter of Danland as a bride."

"Ironic, isn't it?" said the king, clattering plates as he reached for a bread basket. "Commoners clamor for revolution and the end of royal rule. But the moment the neighbors start loading their muskets, everyone runs to the king crying, 'Save us!' I have half a mind to let Stora invade and slaughter a province or two before coming to their aid."

"But you won't, sire," said the queen.

"Of course I won't," he barked back.

The queen nodded and sipped her tea. She was a pale woman with dark hair and strong features whose beauty seemed excessive whenever she uncurled a rare smile.

"An alliance through marriage is often strongest," said the chief delegate. "We have been neglectful of making such a union in the past because the queen bore no daughters."

Queen Sabet dropped her teacup onto the saucer with a loud *clank*. The king placed a hand on her arm.

"The highest-ranking royal girls are His Majesty's cousins," said the chief delegate. "They live in a territory known as Lesser Alva. Three girls. King Fader of Stora will have his pick of them for a bride, if he agrees to our offer."

"I wonder if the girls will have any say in the matter," Steffan said, speaking the question on Miri's mind.

"Royalty has its obligations," said the chief delegate.

Steffan nodded, and Miri noticed his shoulders slump slightly.

"Living in Lesser Alva, I suspect the girls are not very, shall we say, *refined*," said the chief delegate. "The priests of the creator god have called for a princess academy to prepare them, and the delegation approved it. We require this girl to go be their tutor." He gestured toward Miri without looking at her.

Miri choked. "Me? But I . . . I can't . . . I'm going . . ."

The king turned to his wife. "She can barely speak. Are you certain?"

"I am," said the queen, her gaze on her spilled tea.

"Yes, of course, she is the best choice," he said.

"I've completed only one year of study at the Queen's Castle," said Miri. "It takes four years to become a tutor."

"Make her one, Bjorn," said the queen.

The king waved his napkin. "Chief, sign some paper that makes Miri a tutor."

"Yes, Your Majesty," said the chief delegate.

Miri looked at Britta, Steffan, the delegates, searching for someone who thought this idea was as ridiculous as she did. "But why me? There are lots of real tutors—"

"According to our traditions and the dictates of the priests, a tutor for a princess academy must be a princess academy graduate herself," said the chief delegate.

"A more experienced tutor—" Miri started.

"I don't know anyone else," said the queen. "I know you. Please."

"You don't need to say 'please,'" the king roared. "You tell her to go, and she will go."

"*I* have no choice?" asked Miri.

The king shifted in his seat and glared at the chief delegate from under his thick eyebrows.

"She does have a choice," the chief delegate said reluctantly.

Miri opened her mouth to decline so she could hurry and catch up with Peder, but she paused. Would the king be angry and forbid Steffan from escorting her to the camp? No other trader wagons would trek to Mount Eskel until next spring. How could she catch up without the king's permission?

Lesser Alva. She'd read about the outer territory, but at the moment all she could remember was one word: "swamp." The queen and king were ordering her to a swamp to be a teacher to his cousins? She'd been in Asland for a year, and with every letter home, she'd promised Marda and Pa she would return in the fall.

She felt Britta step closer, her shoulder touching Miri's, a faint warmth of encouragement.

"I need to think about it," Miri said.

The chief delegate took a breath to shout, but the king lifted his hand.

"Give her a little time," he grumbled into his beard. "She deserves that much."

The chief delegate pulled Steffan and the king into renewed talk about Stora.

Miri's breath felt tight, as if the walls were pressing in, squeezing. The king's voice begin to sound tinny and high-pitched, as far away as an echo. Miri opened the door and slipped out.

*I spy a dull stone*
*Smartly hidden in scree*
*Now small and unknown*
*Soon polished you will be*
*Carved into a throne*
*In a castle by the sea*

Miri's legs shook, and she imagined she would feel stronger if she just ran. She could run down the corridor, through the courtyard, and into the streets of Asland. Run somehow fast enough to catch up with the wagons. Maybe just run all the way home.

Before she even took a step, the breakfast chamber door opened. Miri expected to see Britta, but it was Katar, Mount Eskel's first delegate to the court in Asland. She was a little older than Miri and a lot taller, with hair so red it seemed angry.

"I don't want—" Miri broke off. She hid her quivering chin with a hand.

"Oh stop it," said Katar. "They're not asking you to cut off your head."

Miri nodded, staying silent to keep the sob in her chest from unsticking.

"Danland needs the stronger alliance a marriage with Stora's king would give us," Katar said. "If Stora invades and defeats Danland's army, then all the changes we worked for—commoner delegates, justice and equality for all Danlanders—all of it will be just *undone*."

Miri nodded again. Katar was right, and yet the loneliness that had pricked her heart when the wagons rolled away without her was spreading outward, chilling her legs and arms.

Katar rubbed her own arms. "It's important, Miri. It's really important. Go, and don't mess it up."

Now Miri felt sick as well as sad.

"There's something else you should know." Katar sighed. "Even though Mount Eskel was made a province, the king still owns all the land. Well, now the chief delegate is encouraging the king to sell his rights to the land to merchants in order to replenish the royal treasury."

"Sell? He couldn't—"

"He could," said Katar. "Merchants would pay the king well for the rights to mine and sell linder. They would move up to Mount Eskel and oversee the quarry."

"Then the Eskelites would work for the merchants, not for ourselves," said Miri.

"Exactly. And the merchants could bring up new workers and fire the villagers, set wages lower than what our people are making now, and really do whatever they please."

"Mount Eskel wouldn't be a town anymore," said Miri. "It would just be a mine. You can't let them."

"I explained that there's no other means of survival on Mount Eskel besides quarrying, so if the merchants fired any Eskelites, we'd have to leave our homes. But the king imagines the Eskelites would be grateful for the chance to move to the lowlands, where *surely* they'd all be *much* happier."

Miri felt tired. They'd fought so hard to improve life on the mountain, and then fought to get commoners in the delegation and improve life in the kingdom, but there was always another fight.

"Miri," said Katar, "you need—"

"I know," Miri said. "I *know*. But right now I need to be alone."

She walked away.

First Miri went back to the chamber where she and the other Mount Eskel girls had slept for the past year. The wardrobes were empty, doors ajar. All her things were packed and bouncing around in the back of a wagon on its way to Mount Eskel. All she had was the hawk Peder had carved for her out of linder stone, a familiar weight in her pocket.

Servants and guards knew Miri, and she wandered freely through the white stone palace as she had always done. The linder stone beneath her feet was as white as cream, with pale green veins, quarried from Mount Eskel generations before. Miri had grown up climbing on rough blocks of linder, breathing linder dust, and drinking from a stream white with it. But the beauty of polished linder still filled her with awe.

She climbed stairs until she reached the top floor and a balcony facing north. She could not see Mount Eskel all the way from Asland, just a hint of purple mountains far against the horizon. The wagons would be miles away by now and take days more to reach the mountain pass.

Dozens of times she had imagined her return—embracing Pa and Marda, giving them her carefully chosen gifts. If she agreed to accept the king's errand, Peder would deliver the gifts with the message that Miri was not coming yet. Despite the new boots and chocolates, there would be no joy beside their little hearth.

"I'm not going home." She whispered the words aloud to convince herself they were true.

# SHANNON HALE

is the author of twenty novels, most of them for young readers, including the *New York Times* bestsellers *Princess Academy*, a Newbery Honor winner; its sequel, *Princess Academy: Palace of Stone*; and the Ever After High series; as well as *Princess Academy: The Forgotten Sisters*. Her first book, *The Goose Girl*, was an international favorite; her adult novel *Austenland* is now a major motion picture starring Keri Russell. She cowrote the acclaimed graphic novels *Rapunzel's Revenge* and *Calamity Jack* with her husband, Dean Hale. They live with their four small children near Salt Lake City, Utah.

www.shannonhale.com
@haleshannon

Look for Shannon Hale's highly acclaimed novel
## BOOK OF A THOUSAND DAYS

Inspired by a little-known fairy tale from the Brothers Grimm, Shannon Hale brings fans of *The Goose Girl* a heartrending tale of mistaken identity and love gone awry.

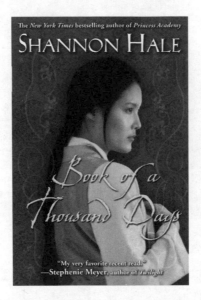

★ "Hale delivers another winning fantasy. . . . Readers will be riveted as Dashti and Saren escape and flee to the Khan's realm where, through a series of deceptions, contrivances, and a riotously triumphant climax, the tale spins out a thoroughly satisfying ending."
—*Publishers Weekly*, starred review

★ "Fans of Gail Carson Levine's *Fairest* will embrace this similar mix of exotic, fully realized setting; thrilling, enchanted adventure; and heart-melting romance." —*Booklist*, starred review

www.bloomsbury.com
www.shannonhale.com
www.facebook.com/bloomsburyteens